SEE ME

WENDY HIGGINS

Love and
Luck, Kim!

♡, Wendy Higgins

DEDICATION

To the Hornback Zoo ~
My brother Frank, sister-in-law Heather,
Davin, Frank Jr., Hanna, Tyler, and Jackson ~
May the winds be always at your back

PROLOGUE

CECELIA MASON HAD NEVER been more frightened. Their infant, Robyn, was fast asleep in the carrier against her chest. Leon squeezed Cecelia's hand as they entered the Fae realm through a lower portal in the Irish countryside. They hadn't wanted to bring Robyn into the land of Faerie, but they couldn't leave her in the U.S.

Cecelia closed her jacket over the bulge of fabric. A lifetime of service to the unpredictable Fae had taught them not to show emotion or draw attention to themselves. They wore their plainest clothes. Cecelia went without make-up and had pulled her brown waves into a low bun. The couple, human except for the magic imbedded in their blood, cringed as they pushed through the thick barrier of atmosphere between realms.

A portal guard recognized the *Dightheach* signatures of the human "helpers" and led them through the vine-covered labyrinth to a clearing. Soft light poured overhead from a sky of pastel swirls and music played like chimes. Cecelia, distrustful of the land's magnetic pull, braced herself against an onslaught of delectable Fae sensory.

They were ushered into a gossamer tent lined with

flowers that reached and wound around one another in dazzling displays of color. On a bed of petals lounged a female Fae with hair like shimmering cinnamon, eyes as vividly yellow as dandelions. Cecelia recognized the Fae woman as Martineth, the Alpha consort who ran the southern regions of Faerie for the Summer King. At her feet, a handsome human man with lost, fanatic eyes lavished her skin with gentle kisses.

The Masons were careful not to show their terror at the sight of Martineth. A light sheen of sweat across their brows and dampened palms could not be helped. They stood very still while Martineth's yellow eyes traveled over them like guinea pigs in a pet shop—possible sources of entertainment. Cecelia, full of new mother ferocity, crossed her arms over her chest to cuddle Robyn closer.

"Leave me." Martineth's voice was lackadaisical as she waved off the human at her feet. He made a pathetic sound and kissed her ankle. She attempted to pull her legs free and swatted at him like a moth, but he mumbled and clung to her, desperate. "Take him," she ordered the guard.

The Fae guard lifted the man with a yank and left them alone. Leon kept a straight face and averted his eyes from the King's consort as he delivered his report of their region in the U.S. over the past year, reciting the numbers of eleven Fae who entered illegally into the earthly realm and the twenty-three human memories that were altered by Leon as a result. The report went better than hoped, faster. To Cecelia's relief, their business must have bored Martineth; she gave a wide yawn and moved to dismiss them.

In that moment, a tiny mew rose from the carrier buried under Cecelia's jacket.

Cecelia turned to leave. Again, baby Robyn made a noise. This time as a whimper that built into a mild cry.

Leon cleared his throat as his wife was set to exit. "Good day, my Lady," he told Martineth, whose head had cocked to the side with curiosity.

"Stop." Her voice carried to them like a bell.

The couple turned their heads, all innocence and nerves.

Martineth's voice was a slow drawl. "What was that sound?"

"I'm sorry?" asked Leon.

Robyn took that inopportune moment to vocalize again and her parents shared a defeated, horrified glance. Martineth's eyes were wide as she stared at the wiggling mass against Cecelia's chest.

"What have you brought into our land?"

"It's only our child," Cecelia explained in an offhand tone. "Probably needs to be changed. Nasty business. We won't keep you, my Lady."

They turned again, only to be stopped once more by the snap of her clear voice.

"I have never seen a newly born human. Show me."

The Faerie was sitting up now, stray petals floating down from layers of gown. Her inquisitive stare and eager tone made Cecelia tremble on the inside. With slow movements, Cecelia opened her jacket and unclasped the carrier from her shoulder. All grace, the King's consort stood and glided forward. Robyn, only weeks old, squinted and quieted as the pleasant light washed over her. Cecelia had a sudden fervent wish that Robyn was bald and funny-looking like so many precious babies she'd seen. Instead, the consort admired an inch-plus of wavy chestnut hair, rounded pink cheeks and the sweetest puckered mouth. Chocolate eyes and black lashes blinked at the Faerie. Beauty.

Martineth's bright eyes filled with wonder. "So small," she marveled. "Her skin appears as soft as down."

Cecelia inched backward, an animalistic intuition of warning rising up in her. As the Faerie woman raised a perfect, slender hand to the baby's cheek, Cecelia yanked the child away and all but shouted, "No—don't touch her!"

The temperature around them rose as the Faerie's eyes shone like fire. Her hand froze in mid-air.

"My Lady," Leon broke in. "Our human physician told us not to let anyone handle her while she's so young. Infants are too fragile. Please forgive my wife. Her body and mind are still transitioning from the birth."

His demeanor was calm, but his wife recognized thinly veiled panic behind his eyes. She fought for composure when all she wanted to do was run.

"I'm very sorry, my Lady." Cecelia pushed out the apology. "I know the touch of a Fae alters a human's mind. We don't know how it would affect a newborn. I would hate for her to lose the ability to be of service to the Summer King someday."

Martineth studied Cecelia, eyes a swirl of sunshine and heat.

"I assume you have reported the birth of this child?" the Faerie challenged.

"Of course, Lady Martineth," Leon said with respect.

To fail reporting a *Dightheach* child would mean death to its parents. Everyone with magical blood was expected to serve.

After another long stare at Cecelia and more greedy

gazing at the child, the consort tapped her sharp chin. An ominous expression crossed her face, as if an idea were hatching.

"I can see why you are attached to the child." The consort leered at the couple and walked a slow circle around them, glimmering hair falling in waves down her back. "She is a thing of beauty." Martineth stopped in front of Cecelia and peered down at the baby. "Beautiful things have a way of disappearing in the night."

The threat bolted through Cecelia with swift understanding. Her knees threatened to buckle as Leon spoke with hardened care.

"What is it that you wish from us, my Lady?"
The consort chuckled. "I have a future mate for her—a binding which will greatly please the King."

As a proud, wicked grin enhanced the Faerie's fiery eyes, a burden of dread settled onto Cecelia's shoulders for her daughter's future. A future which was now as good as sealed.

·ONE

THE END OF HIGH school was bittersweet. My sister and I drove home in the dark from a graduation party to our house in Great Falls, Virginia, a woodsy town of hills and cliffs nestled between cities of concrete. I was so glad to have Cassidy. Even now she sensed my mood as I pulled into our driveway and cut the engine. I stared absently at the porch swing illuminated by the motion-censored light. We'd shared years of secrets on that wooden swing.

"Tonight was fun, huh?" Cass asked carefully.

I nodded. "Yeah. Fun, but… weird too."

"Yeah," she whispered. And then to cheer me she added, "I can't believe the graduating football players streaked. I did *not* need to see all that. My ears still hurt from everyone screaming."

I snorted.

I'd made some great friends, especially my soccer teammates, but I couldn't tell them about my family or the Fae, or the real reason I was going to Ireland tomorrow while they were all headed for post-graduation Beach Week.

"I can't believe it's time for you to go already." Cassidy stared at the house. "No more sneaking to D.C. with my big sis and glamouring ourselves in fancy dresses." I had to smile at the memory. We hadn't bothered doing our hair or make-up that night. We used our magical glamour to sneak into a club and make us look done up. We'd been exhausted after an hour of dancing from the effort of keeping up fake appearances.

I took her hand and my heart tightened with our inevitable separation.

"Let's not get sad," I told her. "Come on."

It was midnight when we let ourselves in. Mom and Dad's luggage sat next to the door, ready to go. Our parents lounged on the couch, Dad reading. If this were a normal night they'd have been in bed hours ago. Mom had apparently been reading, too, but had fallen asleep with her head on his lap and a book on her chest. At the sound of our footsteps, she sat up and pushed back her dark hair.

"There's my girls," Dad said, jovial despite the late hour. He put his book on the coffee table. "Tell us all about the party."

We sat on the couch across from them.

"It was okay," I told him, trying to hide my sadness.

Tension crowded around us. We were all probably thinking the same thing: *This is our last night with me at home.* How weird. I didn't want to think about it. Mom, ever the peacemaker, cleared her throat.

"You said good-bye to all your friends then?" She'd been away from her homeland of Ireland for twenty years but her voice still held a soft lilt and inflection, which I'd always envied.

"Yeah," I said.

Cassidy stretched her mouth wide for a loud yawn, not bothering to cover her mouth. It was contagious—I yawned next, then Mom.

"Look at my tired girls. We should call it a night," Dad said. "Big day tomorrow. Thankfully we can sleep on the plane, huh?"

Nervousness tightened around me like twine.

"I hope you both finished packing," Mom said.

"Mine is pretty much done," I told her. "I just have to bring it down."

"Mine's almost done," Cass said, yawning again.

Mom shook her head and focused on me. "How are you, Robyn? Are you ready for this?"

I gave her a reassuring smile, despite the tightening sensation. "I'm fine. Ready to see what Ireland has in store for me."

"Well, come here." Dad stood, tall and imposing, and opened his arms. The four of us huddled together for a group hug. Mom was shorter than me now. I'd outgrown her last year, and it still felt strange to be the tallest female in the embrace.

We said our goodnights, and then shuffled upstairs. I stood in my bedroom feeling a wave of nostalgia. This room held so many memories. Would I be back again to see the rows of trophies on the shelves? Everything from t-ball to All-State Soccer and this year's Girls' Varsity Soccer MVP. Two large corkboards were tacked full of pictures, ticket stubs for movies, school dances, and sporting events, even a few newspaper snippets about my teams.

I went to my walk-in closet and pulled out the familiar, large plastic storage bin. I placed the bin next to my luggage at the foot of my bed, then sat down cross-legged on the carpet and opened it.

Staring up at me was ten years worth of memorabilia collected to give McKale when it was time to meet.

The mysterious McKale. My "betrothed." A fancy word for "engaged."

McKale was from another family of ancient magic. Mom explained that his people had only been able to produce male children for many, many years now. I was told they needed a special, magical girl to bind herself with one of their special, magical boys to ensure the continuation of their family's bloodline. It sounded extraordinary to me as a child—like I was a princess—special, chosen.

It took a few years to realize the purpose of the union was to have babies.

My friends at school would have been appalled. They all thought I was going off to college overseas. The term "prearranged marriage" was thought of as something from the old days, or something that other societies did. I should have been terrified or indignant, but the way Mom presented my future eleven years ago made me feel important and useful. Arranged relationships were common among *Dightheach*. Normal.

On the night I learned about McKale, Mom told me his clan valued gifts. At six years of age, I remember thinking it was weird that his family was called a "clan," but cool that they liked presents.

I ran my finger over a paddle and ball set I'd gotten at a birthday party when I was seven. I could never get the stupid toy to work for me, but maybe McKale could. That had been the first gift. My favorite was the soccer ball. I smiled at its shiny black and white surface, remembering when Dad landed tickets to the World Cup.

A light knock came as I wrapped tape around the lid.

"Come in," I called. My family knew about the gift bin, but it was still embarrassing, this imaginary relationship I had with a stranger. But he wouldn't be a stranger for much longer, would he?

I shivered with anticipation.

Cassidy walked in and made herself comfortable on my bed while I moved my travel stuff next to the bedroom door and changed into my pajamas.

"How many hours of footage do you think you have?" From her laying position Cass inclined her head toward the video camera on the nightstand that I'd used to record messages for McKale over the past four years.

"I don't know. A lot," I said.

"Mm." Cassidy chewed her lip. She was unusually quiet as she lay there. I sat down and stretched my legs out beside her.

"You okay?" I asked.

"I don't want you to go."

The invisible band around my chest yanked tighter. "You guys are coming, too. We'll get to spend the whole summer together before you go back home."

"Not really. I mean, I'll be there, but you're going to be busy getting to know *him*." Her jealous tone surprised me. She'd always taken my engagement in stride. I began braiding the silky brown hair at her temple.

"I promise to make time for you, chickadee." I wondered if she'd ever outgrow the childhood nickname. I hoped not.

"It's gonna be strange next year at school without you."

"I know."

Cassidy would be a senior. It was a huge high school and we'd both been active in sports and clubs. Cass was even junior class president this past year. But I understood. No amount of friends or activities could replace what we shared. And neither could a man.

She turned her face away and whispered low, "Please don't forget about me."

"Hey." I gasped and pulled her face back to me. It killed me when her eyes filled with tears. I couldn't remember the last time I'd cried.

"If you ever say something like that again, I'll kick your butt," I said. She sniffled and gave me a small smile. "I mean it, Cass. There is no man and no distance that could ever make me forget about you, or stop needing you. I'll do whatever I have to to keep in touch. And don't forget about begging Mom and Dad to study abroad next year."

That idea always cheered us. There was still a shroud of mystery about McKale's clan and what it'd be like there. Mom made it sound like there was no technology. I couldn't even send him letters over the years because mail wasn't delivered there. If Cass could study abroad in Ireland it would make any situation more livable for me.

"I wish he could come here instead," she said.

"Yeah. Me too."

Cassidy wiped her eyes. She nuzzled her head closer to my leg and I continued braiding her hair.

"If he's not a good guy... If he doesn't appreciate you—"

"Don't think like that. Everything is going to be fine."

I'd often been filled with gratitude that this was my fate

and not hers. Cassidy was too free-spirited to handle something like this.

Her smooth hair slid through my fingers and she closed her eyes. The thought of my predicament dampening her spirit broke my heart.

"I wish I could stay here with you longer," I said.

"No, you don't," Cass said without opening her eyes. Her voice was still soft. "You want to go be with him."

Her words shook me. Partly because she was right—I *was* excited to go, to meet the magical boy I'd been chosen for. But that didn't mean I wanted to leave my family.

"I do want to meet him," I admitted. "But I'm not looking forward to being without you." My insides shook just thinking about it. She seemed so young with her head in my lap. I had to remind myself this was an independent girl who always took what she wanted and had kissed way more boys than me. I bent down over her face and cupped her soft cheeks with my palms. She opened her eyes. "You know you're my heart, Cass. Nobody could ever take your place."

She sat up and turned, hugging me around the neck. I gulped back my emotions.

"Now get out of here," I said. "Before you make me cry or something."

"Pfft, yeah right." She gave me a tired smile before slipping off the bed.

"Hey, what if McKale is cross-eyed?" Cass asked, walking backward to the door. Her mood seemed lighter now, but I couldn't forget the jealousy she'd revealed.

"Don't they have surgery to correct that?"

She shrugged, almost at the door. "What if he's got some wicked crooked teeth?"

"Braces."

"What if he refuses to get braces?"

I groaned and threw a small pillow at her. "Go finish packing, dork."

She punched her chest and threw me a peace sign before leaving.

I flopped back on the blankets, feeling uneasy from all the emotion. This whole thing was going to be harder if Cassidy made a fuss. I'd be sure to give her plenty of attention in Ireland.

I switched off the light and set my alarm for the butt-crack of dawn. We'd only be getting a few hours of sleep, so I'd be running on pure adrenaline tomorrow. I climbed underneath the down comforter and snuggled in, doing what I'd done every night since I was six.

I imagined McKale. The guy whose life was tied to mine.

What would he see when he looked at me?

I'd resigned myself to a lot of bad "what ifs" over the years. Cassidy loved to throw those at me for fun. *What if he has a big nose? What if he has halitosis? What if he's got an ugly comb-over and he won't shave it off?*

But in all our imaginings there was one thing I never cared to envision. It was vain and stupid, considering I forced myself to imagine all sorts of horrid scenarios, and yet *this* was the thing that bothered me. Cassidy and I looked very much alike: athletic bodies, ample curves, medium-length brown hair, and round brown eyes. She, like our mom, was taller than average. And at five feet, eleven inches, I was over two inches taller than them.

Of all the truly frightening things worth worrying about, I held one selfish wish. *Please... don't let McKale be too much shorter than me.*

Two

BOARDING THE PLANE WAS SURREAL.

The four of us took our seats in the back row of first class. Thankfully it wasn't a crowded flight. Three other passengers sat in the front, a good distance away. I nestled between my mom and sister with Mom by the window and Cass on the aisle. Dad sat in the aisle seat in the row beside us. I wondered if my father had somehow gotten them to fix the seating with no passengers around us so we could have privacy to talk.

My nerves flared when we pushed back from the gate and prepared for takeoff. I bit my lip to keep from screaming in anticipation. I was on my way to meet McKale! Crazy butterflies dive-bombed inside me. I'd been suppressing uncharacteristic psycho-girly giggles all morning, especially since my family seemed subdued.

I understood why. If I allowed myself to go down the path of how much I'd miss them when they returned home, leaving me in whatever situation I was in, my heart would break and my nerves would shred.

As soon as we were in the air Mom started acting strange, fidgeting, messing with her hair. I watched her stare distractedly out the window while Cassidy read a magazine on my other side. Mom's hand drifted up to her throat and a look of nervousness crossed her face as she shifted her body toward me.

"There are a few things we need to discuss, Robyn. Let's get our drinks and then I'll glamour us so the flight attendants won't pay us mind."

Things to discuss? O-*kay*... What more could there possibly be to say?

When she leaned down to pick a piece of lint from the bottom of her brown trousers she shot a covert look toward my dad that screamed, *Help*! He raised an eyebrow of sympathy to her before shoving his face in a sports magazine.

Uneasiness invaded.

"Uh, Mom?" I said. She fiddled with her tennis bracelet and pushed her hair around some more. "Mom, what's going on?"

She held a finger up at me and politely ordered a glass of red wine from the flight attendant. Cassidy ordered one as well, but Mom shook her head and Cass begrudgingly changed to ginger ale.

Mom guzzled the glass and ordered another. She sipped wine all the time at home, but I'd never seen her drink this fast. I eyeballed Cassidy who shrugged a shoulder. Once Mom had her second glass in front of her she whispered for us to pretend we were sleeping. The three of us slumped down into cozy positions with our eyes closed, and I felt the familiar static-tingle across my skin as Mom draped us with glamour. Now anyone who looked at us would see three people napping while we went about our business under the protective bubble of magic.

"Okay, Mom. You know how I feel about surprises. What's going on?" My brain needed time to process things. She took another big gulp of wine.

"You know that McKale's clan is of ancient roots." She cleared her throat and proceeded to stutter and shift. "Far more ancient than ours. But there are a few things you've not yet learned about them."

Oh no. *Oh-freaking-no.*

"What *things?*" My palms began to sweat as I watched her fiddling.

"Centuries ago, McKale's people were specially chosen to receive magic because of their cobbling talents, er, shoemaking skills. You know Faeries love to dance, sometimes for weeks on end. So, naturally, they need new shoes often, and there are so many of them. Long ago, a country sprite brought this Irish clan of human cobblers to the attention of the Fae, who then offered to bless the clan with magic if they focused their trade solely on providing shoes for the Fair Folk."

Cass leaned over. "McKale's a shoemaker for the Fae?"

Mom nodded, but her eyes were too big.

Tidbits of folklore swirled through my mind, but a hard sense of denial set up camp inside me. It couldn't be the same tale I was imagining.

"Who are they?" I asked.

"Hm?" Mom eyed her almost-empty glass. "Where is that stewardess?"

"Mom…" My heart pounded and I chose my words carefully. "What is McKale's clan called?"

She wouldn't look at me. The cabin space seemed to close in on me. It was forever before she answered in a cracking voice. "They're the Leprechauns."

"That's not funny," I said. Mom stared at her hands. She didn't laugh or say, "Gotcha!"

I was going to suffocate. Cassidy gasped next to me and I flung off my seat belt, jumping up from my seat with my hands in my hair, breaking the magical bubble with a loud *pop* that only the four of us could hear. My father sat straight up, dropping the magazine and looking around with a hardcore expression of seriousness. My action had sent him into work-mode. When he was sure nobody had noticed he gave me a severe look that kind of scared me.

Mom grasped my arm and I shrunk down to the edge of my seat. I couldn't look at her yet. My heart was banging and I could hardly breathe as I fought the wide expanse of emotion.

"Leprechauns?!" I demanded. The word tasted wrong in my mouth, like I was expecting a sip of water and drank lime juice instead.

Cass leaned over me. "As in, *the* Leprechauns?"

"Sh," Mom said, looking around to make sure the people up front hadn't heard. Then she chewed her lip as her eyes flitted to me, a horribly guilty expression on her face. I gaped at her.

I was not marrying a *Leprechaun*! Who thought that would be okay? A sense of betrayal overtook me, worse than any feeling I'd ever experienced.

"Hurry, pretend to sleep again," Mom ordered. I placed my elbow on the armrest and leaned my head against my hand, closing my eyes. When I felt the shimmer of magic I couldn't lift my heavy head. All my life I'd stayed positive no matter what, knowing if I allowed negativity to invade it would take over like a weed. All of my subdued fears and doubts surfaced like a blitz, ignited by my parents' secrecy. I leaned my face into my palms and burst into tears.

Cassidy sucked in a breath, her voice warbling. "Oh, my gosh… Robyn? Mom, you made her cry!"

They both rubbed my back and smoothed my hair. Sobbing was demoralizing and humiliating. I wanted more than anything to stop, but my body wouldn't cooperate.

"Shush, dear. Please don't cry," Mom crooned. "I hear he's the tallest lad in the clan."

Oh, no she didn't.

I looked up through hazy, swollen eyes and choked out, "So he's four feet tall instead of three?" Cassidy had the nerve to giggle.

"Maybe he'll be the funniest and the sweetest wee man in the clan," Cass said brightly. I shook my head in my hands and my chest heaved with another round of uncontrollable weeping.

"Don't say *wee man!*" Mom hissed at Cassidy. To me she whispered, "There, there, love."

"Flying shitballs," Cassidy grumbled. "This is bad."

"Watch your mouth," Mom scolded. "You know I hate that word."

"If there was ever a time that warranted the use of 'shitballs,' it's now, Mom."

"Och! For the love of all things holy, child. Attempt to filter what comes out of your mouth!"

Lost in my own anguish, I barely registered the bickering between them.

I'd always felt like an Amazon woman, standing as tall as the guys at school, and even taller than many of them. Next to McKale I was sure to be an absolute *giant*. How could my parents have agreed to this? I mean, I know it was important to keep the magical bloodlines alive so the Fae secrets could be kept in as few families as possible around the world, but still. There needed to be basic attraction between two people if they were going to bind their lives together and try to have children, right? Everything about this was wrong and unfair.

Impossible.

I took a deep, cleansing breath and sat up with a mild shudder. My practical nature raised its head, composed. Time to stop crying and get answers. I wiped my face and looked at Mom. My voice was thick.

"You should have told me sooner. I need more time than just a day to process something this huge."

I wanted to keep going, to tell her off completely and make her feel the betrayal I was experiencing, but she looked miserable.

"Yeah," Cassidy chimed in, rambling with indignation on my behalf. "Not cool. This is a major detail. I mean, how short are they anyway? Are we talking 'sit on your lap' short or 'sit on your shoulder' short? Because if he's only a foot high I don't know how anyone expects them to *do it*."

Gah! Images of a Ken doll popped into my mind.

"No, no, it's not like that." Mom cradled her forehead in her hand like she did when a migraine was coming on. Something wasn't adding up.

"Why didn't you tell me?" I yelled in frustration.

Dad cleared his throat and rustled the magazine, causing the three of us to turn to him.

"Or you, Daddy!" I wanted to cry all over again. How

could they keep this from me? Why would they pair me with a freaking Leprechaun?!

He spoke without looking away from the pages, keeping his voice low so passengers a few rows ahead couldn't hear him since he wasn't in our magic bubble. "Don't be so hard on your mother, girls. Perhaps we didn't have much choice in the matter. The Fae can be quite… convincing." He looked directly at Mom now. "You need to tell them, Cecelia."

Cassidy and I turned to Mom, who nodded once before draining the rest of the wine. Her lips were stained light crimson. She pushed brown locks away from her face and I noticed a few strands of gray. Those were new.

"The Leprechaun clan is mostly made up of dwarfs, or little people—"

"Midgets?" Cassidy asked.

"Well, yes, but that word's not politically correct and some consider it derogatory," Mom stated. "Anyhow, in order to keep the bloodlines alive, the Fae gathered a sister clan of dwarf females in a nearby town and gifted them with magic in return for their agreement to pair up with the Chaun men. After all these years, for some reason the clans are not successfully reproducing anymore. There've been many miscarriages and stillbirths or babes who die young with internal defects. Some say the two clans have exhausted the variety in the bloodlines and there's fear of accidental incest—"

"Ew!" Cassidy cut in. Mom ignored her and continued.

"They've kept thorough records of family lines, but it's to the point where many of them are related as second cousins and such."

"So, couldn't the all-powerful Fae have found some

other dwarf women in the world for them?" I asked. "Why did they choose a human?"

Mom sighed and looked at Dad who gave her an encouraging nod.

"Fifty years ago when McKale was born—"

Cassidy smacked the armrest. "McKale is *fifty*? Dude!"

"Cassidy Renee, if you interrupt me one more time you'll be sitting with your father away from this conversation." Cass grumbled but shut up. Mom looked back at me. "I've done a lot of digging for information over the years. Fifty is young by their standards. You know magic enables the *Dightheach* to live longer than usual. But the average lifespan of a Leprechaun is a thousand years because the magic is so engrained into their DNA."

A thousand? Wow. My parents would be middle aged for a long, long time before they finally appeared "old." They would probably live between three and four hundred years, which meant Cass and I would as well. Magical families had to periodically move and change identity to keep up the façade.

"When McKale came along there was a lot of talk among the magical people around the world. Supposedly he was the healthiest Chaun to be born in centuries. Some say he was gifted as a newborn by a Faerie of the night. Some say he was born without dwarfism, so the genetics that were hindering the other babies did not affect him." A look of hope must have landed on my face because Mom shot me a cautious look. "It's all hearsay, dearest. I wouldn't get your hopes up." She appeared regretful and my hopes sank again.

"Fact is, the Chaun and Fae both agreed that McKale was their best chance at strengthening the clan lines again, and they wanted a magical female whose bloodlines had never before been crossed with the Chaun. Your father and I were in Ireland seventeen years ago delivering our latest reports to the Fae when all of this talk was going on. I'd just given birth to you three weeks prior, Robyn. You were strapped to my chest in a carrier." Her eyes went dark. "A Faerie woman saw you and laid claim."

"What do you mean?" I shivered and rubbed my arms.

"Laid claim?" Cassidy asked. "That's creepy. Couldn't you tell her no?"

Mom's chin quivered. "Leon, get me another drink, would you, love?"

My father nodded and pushed the call button. A minute later the drink was delivered. When the flight attendant went back to the server alley, Dad passed us the drink, down the line until it reached Mom. I'd never seen her drink like this. She downed half the glass before continuing.

"We tried. The Fair Folk are not accustomed to being denied anything and they're easily offended. They see humans as dispensable, even magical ones like us. Let's just say the Fae woman made a comment about you disappearing in the night.'"

"They threatened you!" My anger immediately switched targets from my parents to the Fae.

"Yes. I knew at that moment they would have you one way or another. Either we agreed to let you bind with the Leprechaun boy for a time, or they would steal you for their plaything. If that happened you would have been lost to us."

"They can't do that!" Cassidy's eyes burned with indignation.

But they could, and we all knew it.

I'd only heard bad things about their race of creatures. Everything they did was for their own good. The humans who helped them, like my parents, did so only as a favor to humanity. They kept humans safe from the beings who thought so little of them. Mom laid a hand on my forearm.

"As a little girl you took the news of your binding so well. I was worried you'd be scared about Leprechauns back then. And then when you got older, I knew you'd be upset about the possible, um, physical issues. I wanted you to be happy for as long as possible, but I let too much time pass."

I desperately wished she would have told me at the same time she told me everything else. Maybe I could have adjusted to the idea. Or, maybe not. Mom's brown eyes were round and imploring as she looked at me.

"Well," I said. "You did save me from being taken. That's... something."

She took my hand and we both squeezed.

"What if it doesn't work out?" I whispered.

Mom wouldn't meet my eyes. I looked over at my father and he stared back at me, offering no sign of false encouragement.

"We're at the mercy of the Fae," he said, keeping his voice down.

"In other words," I stated, needing all the facts laid out, "they could kill us if I don't want to bind with him."

"Or take us into Faerie," Dad said.

Mom closed her eyes and shuddered with disgust. I shared a sickened look with my sister.

"It will work out," Dad said.

I wondered how he could sound so assured. A long, silent pause stretched while we soaked in the information and listened to the drone of jet engines.

"So, what's it gonna be like there?" Cassidy asked.

"Your father and I have never been to their land, but we know a few people who have. The village is guarded with magical wards so humans who stumble across the land will become disoriented and retreat. The Leprechaun have another job besides making shoes. They also keep one of the portals to the Faerie realm. Their lands are vast, and they're surrounded only by farmlands for miles. The dome of magic even keeps the village undetectable to anyone who flies over."

"Are they expecting us?" I asked.

"I assume so. We swore to the Fae woman we'd bring you to the Leprechaun land when you were seventeen and completed your education."

"How far is the nearest town?" Cassidy's voice carried a hint of dread.

"At least an hour by car, maybe two."

"Wow," Cass said. "A giant farm with no tall guys. Sounds... fun."

"Oh, I've heard the Leprechaun know how to have a good time," Mom assured us. "Big parties with music and dancing."

I shot Cass a glance, and nearly snorted at the funny look on her face. A Leprechaun's idea of a good time was not going to be the same kind of song and dance we enjoyed.

"And they do have a cousin clan called the Clourichaun who live on nearby land. I understand there are quite a few average-sized men among them." Cass waggled her eyebrows as Mom went on, slurring her words. "The Clourichaun lost flavor with the Fae, ahem, excuse me, they lost *favor* with the Fae a few centuries ago. I'm not sure what happened there, but they were cursed with infertility. What's left of them will be the last of them."

"That sucks," I said. "They must've done something pretty bad."

"Maybe that's what I'll do for fun," Cass offered.

"What?" I asked. "Get cursed by the Fae?"

"No. I'll get the lowdown on all the clan gossip. I'm not holding out any hope for cute boys, so I've got to stay busy."

"I see." We were semi-joking and I knew Cass was trying to get my mind off the worse stuff, but the air was still thick with discomfort.

"I'm good at being nosy," Cass added.

"You certainly are." Mom finished off her third glass of wine. "I'm knackered. I think I'll go have a lie down next to Daddy."

"You do that, wino," Cassidy said. Mom leaned across me and pinched my sister's thigh, making her holler and jump. Then Mom patted my cheek, warming me with the love in her eyes as she whispered, "I'm sorry, my sweet girl."

With a heavy heart, I nodded.

Looking around to be sure we were safe, she snapped the protective bubble of magic and stood, wobbling on her way across the row to sit next to Dad. He watched, amused, and held out a hand to steady her until she was snuggled up in the seat by his side. He draped an arm across her and looked over at me with question in his eyes. I could almost hear his voice asking me if I was all right. I gave him a small nod; it would be useless for him to worry. His half grin showed that he appreciated my strong act, even though he could see through it. Dad lifted the magazine again and stroked Mom's hair.

Cassidy rolled her eyes at our lovey-dovey parents.

I wondered if I'd ever be able to have that kind of adoration with someone. I wasn't in a position to have such dreams and hopes, especially now. All of my romantic notions had flown out the window and landed somewhere in the Atlantic Ocean, sinking hard, probably lodged in a continental drift by now.

I didn't want to feel angry or cheated or tricked, but I did. I spent the rest of the long flight mourning the loss of the boy I'd foolishly allowed myself to envision for years on end. By the time we arrived in Ireland I'd said good-bye to the dream, and let him go. It was time to move on and face reality. Life was too short to wallow.

Too short. *Ugh.*

THREE

DESPITE THE WHOLE, *"Surprise, you're engaged to a Leprechaun!"* bomb, Cassidy and I were happy to arrive in Ireland. I'd done plenty of research over the years, so I knew it would be beautiful, but seeing it in real life was so much better. It was called the Emerald Isle for a definite reason. The fields and hills were a lush green.

I loved listening to people talk during our layover at Dublin Airport, even when I could hardly understand what they said. I enjoyed the dry, witty senses of humor and openness of the Irish. A few people got excited when they realized we weren't locals. We went for coffee and tea at an airport café, and when a little boy heard me order my mocha latte he said, "Ooh, say that again, miss!" His mother laughed and told me he fancied my accent. I had an accent!

Our next flight was on a tiny, rickety propeller plane to a smaller regional airport in Sligo where I changed from sweats into something nicer. The temperature was comfortable, and a light rain fell. Dad warned us to use the bathroom before we got on the road because we were heading in a direction that wouldn't have any rest stops. Cassidy gave me a fearful look. My little city girl.

We crammed the bin into the trunk of a compact rental car and tied a luggage carrier on top before setting out on our journey. I wasn't the anxious type, but my heart began a steady round of odd palpations. It was going to be a long ride. I clutched my stomach.

Dad caught my reflection in the rear view mirror. "You okay back there?"

"Yeah, fine. Stomach hurts a little, that's all."

Mom turned in her seat to look at me, and said, "Most likely the airplane food."

I nodded, even though we both knew that wasn't the reason.

"Better crack a window if you have gas," Cassidy said. "This car's way too small for that."

"You would know," Dad said. "You're the queen of not cracking the window."

And then laughing like an evil hyena when the smell hit us.

Cass smiled with pride.

Another spasm wracked my insides and I curled forward. When Cassidy awkwardly patted my shoulder I leaned over and lay across her lap. It felt a little odd since I was usually the one comforting her, not the other way around, but I'd never needed her more. For the first time in my life I wanted to complain about my circumstances—I wanted to scream at Dad to turn around. How could he sit up there looking so calm about driving me to my impending doom?

As if sensing my silent judgment, he reached back without taking his eyes from the road and placed a strong, gentle hand on my arm.

"It will all work out," he said.

I heard Mom sniffle. Above me I saw Cassidy swipe a finger across her cheeks.

The car hummed with sadness. I squeezed my eyes shut.

"Um, how 'bout a movie?" Cass asked, her voice thick with emotion. She struggled to get the laptop out of her bag in the small space by her feet, bouncing my head around in the process. After much grunting and several whispered uses of her favorite word, she finally had it out. We crammed it in the tiny space on the console between Mom and Dad's arms. My mind was not on the movie, and a few glances up at Cass's glassy eyes told me that hers wasn't either. But it filled the silence and passed the time.

After an hour I sat up and looked around.

"We are seriously in the middle of nowhere," Cassidy said. "Do you know where you're going, Dad?"

"Of course," he said, tapping his head. "I've got it all up here. One of the few *Dightheach* who's been here gave me directions."

Rolling hills of grass and wildflowers spanned in every direction, with occasional patches of forests and brush. After growing up around the hustle and bustle of D.C., it was serene and even a little spooky to be somewhere so rural and remote. We'd been on road trips before, but even when we passed through croplands there were farms and barns to be seen. Out here, miles passed without signs of homes or life. At least the rain had stopped.

When we went over a particularly large hill and rounded the bend, a giant rainbow appeared, sparkling high in the sky above fields of green grass. I tensed.

Cassidy pointed to it. "Hey, just follow that rainbow and it'll take us right to them!"

Mom and Dad cracked a smile at each other, but their faces quickly straightened when I didn't partake in their mirth.

"Where are we, exactly?" I asked, trying not to sound too grumpy.

"County Leitrim," Dad answered.

"How much longer?" Cassidy squirmed in the cramped seat. "My butt's asleep."

"Sit tight, chickadee. Not much longer." Dad was always so calm. I could see his knees crammed under the steering wheel, but he never complained.

Thirty minutes later Mom pointed to a giant rock up ahead in front of a cluster of leafy trees. Dad slowed and turned directly after the boulder onto a tiny dirt road that cut through the trees.

"We're coming up to the wards now," Mom warned.

Sure enough, a shimmery veil revealed itself up ahead and I braced myself as the car bumped along and crept through it. Sudden pressure squeezed my head and my skin burned. For a frightening moment I couldn't even breathe. When the discomfort eased we all took deep breaths.

The car crept forward into a tunnel of thick trees and it darkened as shade bore down around us. Dusk was beginning to set. Dad had to switch on the headlights.

"I can't believe we're here," I whispered. An ominous quiet fell over the car and all around us. Cassidy took my hand. Mom cast a brave smile at me, but her eyes were tinged with worry.

I'd never been so nervous in all my life. I'm pretty sure even the backs of my knees were sweating, which I didn't even know was possible.

After five minutes of winding through the trees, we burst

out into a vast clearing of grass. Cassidy and I leaned forward with our heads in the middle to see. There appeared to be a faint path in the grass, but we were basically off-roading now. I hoped the car could handle the small ruts. We came up over the largest hill so far, and when we got to the top my sister and I gasped. Mom even reached over and grabbed Dad's hand as he stopped the car.

In the dim setting sunlight, a medieval-looking village was nestled in the valley below: a large, one-story building with a steepled log roof surrounded by many small structures, like thatched huts. The rumors had been true. This place was definitely not modern. There was even a water-well!

Cassidy's mouth gaped open. "Holy shitballs. We're in the Shire."

"Language," Mom deadpanned automatically.

On the other side of the village I could make out a clearing right before another forest began. Flickering lights shone through the leaves and around the huts, like fires had been lit.

"Listen," Dad said.

We rolled down our windows and whimsical sounds spilled in: musical notes, voices and laughter, clapping to a festive tune. Hearing those happy sounds calmed me a little. Cassidy's fingers wiggled in mine. Our palms were damp, but neither of us let go. Mom turned to me.

"Are you ready, love?"

"No." I laughed shakily. It took every ounce of my will power to say, "But I'll be okay. Let's go."

Dad shifted back into drive and coasted down the hill. He parked on the closest side of the village, rather than pulling around and driving up to their party, which I was glad about. I'd hate to scare them to death if they'd never seen a crazy vehicular contraption. Surely they'd seen cars with previous visitors, right? After setting sight on this village I had to wonder.

"You're looking kinda rough," Cassidy told me. "Do you want to brush your hair or something?"

I patted my crazy waves and shook my head. What was the point? Cass shrugged and applied some shimmery lip gloss. At the last second I snatched the lip gloss from her and swiped some on with a trembling hand.

We climbed out and moaned, stretching and cracking. I attempted to smooth my hands over the wrinkles in my white linen blouse, but there was no use. At least my khaki skirt survived the car trip well. I sighed and tried to relax as Cassidy combed her fingers through my hair, scrunching it a little. Then my parents came forward and simultaneously kissed me—Dad on my temple and Mom on my cheek. They led the way around the village, holding hands, while Cass and I followed close behind, linked arm in arm.

I don't want to go. I don't want to do this. Please don't make me.

My body took on a mind of its own as I walked: clumsy feet, fluttery heart rate, jittery knees. I probably would have wobbled to the ground like some fainthearted actress if I didn't have such a tight hold on Cassidy's arm. I couldn't wait to meet McKale and get it over with so my body could go back to normal. Weak did not suit me.

As we rounded the corner, the four of us stopped. The sky had darkened, illuminating four giant bonfires at each corner of the expansive clearing. The back of the flat field was lined with forest, and on the other two sides were tall rows of flowering grasses. At least a hundred little people were gathered, both men and women. There were long rows of wooden tables with benches along the edges of the fields of grasses where people ate, drank, and conversed. In the center was music and dancing.

My first thought was that I'd been wrong. The Leprechauns definitely knew how to throw a party. The atmosphere was festive and lively. I bit my lip against a smile at their outfits. They weren't wearing green top hats and buckled shoes, but some of the older-looking men did have on little gray suits with waistcoats, the kind with tails that hung lower in the back. Others wore tunic shirts with plain pants, like woodsy hospital scrubs, only in natural colors like tan, brown, and forest green. Nearly everyone was barefoot. Some of the males wore little caps that resembled berets. The women wore simple peasant dresses with their hair pinned up.

Everyone looked so *happy*. I wanted to feel happy, too. Not this sense of despair.

Two bearded men in suits sitting at the end of a table noticed us and jumped up, hurrying over. They went straight to my father, looking way up and shaking his hand with exuberance.

"You must be Mister Mason, then!" said the older little gentleman with a long, white beard. He wore a matching charcoal cap, which he took off to reveal a shiny bald top with tufts of fluffy gray hair around the sides.

"Yes, sir," Dad said. "That's me. Call me Leon, please. This is my wife, Cecelia."

"So nice to have you! I'm Brogan, the father of McKale, I am." He bowed toward my mother and she inclined her head to him in return. Then he looked toward Cassidy and me.

"This is Cassidy, our youngest," Mom introduced. "And this… is Robyn."

Brogan nodded at Cassidy and then came forward to stand in front of me. He bowed low and I let go of Cass's arm to do a curtsy/bow combo, which felt absurd. He straightened and smiled big, wrinkling his whole face and eliciting a smile back from me. I felt like I should squat to talk to him because of the height difference, but stood straight for fear of appearing condescending.

"Ye've a pretty face, Robyn, that's fer certain," he said.

"Thank you, Mister Brogan."

He gave a hearty laugh. "Just Brogan is fine by me. I suppose ye'll be wanting to meet my McKale, then, eh?"

No! Not yet.

The moment I'd waited for all these years was here, and now all I wanted was more time.

Brogan winked up at me. Why did he seem so happy? Couldn't he see this was a bad fit? Didn't it bother him that his poor son was being forced to marry a behemoth female? I bit my lip as he peered around at the crowd. He pointed to the middle.

"There he is, back there fiddlin'. Soon as this song ends I'll call to 'im. He's our best fiddler, he is." Brogan grinned up at me with pride and I followed his gaze toward his son. My face wore a neutral expression that I'd practiced to perfection. I didn't want to give away the fact that my heart was going ballistic or that my insides had all but liquefied.

I'd spent my life dreaming of him. And then I'd spent every moment of the last day *un*dreaming him. As much as I prided myself on emotional control, it all fell to the wayside as I weaved my sights through the sea of dancing little people, seeking out the sound of the fiddle, and finding the source sitting on a tree stump.

My hand flew to my rapidly pounding heart in my throat as I stared. Sitting on the stump with his long legs stretched out before him, crossed at the ankles, was a redheaded guy playing his heart out—an average-sized man among the little people.

I think I made a really weird squeaking sound, but I couldn't be sure.

His eyes were closed. His wrist moved back and forth over the polished fiddle at high speed, ringing out pure notes of sunshine in the darkness. I would remember every detail of those few seconds for the rest of my days. I'd expected to feel emotional when I laid eyes on him. But I hadn't expected the emotion to be so intense that it would impact me physically. Blood rushed through my veins at an alarming speed. My mind swirled and I swear I tilted to the side, off balance and unable to fully fill my lungs.

Cassidy was the drama queen, not me. To be so out of control was disorienting.

"Ohmigosh, ohmigosh, *ohmigosh*!" Cassidy squealed, and started jumping up and down and clapping when she saw him. Mom grasped her by the wrist and begged her not to make a scene. My family beamed at me and my eyes stung.

I looked back at McKale. His father had been right to brag; he played beautifully. I'd never known anyone who played a violin. I loved the bursts of tinny sound, especially when combined with the high-pitched wooden flute of the Leprechaun boy next to him. It was a lively tune that had everyone kicking up their heels, clapping, and spinning one another round.

Brogan turned and caught my expression.

"No' bad, eh?" he asked. I smiled and nodded my head. I was afraid if I opened my mouth I would squeal idiotically like Cassidy. I looked over and saw her wiping tears from her face. Oh, man, I wished she wouldn't do that. When she caught my eye she gave a great laughing sob and reached out to hug me. I was such a firmly wound bundle of emotion that I had to lock my jaw and swallow hard. We pulled away as the song ended, and my heart began doing that slamming thing in my chest again.

The crowd cheered and Brogan hollered McKale's name, waving his arms at him. I held my breath as McKale lowered his instrument and peered around the crowd, searching for the caller. As soon as he spotted him, Brogan motioned toward me. Cassidy stepped away, nearer to our parents, leaving me as the lone beacon for McKale's sights. His eyes moved slowly from his father… to me, and stuck there.

Later, I would ask Cassidy how long we stayed like that, just staring at one another across the field, and she swore it was only for a few seconds. It felt much, much longer to me, like forever. I schooled my face into its careful, expressionless pose and he seemed to do the same.

He stood, and as he made his way toward me in long, graceful strides, a hush dropped over the party. He towered over the other people, walking with purpose. The closer he got, the more apparent it became that he was gorgeously, blessedly *tall*. I pressed my lips together against the geeky grin that was trying so hard to appear.

McKale wore a dark green tunic with brown bottoms that went to his mid-calf, and his bare feet swished through the grass. His dark red hair hung in waves about his head. He had sideburns that turned into a thin beard running neatly along his jaw line down to a slightly pointed chin. His nose was straight and narrow and when he stopped in front of me I could see his eyes were hazel. I couldn't look away from him.

"This is Robyn, son," Brogan said.

He needn't introduce us because we hadn't taken our eyes from one another since locking gazes across the clearing. McKale inclined his head toward me. His expression had not changed, but his eyes searched my face with a pleasant, bashful curiosity.

"This is her father, Leon," Brogan continued, introducing my family. "Her mother, Cecelia. And their youngest girl, Cassidy." McKale gave a small bow of his head in greeting to each of them before turning back to face me, stepping closer. I got a whiff of something sweet just then, but I couldn't place the scent. A natural aromatic of some sort, distantly familiar.

"Very pleased to make yer acquaintance, Robyn." He spoke in a soft, lilted tenor.

I opened my mouth to say something amazingly intelligent, but what came out was a short burst of joyful laughter. The grin I'd tried to contain stretched across my face.

My laughter seemed to take him by surprise. I forced the smile away.

"I'm sorry," I said. "It's just that… you're so… tall."

Nearby little people gasped. A hot blush flooded my cheeks at the stupidity of my remark, and McKale's face darkened.

"Aye. That I am." He cleared his throat, looking away. An awkward silence fell, and I knew I'd screwed up, though I couldn't understand why. Sure, it had been a lame thing to say, but he acted like I'd insulted him or maybe I'd insulted his people. I felt terrible.

The music still played, but stray clan members were beginning to assemble around us. I opened my mouth, not sure of how to fix the moment, but McKale beat me to it.

"I'd best be returning." He motioned to the musicians who'd started a new song without him. "I bid you good evening." He gave me one last reluctant look, as if he'd been shamed, then he turned and bowed toward my family and walked swiftly away from us. My mouth fell open as I stared after him.

Brogan stepped up, smoothing his beard down several times.

"I'm afraid ye've found the boy's tender spot."

"What do you mean?" I asked.

"He's a tad sensitive about his height, is all."

My sister and I shared a shocked glance.

"I didn't mean it in a bad way," I told Brogan. "I mean, look how tall I am!"

He cocked an eyebrow as if it wasn't exactly something to be proud of. I felt myself frown.

"We Chaun men pride ourselves on being small of stature. I'm afraid he's had a hard time of it. Forgive the lad, please." People from the crowd stared at us. Brogan stepped away to shoo them, saying they'd have a chance to meet the guests after we got settled.

"Geez," Cassidy whispered to me. "He got all weird about being called *tall*? That's kinda… sad. Maybe he's like

Rudolph or something. I bet he can't join in any Leprechaun games."

She started to giggle at her own joke, but Mom elbowed her in the ribs.

"I can't believe I said that," I muttered, still staring out into the crowd. I couldn't even spot where Brogan had gone now. I looked pleadingly at my parents.

"He'll come around." Dad patted my shoulder. Mom nodded in agreement, but her face appeared distressed about how fast our first meeting had soured.

"He could have been a little nicer about it," Cassidy said.

"I think he's shy." I couldn't help but defend him, even though I was shaken by the brief introduction. Nobody could possibly understand how stressful that initial meeting had been for McKale and me.

A sudden cacophony of strange noise came from the field to our right. It sounded like swishing grass and stomping feet. And something else… bleating? One of the Leprechaun men hollered something and the crowd surged to get a look at the field. The musicians began playing faster and louder, giving each other amused, knowing glances.

"What's going on?" I asked.

"I've no clue," Mom said, keeping a wary eye on the field.

A single white, fattened sheep ran through the high grasses with something dangling off its back. Another sheep followed behind it. After a few beats an entire flock of sheep came barreling through the field, all with these strange wiggling little things attached to their tops. A great roar of laughter rose up from the majority of the crowd, while the older, bearded men of the clan shook their heads and pounded their fists, red in the faces.

"What in the world?" Dad murmured. He took a protective stance in front of us three girls and motioned us to step back. We backed up as far as we could against the building just as the herd of sheep came stomping into the clearing in front of us.

One of the little things jumped off of its sheep's back and ran right in our path. My eyes bugged out as I tried to comprehend what I was seeing. Cassidy screamed, dancing on her tip-toes as if it were a snake. Dad threw his head back in laughter.

"Is that… was that…?" I stammered. No freaking way. It looked and moved *exactly* like a man—a foot-tall man.

"I don't believe it," Mom said. "It's the Clourichaun making a grand entrance, same as they did in the tales of old."

"I thought you said some of them were normal sized!" I said.

Everywhere we looked miniature men were jumping off the backs of sheep, scurrying up on tables and dunking their heads into people's mugs or dancing little jigs. Once Cassidy and I got over our initial confusion we laughed at the spectacle. Some were climbing the Leprechaun men and sitting smugly on their shoulders or heads. Cassidy pointed to one who sat on a woman's shoulder and dove down into her cleavage, only to be pulled out and flicked away by her frowning male friend.

Leprechauns shooed the sheep out of the clearing, trying to herd them back into the direction from which they'd come. Cassidy elbowed me.

"McKale's looking at you!" She spoke through the side of her lips.

I spotted him sitting at one of the long benches on the far side, leaning back with his elbows on the table behind him. A dark-haired little Clourichaun sat straddling his shoulder. McKale quickly dropped his eyes when he saw us looking.

Without hesitation, I turned to my parents. "Be right back," I told them.

They nodded in agreement when they saw McKale. I started in his direction before I could lose my nerve. Cassidy caught up and walked by my side. McKale glanced up once and his eyes widened, but he looked back down again. I think the mini man was asking him something because he kept giving his head little shakes and nods. McKale had something sticking out of his mouth, like a large toothpick.

I weaved through the crowd and stopped, standing between his feet. He stared at my legs for a moment before timidly lifting his greenish-brown eyes to mine.

"I'm sorry I brought up your height," I told him, opting for openness. "To be honest, I meant it as a compliment. I'm glad you're taller than me. *Really* glad." *Okay, shut up now, Robyn.* I clasped my fingers together behind my back.

His face softened and he appeared embarrassed, eyes flickering around me. I became a little distracted by the man on his shoulder who hadn't stopped moving, trying to get my attention. At the moment I could have sworn he was pretending to do something naughty to McKale's ear. Cassidy's giggling confirmed it. McKale pulled his head to the side and his red eyebrows drew together. He pulled the little stick out of his mouth.

"Cut that out, cheeky bugger."

The little man gestured to us girls, then pointed at his

self. McKale sighed and tossed the stick in the grass.

"He wants to meet ye."

"Oh," I said, squatting a little to see him better. Being so close to McKale's face, I caught the flavorful scent again and recognized it this time. Licorice.

The Clourichaun looked no older than McKale, with a head full of curly brown hair. I smiled at him and said, "I'm Robyn."

He extended his arm and I put my fingertip in his hand, which he shook up and down, then to my amusement he kissed my finger. I heard him holler in a squeaky little voice.

"The name's Rock! Yer quite a looker, there, Robyn!"

"Wow," I laughed. "Thanks… *Rock*." I moved to the side. Cassidy shot me a nervous look when I beckoned her toward him. She leaned down, putting her hands on her knees and examined Rock with wonder.

"My name's Cassidy. I'm Robyn's sister."

He waved her closer, using his whole arm for the gesture. She leaned in, but he waved her closer still.

"Careful now," McKale warned.

"He won't bite, will he?" I asked.

"Somethin' akin to that," he mused.

When Cassidy got close enough, Rock grabbed her cheeks with his outstretched palms and pulled, pressing his whole face into her lips. I'd never seen her eyes so big before. I snorted out a laugh, and to my surprise Cassidy did not try to stand up or move away. She waited until Rock released her and then she beamed him a pretty smile. He pretended to grab his heart and tumble off McKale's shoulder to the table, dying of love sickness. Cass laughed like it was the funniest thing she'd ever seen. She had the sweetest, bubbly laugh.

Unfortunately I'd inherited my mother's strange, mostly-silent chortle.

McKale scratched his cheek. "Sorry 'bout that. He's a bit forward."

"He's so cute," Cassidy said. She sat down on the bench and Rock walked to her, putting his elbows on her shoulders and resting his head in his hands to gaze up at her, starstruck.

"Don't encourage 'im. Trust me. Ye won't think he's as cute full grown."

"That's right!" Rock yelled. "I'm even cuter!"

"You mean he won't stay this size?" I asked.

"Nah. All Chaun can shrink and grow."

"Even you?" Cassidy sounded as surprised as I felt. McKale nodded like it was no big deal. I pointed at Rock.

"You mean you can get *that* small?"

"Well, I suppose a tad bigger since I'm larger than 'im in actuality, but aye."

It took a second for me to comprehend all of his heavily accented words.

I sat down on the other side of McKale. I felt like I was making him nervous or something. He wouldn't meet my eyes for more than a brief second, and then he would find excuses to look elsewhere. He kept rubbing his hands on his pants and crossing his arms, then uncrossing them. I wanted to take his hand or touch him somehow to reassure him, but it was too soon for that. So instead I climbed up and sat on the table top, resting my feet on the bench next to where McKale sat.

He looked down at my feet, examining them so long I began to feel self-conscious about how big they were. At least my brown sandals were new and cute, bejeweled with cream flowers along the straps. He surprised me by reaching down and running a fingertip across my big toenail, then looking at his finger.

"How'd ye do that?" he asked, sounding fascinated. "Make it red, like?"

"Oh, um, it's called nail polish. It's a special type of paint. I can show you later, if you want." He nodded and looked back down at my feet while I gazed at his full head of red hair. I'd always pictured him as a brunette like me, but I liked this better. Only a guy would be lucky enough to have such natural color variations: shades of red with nutmeg brown undertones. Autumn colors. The world was so unfair.

Cassidy and Rock were watching us. Rock said something that made her stifle a laugh, but I couldn't make it out.

"May I?" McKale's imploring eyes were looking up at me and I realized he was motioning to my shoe.

"Sure, yeah." I slipped one off and he picked it up, turning it round and round to see the specimen from every angle.

"Have you ever seen flip-flops before?" Cassidy asked. McKale shook his head, feeling the strap. Then he held it on his outstretched hand and wrist, appearing to measure it. I worried that he'd scoff at the size nine, but he showed no reaction. He ran a finger over the imprint my foot made in the squishy sole, and I began to feel tingly from the indirect attention. I wiggled my toes absently.

"Go ahead then, mate!" shouted Rock. "Give the shoe a snog—ye know ye want to!"

I blushed and McKale blanched, slipping the flip-flop back on my foot and crossing his arms.

"Git," he mumbled toward our wee companion. Rock was undeterred by the insult.

After that, we sort of kept our attention on Cass and Rock who were quite the silly pair. He had to holler to make his voice heard over the raucous laughter and music around us.

"So you can get big, like us?" she asked her tiny admirer. He nodded. "Can you do it now?"

"Only for another kiss!"

Cassidy laughed, a glint in her eye. "My lips are too big. I almost suffocated you last time."

"Kiss me when I'm big!"

"My parents are standing right over there." But when we looked, they weren't there anymore. "Hey, where'd they go?" Cassidy and I both stood up and searched with our eyes. They were nowhere in the crowd. A short blast of tingling magic hit us at our backs and we spun around. There on the top of the table sat Rock, full-sized, limber legs crossed. Cass let out a little scream in surprise.

"Ladies," he said, inclining his curly head and flashing a cute grin.

I looked at McKale and caught him studying my face again. I gave him a small smile. To my surprise he flashed me a quick one in return before looking away again. It was the first time he'd smiled at me and it sent a buzz of warmth through my body.

Rock stepped nimbly down from the table, past McKale. The Clourichaun was my height, I couldn't help but notice. Rock bowed to me first before turning to my sister. He took Cassidy's hand and kissed her fingertips. Definitely a charmer. Then without asking, he leaned down and kissed her on the lips. She did not pull away. Instead she went up on her toes. Thankfully the kiss ended before I started to feel embarrassed, but it left Cassidy with a dreamy look on her face.

Her dream-state was quickly shattered when Brogan broke through the crowd, swinging his arms at Rock, who jumped back. Brogan's assault kept coming, landing punches anywhere he could on the Clourichaun. Rock cupped his hands over his crotch, laughing as he begged Brogan to take it easy. McKale shook his head and chuckled as his friend climbed up and over the table, escaping Brogan's wrath.

"What are you on about, old man?" Rock asked, extending his arms in question from the safety of the other side of the table. He had a mock-pained expression on his smooth face, underscored with amusement. McKale's father was pink in the cheeks and had his small hands balled into fists.

"Our guests have hardly been 'ere an hour and yer already making advances at their youngest? I think not! Keep your no-good hands to yerself and don't be causing trouble among us. Do ye hear?"

"Aye, crystal clear. I'll be a good lad. Promise."

Brogan gave a deep, barrel laugh. "You don't know how ta be good. Gather yer troublesome clan and leave us be. Go on!"

"All right then," Rock said with an easy shrug. Brogan eyed him with distrust and put his fists on his hips.

"I'd best be off, then. Night everyone." Rock bowed to us and put two fingers between his lips, ripping an ear-shattering whistle. With a wave of his arm the tiny Clourichaun came bounding over from their various places.

All of them but Rock had stayed small. They climbed him, some going up to his shoulders and others swinging on handfuls of his tunic. He gave Cass a stealthy wink before ghosting away into the field with the others. Once satisfied, Brogan turned to us.

"Please forgive his indiscretion. Their ways are not our own. 'Tis getting late and I know yer both travel-weary. I've shown yer folks to their rooms, and I'll show the two of ya to yers as well. We'll be having more festivities on the morrow. Everyone's itchin' to meet ye."

"Thank you," I said.

McKale stood, rubbing his palms down his pants again.

"Good night, McKale," I said.

"G'night, then, Robyn." He watched my face.

I liked when he really looked at me, as if he didn't want to stare, but his eyes would get stuck against his will. When he became aware he tore his gaze away and scratched his cheek self-consciously.

As Cassidy and I left to follow Brogan, clan eyes turned toward us. I realized then that nobody approached us while we sat with McKale, out of respect. I smiled and nodded at the people as we passed, excited to find our room and return tomorrow to meet them.

I peeked back at the shy guy who was staring at the ground, deep in thought. Lots of girls didn't care for the quiet type. Even Cassidy, who was a smart girl in so many ways, often lost all proof of intelligence when it came to guys. Most girls I knew wanted boys like Rock: the confident and outgoing "bad" boys. But there was something endearing to me about McKale's quiet, introverted demeanor.

I looked forward to gently cracking his shell and seeing

what lay hidden underneath. We had to gain one another's trust before we could bind. I welcomed the challenge.

FOUR

WE FOUND MOM AND Dad coming out of one of the bungalow rooms.

"We were just looking for you girls," Mom said.

"Are the accommodations satisfactory?" Brogan asked.

"Oh yes," Mom answered. "Everything is wonderful. I wish we could stay up later to enjoy the party."

Brogan assured her with a scrunched-faced grin. "Rest up. Things are winding down fer the night. There'll be plenty festivals to come this summer."

My parents gave him an appreciative smile. They both had circles under their eyes and looked like they might collapse.

"You girls okay?" Mom asked. She searched my eyes.

"We're fine," I said, giving her a hug. "Don't worry."

"Enjoy yourselves and get some rest tonight." Dad hugged me next, squeezing me extra long before whispering goodnight.

I waved as they went back into their room. Brogan led Cassidy and I to another bungalow and opened the door for us.

"'Tis a guest room," he explained. "Ye have yer own

washroom over there. Someone'll come around each day to refresh the water and clear out the waste. Of course, Robyn, this room is only temporary since ye'll share McKale's abode after the binding, whenever that may be."

My face lit on fire as I nodded my understanding.

Cassidy poked me in the back, but I refused to look at her. She was, no doubt, holding back her humor about Brogan's frankness regarding sharing McKale's "abode," a thought that thumped around inside my head. Soon I would share a room with a boy and… and… *ack!*

I cleared my throat and thanked Brogan.

"My pleasure, it is. Let me know if ye be needing anything further."

We stepped into the room and he bowed low before leaving us. Cassidy and I looked around the space for a moment until we knew Brogan was far enough away, then Cass whispered, "I can't believe it! This is awesome!"

In a moment of jet-lagged, expounded relief, we grabbed each other and jumped up and down in a circle, giggling and carrying on as quietly as we could. We squeed and stamped our feet a few seconds more before gaining control and taking deep breaths. I would've never behaved that way in front of another soul.

"What do you think of McKale?" she asked. "Don't you think he's too quiet?"

I shrugged. "He doesn't even know us yet. But I prefer quiet over someone who's a loose cannon anyway, no offense."

She let her head fall back, unoffended. "Ah, Rock. What a nice surprise. I like Ireland."

Now that we were calm I checked out our room, which

was lit by a gas lamp, like a lantern. The room was smaller than mine at home. Our luggage was by the door, including the storage bin for McKale.

There were two small beds close to the ground. I squatted down next to them. They didn't have mattresses, exactly. They looked like giant, fluffy pillows encased in wooden sides. I hoped they weren't full of straw and lice like the beds I'd read about in the Dark Ages. I pressed on one of the makeshift mattresses and was pleasantly surprised to feel it was full of downy feathers. Lifting it, I saw that underneath was a thick layer of sheep wool. Cassidy flopped down onto her bed and sank in.

"Oh. My. *Heaven*," she moaned. "It's not very easy to move around in, but you don't really need to." She tried and failed to sit up, being sucked into the softness. "Help!" She flailed her arms, laughing. I grasped her hands and pulled her out of the bed.

Next we peeked at the washroom, which was partitioned from the sleeping area with a hanging drape.

"Oh," Cassidy stated.

Oh. That about covered it. No indoor plumbing. An oval wooden tub sat against the wall with a wooden bucket overhead. We'd have to kneel or sit in the tub and pull a lever to release a stream of water. Next to the tub was another wooden bucket, which I could only assume was for squatting. It had a lid next to it. And then there was a raised basin full of fresh water.

Cassidy scowled. "Geez, the Leprechauns really need to get up to speed."

"This looks way worse than camping." I was not looking forward to this adjustment.

"They talk funny here," she said. "They sound different from the Irish people we met."

"Yeah," I agreed. "They sound a couple centuries behind or something."

"Guess that's what happens when you live in the boonies with no plumbing."

"Come on." I pulled her from the bathroom area. "Let's go to bed."

I changed into pajamas and felt butterflies at the thought of McKale.

"Do you think Rock will come again tomorrow?" Cassidy asked, sliding into her bed.

"I don't know. I wouldn't if I were him. Brogan seemed pretty pissed."

She crinkled her nose with disappointment and I fiddled with the lamp until I figured out how to turn it off. Cass hadn't been exaggerating about the bed. The softness had a way of dredging the day's anxiety from my muscles and lulling me to sleep, content. For the first time in eleven years I had a real face to imagine as I drifted into slumber. And I liked it.

✤

When I woke, the soft light through our window told me it was early. I struggled out of the snuggly bed and got ready as quietly as I could. Cassidy was still asleep when I slipped out the door in my shorts and flip-flops.

The sun was still only peeping through the trees. A few little people bustled past, nodding at me with curiosity and saying, "G'morning, miss" as they went about their work. A couple of the younger guys stared wide-eyed at my bare legs, making me feel like a naked giraffe or something.

"Excuse me," I said to a female with a basket full of eggs. "Can you tell me where I might find McKale?"

"Aye," she said. "He's in the Shoe House. But 'tis early for them still."

She pointed in the direction of the biggest building and went on her way.

The Shoe House was an odd structure, somewhat like a barn with large openings on either end, but nicer like a meeting hall with a steepled roof. I had to cover my nose when I peeked through the doors, though. It smelled gross—faintly putrid with floral undertones. This must've been where the tanners made leather.

Nobody was inside yet. At one end was a giant wooden barrel with a crank, and scattered through the room were stations for differing stages of the tanning process and shoe making. Racks of fresh, soft animal pelts lined the walls.

"Oh!" came a voice from behind me.

I spun to face a startled little man with breadcrumbs in his beard. "Hi," I said.

"Er… hallo. My apologies, miss. I'm not accustomed, ye see, 'tis not usual fer women folk to be in the Shoe House."

The smile fell from my face and I quickly stepped out of the entrance, back into the sunshine.

"Sorry," I said. "I didn't know." I tried not to feel offended, but geez.

Someone else approached now and my insides leapt at the sight of McKale, dark red hair hanging damp about his face. He blinked several times.

"Och, Mac, yer not being a superstitious old bag, are ye?" McKale asked him.

The man's cheeks reddened. "Certainly not. As I said, I'm just no' accustomed to seein' a female here, is all." Mac huffed and gave me a polite nod before disappearing into the Shoe House.

When I looked back at McKale he was totally staring at my legs. In a good way, not the giraffe way. Which gave me a nice feeling.

"Sorry," I said, making his eyes jump up to mine. "I didn't know I wasn't supposed to come here. I was curious about where you worked."

He shrugged. "'Tis no rule against it. Just habit or tradition, I suppose. Did ye want to look inside?"

"Oh, no. I don't know." I smoothed the hair back on my ponytail, nervous and embarrassed by my apparent faux pas. "I don't want to get you in trouble. Or curse the Shoe House with my girliness."

He kept a polite expression while his clear hazel eyes studied my face. I hoped he knew I was joking.

"Ye don't look like bad luck to me," he said in a soft voice. "Come on. In we go."

I bit my lip and followed him into the open building to the far side with the gigantic drum barrel on its side. Next to it was a ladder. Without thinking I covered my nose against the strange smell permeating the area—not rotten exactly, but definitely unpleasant. When McKale turned I dropped my hand.

"Does it smell bad to ye?" he asked.

"A little," I admitted.

A tiny grin traced his mouth. "Ye should get a whiff of

the main tanning house. It's kept clear on the other side o' the property. That's where the lads do the slaughter and skinning and soaking—" He broke off when he saw the grimace on my face. "Aye. My apologies. Here we extract the essential oils from flower petals usin' steam to make tanning liquor." He pointed at some barrels and contraptions around the room. He went on to explain the process with words like "thinned, dried, conditioned, and buffed" but I was lost to it all.

"You guys kill… cows?"

"Deer," he said. "And naught goes to waste."

I wasn't a vegetarian, but the thought of all that "fresh meat" on the premises was still unsettling.

Little men were starting to trickle in now. Some gawked and nudged each other when they saw McKale and me. I sent McKale a worried glance, and he bent his head toward the drum barrel for me to follow. On the other side of it we were out of sight from the men. McKale led me forward and stood behind me, pointing at the parts. On top was the opening. We could both reach it, but the little men would have to use the ladder.

"The skins soak in the tanning liquor and we crank the barrel… here, give it a go."

I couldn't get it to move at first, so I threw my weight into it until it gained momentum. Once it got going it was kind of fun. I got a bit carried away until I wondered what McKale must have been thinking. I became suddenly aware of his presence close behind me. I felt my ponytail lift and I stopped cranking. A slow turn of my head caught McKale letting the hair fall from his hand. He'd been smelling my hair. And now he wore an expression like a boy who'd been caught with his hand in the cookie jar.

It probably should've been creepy, but the small gesture of intimacy made my scalp tingle in a not-at-all creepy way.

He stepped away, his cheekbones pink. "I... yer hair... how do ye get the scent into it?"

I had to smile. "It's this stuff called shampoo. It's liquid soap and it's scented."

"Ah." He looked confused.

I remembered now the bar of soap in our bathroom had been unscented, but I assumed they knew how to make scented soap if they'd wanted. A little man came around the corner and gasped out loud. He jumped back and shouted something in Gaelic when he saw me, then skittered away. McKale's eyebrows went up.

"I should go," I said.

"I'll show ye the back way out."

He led me the opposite direction from where I came in, and we stopped at the door. My heart gave a nervous sputter as we faced each other. He held my eyes and scratched his cheek.

"Robyn?"

Oh, my. The way he said my name...

"Yeah?"

He didn't respond. His eyes dropped and roamed the ground as if he were struggling for words. And then with a forward rush of air he said, "Ye should know... a forced binding is not the way of our people."

Okay...? Thoughts stuttered through my mind. "It's not the usual way of my people either," I said. "At least not the forced part."

Magical boys and girls were usually given a chance to get to know one another, starting from childhood, before any sort of agreement was made by their parents. What we had was different. I wondered if he had any idea we'd been set up by a Faerie.

I wanted to assure him I wasn't a fan of our exact predicament either, but the words wouldn't come. We were still strangers, and I couldn't read him yet.

He finally looked at me again, a plea in his light eyes. Sudden panic struck my chest. Did he want out of this? If McKale didn't want to go through with the binding, would the Fae still come after *my* family? I would do anything in my power to keep them safe, but if he refused, what could I do? He needed to know what we were up against.

"Look, McKale, I understand how you feel, but a Faerie claimed me to bind with you when I was a baby. It's not something that we—I—can easily back out of."

His lips pursed and his head dropped. He scratched his cheek again. This was coming out all wrong.

"I'm not saying I don't want to—I mean, not right this second, but if you don't want to, then… *Crap.*" I shook my head. "I'm not making sense."

"They're forcing you?" he asked. "The Fae?"

I exhaled. "Yes."

And now he looked sad, or hurt, or maybe worried. The pressure between us was awful. I should have never let myself imagine it would be as natural and easy as my parents' getting together had been. They'd been forced to meet, but they had other options if they hadn't liked one another. It sucked not to have a choice. But was I really so bad that he'd want to call it quits before he got to know me? Or maybe we were having communication problems. My hands were shaking, so I crossed my arms.

"*McKale!*" someone called from inside the Shoe House.

"I must go," he whispered. His eyes met mine at the same time as the warm morning sun shifted through a break in the trees.

I had so much to say, but the only thing that came out was, "Will I see you tonight?"

"Aye." He gave me an apologetic look before stooping to disappear through the open doors.

I spent the rest of the day pressing down paranoia that wanted to grow. Underneath it was a seed of hatred for the Fae. Such emotion was futile and would only cause bitterness, and yet the roots had sprouted.

"Maybe it was a misunderstanding," Cassidy said at lunch, though she didn't sound certain. "You guys will work it out when you talk tonight."

"Yeah, maybe." I chewed my grainy roll. "We just need to get to know each other. Right?"

"Mm-hm." Cassidy glared across the field to where McKale walked, head down.

I knew she was thinking the worst. That he didn't want me. And that hurt more than I cared to admit.

FIVE

THE PARTY WAS IN full swing when we made it out that night. My eyes did a quick scan of the clearing until finding McKale among the musicians. As we entered the gathering, people began to approach and introduce themselves. I'd met a few people that day, but most had been busy working.

I stood with my family, shaking hands or hugging each male and female who bounded up to greet us. Brogan stood nearby, receiving claps on the back and hearty handshakes of congratulations from the men. I'd never be able to remember all of the names just yet, but they were all so friendly that my face hurt from smiling by the time we were through.

We found an open spot at a table near the musicians and sat, watching McKale on his fiddle and the people dancing. Other Irish instruments were played: wooden flutes, tin whistles, and even a small harp. McKale caught my eye between songs and held it for a few beats before giving me a bashful grin, turning me all toasty warm and confused inside. Maybe I'd made too much of our conversation that morning. Maybe he'd just been giving me an out if I wanted it. Cass saw the exchange and bumped my ankle with her own.

Across from us, Dad took a sip from his wooden mug

and slapped a hand to the table, shaking his head before letting out a "Woo!" He leaned over the table and whispered, "Girls, do *not* drink the moonshine!" And then he took another drink.

"It'll put hair on your chest," Mom said, patting Dad's pec.

"Ew." Cassidy pulled a face.

Two Little Men with short blond beards approached Cassidy and me, asking us to dance. We looked at one another, hesitating.

"I don't really know how…" Cassidy stammered.

"Och, not to worry!" said the one closest to her. "We'll teach ye the steps."

"Sure, why not," I said. We'd most likely make fools of ourselves, but we were going to spend the summer with these people and we needed to make an effort. Better to look like fools than snobs. The men held out their small hands and we took them, allowing ourselves to be led onto the "dance floor," which was essentially a circle of stamped down grass.

We lined up with the others and took their hands. I peered over at the musicians and McKale gave me a slight nod of approval as he raised the fiddle under his chin.

The dance required us to skip to the side, then skip to the other side. Our partners were supposed to spin us around, which was funny because we had to squat down and pivot. By the end, we'd gotten the hang of it and we were laughing and breathless. The song ended and everyone cheered. It took a moment to realize they were cheering for Cassidy and me. When I glanced at McKale again he was half grinning, the fiddle resting on his knee.

Cassidy and I smiled at the people and one another, but

declined a second dance because we were thirsty. She and I headed to the corner of the field where a Little Man stood on a stool scooping drinks from barrels with a fire roaring at his back.

"Fine dancing!" he said when we approached. "What will ye be drinking? We got ale, mead, and a bit o' fire water."

Fire water sounded bad. It had to be the moonshine Dad warned us about.

"What's mead?" Cassidy asked.

"Fermented honey," I said. "You'll learn all about it when you read *Beowulf* next year."

She didn't look excited.

"Refreshing after a good dance, it is." He filled two wooden goblets and handed them over. We thanked him and tasted the mead. There was slight bitterness from the alcohol and a light, sweet aftertaste. I expected carbonation, but it was flat. All together not bad. He smiled at our approval and refilled our mugs before we walked away.

As we made our way back to the table I wondered what time it was. I'd always used my phone for the time, but I didn't bother to turn it on here. No signal. No electricity to charge it.

The crescent moon was high in the night sky and there seemed to be a million more stars than there were back home. I felt content and sleepy, especially after my first glass of mead.

I wasn't the only one who was tired and still jet-lagged. We hadn't been out there very long before our parents retired for the night. I guess the firewater did Dad in.

Cass and I stood for a while and clapped to the music. I was admiring McKale's swift movements of his bow across the instrument until someone from behind tapped our shoulders.

"Hide me from Brogan, would ya?" asked Rock in full form.

"Hey!" Cassidy's face lit up and she bounced on her heels.

"Hallo again, gorgeous."

And with that she was mush. In all honesty I couldn't blame her. There was something fun about being in his mischievous presence. The three of us stood there bantering at the far edge of the clearing.

"So, what's your real name?" I asked him. "It can't be Rock."

"Nah. Pop used to say me head was full o' rocks and just as hard." He knocked on his skull for effect and Cassidy smiled. "The real name's Ronan, but 'tis far too proper."

When Cass giggled I rolled my eyes at her. She lifted her hands and mouthed, "*What?*"

Before I could respond, a burst of magic stronger than any I'd ever felt flashed through the field. It sizzled my skin and I almost lost my balance. Cassidy fell back onto the bench. The music stopped and people ran, shouting about Fae and the Portal.

Rock whispered something in a sneering tone under his breath and took off.

Cassidy hurried back to my side and we grasped hands, freaked out as we stared in the direction of the field where the Clourichaun Men had arrived last night. I watched in horror as an invisible knife seemed to stab the air and slice downward to the ground, opening a dark slit between our worlds. I looked to McKale, but he simply stared at the portal like everyone else, his instrument dangling from his fingers as he stood.

"*Pssst!*" A hissing call came from the woods beside us, not ten feet away. Cassidy and I looked to see Rock stick his curly head around a tree trunk and urgently wave my sister to him. She ignored my efforts to cling to her fingers, letting go and running.

"I'll be right back!" she whispered.

I stayed where I was and crossed my arms, chilled to the bone. I was too terrified by the unnatural sight of the portal to worry about what Rock might be up to.

A murmur swept through the crowd and people lowered their heads in reverent greeting as five beings came through the portal. I couldn't make them out completely, but I was awestruck. They moved in our direction, two smaller creatures flying around them.

Whispering stopped as they got closer, and tension filled the surrounding air. I was able to see them now—four males and one female, though the faces were still unclear from this distance. The winged creatures flew ahead of them and began to flit around above the Leprechauns, snatching off hats and dropping them on other people's heads, even pulling hair. They had naked green bodies with fat bellies, and they cackled in high-pitched voices that hurt my ears. I heard someone near me whisper, "*Bloody pixies.*" Everyone looked annoyed, but nobody spoke out against the pixies' behavior.

A little woman sidled up next to me, seeming terrified with big eyes and hands on her cheeks.

"Can the Fae just come and go whenever they please?" I whispered to her.

"Aye. We cannot stop them."

I looked back toward the Fae, who had reached the edge of the field now, and my abdomen tightened. Each of the four men had long, shimmering hair of metallic colors that fell to their shoulders: silver, gold, bronze, and copper. Their skin gave off eerie, iridescent glows. Their bodies and faces were symmetrical to the point of being unnatural. Too sharp. Too perfect. Like life-sized animated dolls.

It was the petite Fae girl at their side who stole my attention. Her tiny oval face was made of delicate features that would break any girl's heart with envy. I was mesmerized by her big, almond shaped eyes of icy blue and her round, innocent flower of a mouth. Her hair was amazing: long, past her hips, straight and thick without a single hair out of place. The color was like white gold: the ultimate platinum blonde. I was utterly humbled by her beauty. All of the Chaun were on their feet now.

Brogan stepped forward through the crowd and bowed at the waist.

"Good evening, sires and miss. We welcome ye. To what do we owe this pleasure?"

"This is to be a special summer for the Leprechauns." It was the bronze-haired male who spoke. His voice reverberated with power. "Has the betrothed of your son arrived as sanctioned by Lady Martineth?"

My stomach plummeted and for a split second I contemplated diving under the table. I hadn't expected the Fae to show. I did *not* want their attention, and I suddenly yearned for my parents' presence. The entire field was stiff. Music had stopped and everyone peered around, large-eyed, unmoving, eyes stopping on me. I looked at McKale, who stood tall. His eyes flashed to me for one seemingly paranoid second, then turned back toward the Fae, rapt. I peered toward the trees and found the faces of Cass and Rock peeking out from the shadows, watching.

"Why, y-yes, she has arrived," Brogan confirmed. "'Tis a special time, indeed. We hope the binding will commence soon."

"Very well. We bring goodwill from our realm, Brogan of the Leprechaun."

"Oh, thank ye." Brogan bowed again. "We are very much obliged."

"Should there not be music and dancing on this momentous occasion? Please, commence the festivities."

The bronze-haired man snapped his fingers and the pixies flew to him. He looked toward the Faerie girl, as if seeking her approval, but her freaky eyes were busy scanning the Chaun people. Brogan signaled the musicians who exchanged glances before raising their instruments. All except McKale, who had moved further into the clearing away from the musicians, appearing dumbfounded and dazzled. He'd left his fiddle next to the stump. The other musicians began a song.

Watching McKale, a knot slowly formed in my stomach. I followed his stare to the Faerie girl who was intently watching him in return. The knot grew larger and curled inside of me.

The four Fae men dispersed as the music began and the girl drifted seamlessly through the clearing, straight toward my betrothed. I watched, frozen, as she approached and stopped in front of him, not ten feet away from me.

"It has been too long, McKale of the Chaun." Her voice was a soft caress.

He bowed his head and said, "Indeed, Khalistah."

She held out a dainty hand and McKale hesitated. When he took her fingers in his palm, he shuddered and closed his eyes, but it wasn't pain he was experiencing. His expression was euphoric. The knot in my stomach exploded like hot lightening. Warning sirens blared in my head. Every cell in my body desperately wanted to get him away from her. She gave the smallest smile of satisfaction before releasing his hand.

The Fae girl, Khalistah, looked past him to where I stood. Her lips tightened as her eyes took in every detail, from my flip-flops to the top of my head, which surely had stray hairs and frizz.

"This is her?"

McKale, who didn't seem to want to take his entranced attention from the Fae girl, turned enough to verify that I stood there, and confirmed who I was with a nod.

"Wait," he said, blinking when she stepped around him and moved closer to me. A small crowd formed, their faces worried.

Khalistah's eyes reached the top of my tall frame.

"I didn't realize human women could grow so *large*." There were a few gasps from the crowd as Khalistah laid down the ultimate insult by Leprechaun standards. I already felt like a gigantic oaf here, so the smack-talk was unnecessary. She continued to speak to McKale about me, right to my face.

"You will bind with her?" she asked in a distasteful way.

I looked to McKale, imploring, but he appeared dazed. He blinked again and swallowed hard.

"I will do my duty for the clan," he said quietly. Bile rose in my throat.

"Hmph," Khalistah breathed.

Yeah. I didn't like her. And I wasn't his biggest fan right now either.

I clamped my teeth down hard. As visions of violence danced in my head, I had to remind myself that this Fae witch had the power to curse my family and me.

I didn't feel so good.

"Excuse me," I said. With a humble bow of my head, I turned on my heels, and pressed my way through the crowd. I heard the tinkle of her laughter behind me. Onlookers gawked as I passed, picking up speed as I headed toward our bungalow. I contemplated going to my parents, but decided I'd tell them everything in the morning. Right now I needed to be alone to think this through.

Something was going on with my betrothed and a beautiful, cruel Faerie. I wouldn't go so far as to say he was in love with her. It looked more like infatuation. He'd *better* not be in love with her. Infatuations were bad enough.

Could she be the reason he'd brought up our binding the way he did this morning?

Acid burned the back of my throat. How was I supposed to compete with *that*?

Wait, compete? I didn't want to compete for a guy! It went against my basic morals. If a guy didn't want me, then screw him. But this was different. I couldn't just walk away from this like some silly crush in high school. My family's lives depended on McKale and I together. If this binding didn't work out, the Fae wouldn't care about the reasons.

I walked into my bungalow and shut the door a little too hard. I kicked my flip-flops across the dark room. Then I pushed down my shorts and yanked off my blouse, throwing them to the floor and falling into the squishy bed in my tank top and panties. I curled up small, and my bra dug into my sides, but I was too ticked to move. I willed the bile back down to my stomach.

I wanted to go home.

I regretted leaving Cassidy in the trees with Rock, and I hoped she'd come to me soon. I felt stupid and out of place here. I needed my sister.

The memory of McKale kissing the Faerie's hand kept resurfacing, making me ill and something else—something bitter. Jealousy. He'd seemed so... overwhelmed or something.

After seeing that, I felt apprehensive of what else I might find out about McKale. I was scared of his possible secrets and past. But getting to know him was the only chance I had in this battle. Khalistah had taken the first round, but I wouldn't go down without a fight.

Unfortunately, I had a feeling Faeries wouldn't fight fair.

SIX

I HADN'T FULLY CALMED yet when I heard voices and the door swooshed opened.

"Robyn!"

I exhaled with relief at the sound of Mom's voice.

"It's so dark," Cassidy whispered. "Robyn? Are you in here?"

"I'm here," I replied. I wiggled around until I was able to push myself up on the bed with my legs crossed. Cassidy stumbled through the dark and sat next to me while my mom found the oil lamp and turned it on. She wore flannel pajama pants and a pullover fleece. Her face was tight with worry as she came and sat next to me. Having both of them was a comfort, a balm for my agitation.

"Why didn't you wake me? Cassidy says there were Fae about? I was so hard asleep I didn't even sense them. Did they hurt you?"

"Not exactly. But... I think there's something going on with one of them and McKale."

My mom sucked in a shocked breath. "*No.*"

"Freaky Fae girl," Cassidy brooded. "What did she say to you? I couldn't hear but I could tell it was something bitchy."

Mom glared at her and Cassidy amended. "I mean something not nice. I wanted to run after you, but Rock held me back—"

"Rock was there?" Mom asked.

"Yeah, he was hiding, though." Cass looked at me. "I'm sorry I didn't come right away. I really wanted to, but Rock made me wait until the Fae left."

I shook my head. "It's okay. It was smart of him not to let you draw attention to yourself."

Even Mom agreed. "What else happened?"

The last thing I wanted to do was rile up my mom and sister. I wouldn't tell them about how Khalistah called me "large," but they did need to know the basics of what was going on, and what I was up against if I was going to attempt to build a healthy relationship with McKale.

"She asked if McKale really intended to bind with me and he said he had to do his duty for the clan."

Cassidy's eyebrows flew together. "He called you a *duty*? Ouch."

"That's what this is, Cass," I reminded her. "It's a duty for both of us."

"Yeah, but look at you. He should be happy and honored that he gets to bind with a hottie like you. I'd just hoped… you know."

We were all quiet. My parents' marriage had been arranged, but they'd met first as teens and got to know each other through letters. What started as a duty became a joy they both shared.

"This is dangerous territory, girls," Mom said. "Where the Fae are involved, one can never be too cautious. Tomorrow we will sit down with Brogan and McKale, and have a family discussion. McKale is only human, no matter how ancient his magical blood may be. The touch of a Fae manipulates the human mind. A single kiss from her could make McKale obsess. If a human fully gives themselves to a Fae, they are lost to anything but that Faerie. They become mindless slaves. We need to find out what we're dealing with."

I trembled inside remembering how McKale reacted to such a small touch from her.

"I don't think he's, like, *done* anything with her," I said. "I don't know. He seemed pretty normal until she showed up."

"Yeah, and then he couldn't take his eyes off her," Cassidy added.

"Faeries can be mesmerizing," Mom said. "But don't jump to any conclusions yet. Let's hope they've done nothing more than share simple touches, though even those are dangerous." She sighed. "They're capable of ruining our lives with no thought or remorse, so do not say a word to the Fair Folk unless you are politely responding. Use great care. Especially you, Cassidy."

"But—"

"No buts!" Mom's voice boomed and her face was fierce. "You don't tangle with them, child. Ever. I don't care if they anger you. Bite your tongue off if you have to. Understand?"

"Fine, okay, but McKale better get his act together because I *will* give him a piece of my mind."

"I'll handle McKale," I said.

Cassidy crossed her arms and gave me a "yeah right" glare that I ignored.

"Get some sleep, girls. We'll deal with this in the morning."

She stood and kissed the tops of our heads, waiting for us to climb under the covers before blowing out the flame and leaving. Cass rustled around, getting comfortable.

"What did Rock say when you were in the woods together?" I whispered.

"He was warning me to stay away from the Fae."

"That's it? Did he say anything about that Fae girl and McKale?"

"No. Nothing. He told me that his clan wasn't even supposed to be seen by them. I asked him what his clan did that was so bad and he said the Clourichaun have always liked to have too much fun, and the Fae are overly sensitive about their rules being broken."

"Hm. That's probably true, but I'm sure there's a lot more to it."

"Yeah." We were both quiet for a while before she asked, "You don't think Freaky Fae Girl is going to be a problem, do you?"

I did, but I didn't want to admit it. "I don't know what to think. I'm trying not to worry anymore until I talk to McKale tomorrow."

"When will you give him all of his presents and stuff?"

Ugh. The bin.

"I don't know. I can't think about that yet. Let's just go to sleep."

It didn't take long for Cassidy to doze off. I lay there for a while trying not to think about the Freaky Fae Girl. I liked Cass's name for her. The FFG. It was nice and ugly.

No matter which way I looked at the situation,

something very unsettling was going on.

I thought about the bin of gifts. At this point it would be completely awkward and uncomfortable to give it to him. He couldn't possibly appreciate them yet. I would give McKale the presents if and when we earned each other's trust.

I could tell it was really early when I woke. Our room was still dark and my head throbbed with tiredness. But now that I was awake I couldn't fall back asleep. I struggled out of the bed and slipped on shorts, flip-flops, and a pullover hoodie. The fresh morning air might do me some good.

I quietly left the room and walked toward the clearing, dewy grass dampening my toes. Busy birds chattered and a few crickets still chirped. Halfway to the clearing I thought I heard music. I stopped and strained my ears, listening. A violin. I headed in that direction, heart quickening.

The sound led me to the woods. As I got closer and could make out the sound of the sad ballad, so beautifully wrought, goose bumps prickled my skin. I slowed, entering the trees, and saw him sitting on the ground against one of the larger trunks. His eyes were closed as he played the heartbreaking melody. When it ended he lowered the instrument and peered over his shoulder. His eyes only met mine for a moment before looking away.

Apparently the song fit his mood.

I moved forward and sat down near him in the dirt and fallen leaves. He didn't move, just hung his wrists over his knees, the violin and bow dangling from his fingers. I picked apart a leaf into tiny particles. What I wanted most from him was the truth.

"Do you love her?" *Please say no.*

He looked up at me, appearing startled by the forward question.

"No. I suppose not, exactly. She's…"

"Beautiful?"

"Well, there's that, yes. But 'tis more than that." The words sounded as if they were being pulled out against his will. He wasn't comfortable sharing, but this was necessary. We needed to talk.

"Go on," I urged.

He sighed and swallowed. "When I was a wee lad, I dreamed of running away. I didn't understand why I had to be different. Not just my height, but also that I was bound to someone while the other lads were choosing lasses of their own free will. No offense." He looked at me. When I shrugged, he continued. "But when Khalistah would come, she made me forget about it all."

I pushed aside the nagging jealousy and hurt feelings that he hadn't been looking forward to meeting me. "So, you're saying she's nice to you?"

"In her own way. When she is, 'tis real, not born of obligation."

Ouch. First of all, I had a hard time believing anything from her was "real," but I was more bugged by the obligation comment.

"You think I'm being nice to you out of obligation?"

"I don't rightly know."

"Well, I'm not."

"Robyn." He sighed and set down his instrument,

moving his hands over his hair. "Ye don't have to say that. Ye told me yerself that the Fae are makin' ye bind wit' me."

I scooted onto my knees in front of him, needing him to see my eyes and understand me.

"McKale, I only found out about the Fae's involvement while I was traveling here. I didn't know before that, and I grew up thinking about you. I've looked forward to meeting you since I was six-years-old—"

A derisive laugh burst out of him, cutting me off and taking me by surprise. I sat back on my heels. "You don't believe me?"

He shook his head at the ground. "I believe ye want to keep yer family safe from the Fae, and I can respect that. Ye do no' have to pretend."

He was so jaded. It made my heart ache.

"McKale, you were the one who brought it up about how your clan doesn't usually force bindings. How was I supposed to feel?" He opened his mouth to say something, but I kept going. "Look. It sucks that we're being forced, and maybe I'm being naïve, but I want to make the best of this, don't you?" When he didn't answer, I asked, "Do you want me to leave? Go back home?"

"Are ye ready to leave so soon?" The look he gave me was tough, but I could sense the hurt underneath.

"No." This was frustrating. "But I was ready to leave last night. I wasn't feeling very welcome."

"Has the clan not welcomed ye openly?"

"I meant welcomed by *you*."

He dropped his eyes again, touching the smooth wood of his violin.

"Forgive me," he whispered. "I…"

Before he could finish we heard Brogan calling him. McKale sighed and we both pushed to our feet. I wiped debris from my bottom and followed McKale out to the clearing. Brogan uncrossed his arms and softened when he saw me.

"Top o' the morning to you, Robyn."

No, he did not just say that. Cass was going to flip when I told her.

"Good morning, Brogan."

"Yer father's requestin' that we have a discussion first thing this morning. We'll break our fast soon after."

Break our fast? Oh, my gosh—*breakfast!* Another cute thing to make Cass happy. The seriousness on Brogan's face kept me from smiling as he turned and headed back in the direction of the huts with McKale and me following. Before we got there, my family came walking out. Cassidy hadn't even bothered to change out of her pajamas for the family meeting.

Brogan led us all to the end of a row of tables under a thin canopy. A palpable tension banded around our group. Brogan and McKale sat together on one side of the table. When I came around the other side to be with my family, I caught the not-so-friendly look on Dad's face as I sat next to him. Uh-oh.

McKale and his father made quite the pair. Brogan sat up tall and McKale slightly slumped, as if he didn't want to loom too much higher than the older man. They both propped their forearms on the table and linked their fingers in the exact same way. Brogan looked up at his son.

"The Masons are concerned about yer commitment to this pairing, and rightly so. Last night was the first time I'd ever noticed the interaction between ye and the Shoe Mistress. Have ye compromised yerself, son?"

The Shoe Mistress? What the heck did that mean? And I squirmed a little at the question about being "compromised." Yuck.

"My commitment to the clan has never wavered, Father." McKale's voice was quiet and careful. "I cannot ignore the Shoe Mistress when she speaks to me, or deny taking her hand when she offers it. Ye know we cannot slight their kind."

A sarcastic cough sounded from Cassidy at the other end of the bench.

"McKale, dear." Mom reached across the table and patted his hands. He lifted his eyes to her with politeness. "We all want this to work out. As for Robyn's father and myself, we are mostly concerned that the two of you will be *happy*. That means there can be no future… *relations*"—insert cringing from me here—"with this Fae, no matter how great or small."

McKale nodded and lowered his eyes as if humiliated.

Brogan clapped his hands together and puffed out his chest. "Now that we've cleared that up, when can we expect the binding ceremony to take place? The Summer King's mistress will want to be notified."

Gee, no pressure or anything. McKale and I shared an embarrassed look before both staring down at the table again. Dad cleared his throat next to me.

"Robyn will turn eighteen in less than a month's time. We would prefer if they had at least that long to get to know one another."

Brogan's tense brow showed that he worried the

timeframe was excessive, but he nodded his agreement anyhow.

"Very well, then. Please accept my apologies for the unpleasantness of last eve. Surprise portal openings never bode well. They usually occur but twice a year—once for ordering shoes and once for delivery of the goods. We weren't expecting them again until summer's end."

"Things happen," my father said, and though the words were pleasant, his face was still in scary-mode. "I believe they came to make sure Cecelia and I honored our agreement. I'm sure the rest of the summer will work out just fine. Won't it, McKale?"

Oh, dear. That was dadspeak for stay-away-from-the-Fae-and-don't-hurt-my-daughter.

Or else.

I wanted to crawl somewhere and hide. Or better yet, shrink into a mini Robyn-chaun and jump on the back of the nearest sheep that could whisk me off somewhere where boys weren't forced into being with me.

McKale straightened and met my dad's eyes. "Aye, Mr. Mason."

Brogan stood. "Well, then. Glad that's all settled. I do believe I smell our morning meal preparing. Let us visit the kitchens and then we'll eat in the open air this fine morn."

My parents thanked him and followed.

"I'll be right there," I told them. Cassidy scooted closer to me and McKale didn't move from his spot across from us.

"Well, that was awkward," Cassidy said once the adults were out of hearing distance.

I looked at McKale, but he was intent on studying a groove in the wooden tabletop, running his thumb along it.

"Can I ask you something, McKale?" Cassidy spoke, then she forged ahead without waiting for him to answer. "What do you think of my sister so far?"

"Cass!" Could my family possibly humiliate me any further this morning?

"What?" She eyed me before turning back to McKale. "So? What do you think?"

I clenched my teeth.

"I don't believe it truly matters what we think of one another," he said.

"Wrong." She leaned forward. "There's no time to be negative and bitter. It may not matter to your clan or the Fae what you two think of each other, but we Masons are not a clan, we're a family, and it matters to us. So tell me. What was your first thought when you met her?"

My breathing went shallow. As uncomfortable as this was, I wanted to hear his answer. Plus, he had to pass this "test" in order to gain Cassidy's approval, which meant a lot to me. Would he even play along?

Please play along.

His Adam's apple bobbed as he swallowed, and then his jaw rocked back and forth slowly, highlighting the line of red hair that ran along its edge. Other Chaun men began to filter into the clearing, carrying their plates. I felt Cassidy getting uptight next to me. Just as I was about to tell her to forget about it, McKale whispered.

"She reminded me of the Irish Hollyhock."

"The what?" Cassidy asked.

He shook his head. "Nothing. Never ye mind."

She crossed her arms and glared at him. A Little Man was walking nearby and she called out to him.

"Excuse me, sir?" She smiled and waved him over. McKale's face froze. "Can you please tell me what the Irish Hollyhock is?"

"Well, certainly then. It's a flowering plant that grows taller than meself. The bigger it gets the more it blooms with color. They're sturdy and quite stunning, really. Does that answer yer question, miss?"

Cassidy beamed a large smile at him. "It sure does. Thank you so much." He nodded and walked to his table. With her arms still crossed, Cassidy faced McKale and cocked her head.

"You could have just said you thought she was pretty, but I like the Hollyhock thing even better. And just in case you're wondering, she thinks you're cute, too."

Kill me, please.

A slight tint colored McKale's cheekbones as Cassidy tapped my arm. "Come on, Robyn. I'm hungry."

"Wait," McKale called. We stopped. He captured my eyes and my insides cartwheeled. "Robyn… about last night. I hope ye'll accept my apology."

His brow was creased with the strain of everything. Filled with a strange mix of trepidation and hope, all I could do was nod. I was too shaken to chance a look backward as we walked away. Cassidy bumped my hip with her own, and I pressed my lips together.

"See, aren't you glad I asked? He thinks of you like a flower!" She giggled.

"Not a flower," I corrected. "A sturdy plant."

"Covered in beautiful flowers! And sturdy is good. I'll cut him a little slack for now. I'd hate to have to embarrass him in front of the clan."

I bumped her hip back, hoping more than anything there would be no need for anymore embarrassing confrontations at all, this summer or ever.

SEVEN

In the hot kitchen, women bustled around with aprons, cooking in pans over open coals in giant fireplaces along the wall.

A pretty, younger girl with long golden hair and a round face approached Cassidy and me, smiling.

"Mornin' Robyn and Cassidy! I'm Leilah. Let me fix yer plates."

Half a minute later she handed us both tin plates and we thanked her, stomachs growling at the sight of fried eggs, a slice of what she called bacon, though it looked like ham to me, and a thick piece of flatbread spread with purple jam.

"My pleasure. Come back and see us. There's always talk to be heard in the kitchens for anyone with an ear." She winked at us, wiping her hands on her apron and moving on to serve the group of men who'd come in behind us.

"Everyone here sure winks a lot," Cassidy whispered as we walked with our plates back out to the clearing.

I thought about Leilah's offer to come back and talk. A lot could probably be learned from the females. Visiting the kitchen topped my agenda list for today.

I was surprised to find McKale sitting at the end of a

long table across from my parents, seeming to exchange pleasantries. My parents had plates of food, but McKale didn't. I boldly sat down next to him and smiled when he looked at me. The goal was to get to know him. No time to waste.

"Aren't you eating?" I asked him.

"Aye, but I'm in the habit of taking mine an' eating on the way to the Shoe House."

"The Shoe House?" Mom asked.

"Aye. Our largest structure. Most of the men folk spend their days working on the shoes. My job is tanning hides for the leather. In fact, I'd better be off. My partner is cranky when I'm late."

He stood and inclined his head to the four of us, lingering longest on me, before walking in the direction of the big building. I watched him go, noting his long limbs and thin frame. It was hard to believe he was fifty-years-old and his body still had some filling-out to do. I turned my attention back to my breakfast, which was as delicious as it looked.

"Well, he can certainly be polite when he wants to," Mom noted, sipping her hot tea.

"What kind of trouble will you girls get into today?" Dad asked. Cassidy and I thought about it.

"I'd like to meet some of the women," I said. "Maybe take a walk around the area or something."

"Yeah, your mother and I will probably explore the land, too. I might have a look in the shoe factory later. See if I can make myself useful while I'm here."

"It's the Shoe House, Dad," Cass corrected him. "You have to use their lingo."

"Ah, yes. Shoe House."

"And Robyn says they're anti-women over there," Cass warned him.

Our parents looked at me, interested.

"Yeah, I went by yesterday and they seemed a little spooked to see a girl inside."

Dad laughed. "Feminine wiles would distract the boys from work."

"Nah," Mom said. "Harmless superstitions, is all. Don't get your feelings hurt."

After breakfast, Cassidy and I set off for the kitchens. I felt shy when we got there. I'd always been somewhat intimidated by other females, feeling like I wasn't girly enough and I couldn't catch on to the passive-aggressive subtleties many girls lived by. I'd always gotten along better with boys. In general they were simpler to understand, although McKale was giving me a run for my money.

Six women hunched over shallow barrels scrubbing dishes and pans. They had an assembly line going. The oldest woman with a head full of short, curly gray hair held out a soapy hand for our dishes without looking at us.

"We can wash them," I told her, feeling bad.

"Och, just give 'em to me." She snatched them from my hand and began scrubbing with zeal.

Leilah and the other young girl were at the rinsing station, dunking sudsy dishes into the clean water.

"Here." Leilah tipped her chin toward a stack of towels. "You can dry."

Cassidy and I went over and grabbed towels, drying and stacking. Those ladies moved fast and we worked quickly to keep up, fumbling a little and making Leilah and her friend giggle. I decided I might write an ode to the awesomeness of electric dishwashers and indoor plumbing.

"This is my friend, Rachelle." Leilah's friend had curly dark hair that she pulled back in a bonnet.

"Do you two room together?" I asked them, wiping my damp forehead with my arm.

"Aye. Most of us wee women live together except the ones currently bound."

"How old are you, Leilah? Sorry, not trying to be nosy. I'm just curious."

"Not at all. I'm one-o-nine. Rachelle here's the babe of the women. She's only ninety-eight."

We finished up the dishes and the four of us girls left the hot kitchen. It was warm outside, but at least there was a breeze and occasional clouds.

Leilah and Rachelle took us through the village, into a part we hadn't been yet. We ended up in a fenced farm area with partitioned spaces for goats, pigs, and chickens. The girls scooped feed from a barrel to feed the animals. I watched them work, noting every detail in hopes of eventually "making myself useful" like Dad had mentioned. They walked us through their morning chores, mostly caring for the animals. I could deal with farm animals way easier than something like, oh, let's say, dumping the chamber pots. Blech.

When they were finally done they led us to a nearby patch of soft clover where we all sat.

"What do ye think of our McKale?" Leilah asked.

I was so glad she made the first move.

"I like him," I told her. "He's shy, but we just met, so hopefully that'll pass."

"Ye don't think he's too…" Rachelle's little voice was a

cute, squeaky sound. She motioned upward from the top of her head. Leilah poked her in the side and frowned. Rachelle slumped, shamefaced.

"Too tall?" I asked. "Not for me. I prefer men who are taller than me."

"Oh?" Rachelle's eyes rounded, disbelieving. "Ye don't say."

"What can you tell us about him?" Cassidy asked. "Just between us girls." She sounded easy-going, but I knew she was itching for info.

"Well, I'm not one to talk down about the clan," Leilah began. "But McKale's not exactly had it easy. He surely feels a bit o' pressure being the clan's 'last hope.' Ye can be certain the elder men don't let him forget it, either. But at the same time, they're careful not to let it go to his head. He might have the blessing of the Fair Folk, but among the Chaun he's the odd man out."

"Because he's tall?" I asked.

She nodded, looking ashamed to admit there was such a prejudice among them. The height issue seemed stupid to me, but I supposed every culture had their ridiculous prejudices. Not that that made it okay.

"If he doesn't want to be tall, can't he just shrink himself down to everyone else's size?" Cassidy asked.

"Och, no. They can only be normal sized or tiny." Leilah held her hands about twelve inches apart. "Nothing in between. And the Leprechaun don't take well to unnecessary shifting, such as the Clourichaun do fer fun."

"I don't get it," I said. "What's the point of being able to shift? Can they glamour to disappear, too?"

"Aye." Leilah settled back onto her hands, crossing her

short legs in front of herself. "The Leprechaun were the first humans ever to be gifted with magic by the Fae. It was a test of sorts. The Fae didn't want to give men too much power at first, but they wanted them to be able to easily hide in the grasses and forests if necessary. Besides making shoes, they had the job of tracking Fae who came out of the portal to mingle among humans. The Fae could not be stopped, but the humans who had interaction with the Faeries had to be wiped clean."

"Wiped clean?" Cassidy and I asked at the same time, making the girls laugh.

"Surely ye've heard of Trackers?" Rachelle asked. I shook my head. "Well, they're able to use magic to make humans forget moments. They follow the Fae and wipe the memories from humans who come into contact with them. Eventually the Fae bores and returns to their own realm. Only two Chaun Trackers remain, and there's nary a bit o' use for 'em anymore."

I absently plucked bits of clover and grass as we digested the information, which was all fascinating to me. For years Mom and Dad said, "We'll tell you everything someday when it's time." They loathed speaking of the Fae and their realm.

"Do you guys know anything about McKale and that Freaky Fae Girl?" Cassidy asked. "The Shoe Mistress?"

My stomach clenched at the mention. Leilah and Rachelle shared a grimace.

"You can tell us," I said.

"It's all rumor, of course." Leilah lowered her voice. "Some say the Shoe Mistress has sneaked into the earthly realm alone… to see him."

Again my stomach spasmed, and I curled an arm around

my waist. "Wouldn't everyone know if she opened the portal?"

"No' necessarily," Rachelle squeaked. "She could bribe their doorman and open the tiniest crack, which could only be felt by people standing nearby at the moment of the opening. If she snuck in during the night there would be no one around…"

I gritted my teeth together at the thought of her gliding unsuspectingly into McKale's room whenever she got the urge.

"Well, they obviously haven't done the diddy or he'd be brainwashed," Cassidy blurted. "Right?"

"Really, Cass?" I shot her a look and Rachelle covered her face to hide a scandalized expression.

Leilah continued unfazed. "If you mean what I think, he's definitely not given his full self or she'd have taken him over to Faerie for keeps. That's the only way humans are accepted over there: as property."

"I don't understand why she has to sneak," Cassidy said. "Can't Faeries do whatever they want, anytime they want? Why does she care what the Leprechauns think?"

"Oh, no," Rachelle piped in. "It's no' because of the Chaun that she sneaks. It's the Fae who would no' accept her extended interest in a human. They think of us as working dogs. She'd be shunned by her own kind, she would." The little woman nodded her head vigorously, curls bouncing on her round shoulders. "And besides, Lady Martineth and the Summer King would be naught too happy to find she's taken to the Chaun's 'last hope.'"

Cassidy's sickened expression mirrored mine. This did not bode well. I didn't want to talk about it anymore. Thank goodness for my sister who knew me so well. She cleared her throat.

"Well, we're not going to worry about her right now. What do you know about the Clourichaun?"

"Crazy Clours," Leilah said with amusement, picking a clover bloom and fiddling with it. I ran my hands over the clovers as Leilah told us the story.

"They've always been a rowdy bunch who drink far too much. Some say it's 'cause they're mostly average-sized blokes with no control. No offense." She stopped to look at Cassidy and me, but we just shrugged it off. She smiled, relieved. "The Clour share this land. They're on the other side of the forest, and they used to share shoe-making responsibilities. Too often they were behind on orders, and the Leprechaun had to step in and do their work for 'em in a rush like. Besides that, the Clour were leaving the lands and being careless around humans. Especially females. They'd been warned by the Fae, which was lucky because they're no' usually the type to waste time on warnings.

"About two hundred years ago one of the Clour impregnated a nearby farmer's daughter. It certainly wasn't the first time, but the Chaun had become good at hiding incidents of their kin's indiscretions. Ye can only imagine the surprise humans experience when they discover their child can do magic! It was terrible business, switching babies and the like. This one particular time was being dealt with when the portal opened a day early and the Faeries discovered what had happened. It was the last straw. The Fae cursed their bloodlines into extinction."

"Why didn't they just take away their magic?" Cassidy asked.

"The magic is so deep in them. To pull it out would require a lot of Fae energy, and t'would make the Clour lose their minds, but the Fae wanted them to live and suffer."

They didn't seem to be suffering much to me. But maybe it was all for show. It was kind of sad to think of them watching their family die one by one with nothing but shame to show for it.

We all plucked at the clover for a minute until Leilah spoke.

"Have ye seen the waterfall yet?"

"No, we haven't seen much of anything," I answered.

The girls had to get back to work, but they explained how to get to the waterfall. We thanked them and shared a round of hugs with our new friends before going our separate ways.

It was a serene fifteen-minute walk uphill through the edge of the forest, but Leilah had been right. A light path made from frequent footsteps made it easy to find. We heard the rush of water minutes before we saw it.

By the time we came to the gorgeous sight, we were both sweating lightly from the hike and the warm summer air. Down a little farther was a small rocky cliff with the waterfall.

"Wow," I said. We jogged up to the marshy edge of the fattened stream. Clear water ran crisply over smooth rocks. Some parts looked as shallow as one foot, while other darkened pools closer to the waterfall looked deep. I kicked off my flip-flops and walked into the shallow water. It was warmer than I expected. I sighed and let my head fall back, looking up at the canopy of shading trees overhead and taking in a deep breath of air.

"This is awesome!" Cassidy said. "Let's walk down to the waterfall and go swimming!"

"Um, hello, no bathing suits," I pointed out.

"Um, *hello*," she said, pulling her shirt over her head and wiggling out of the pajama pants, then standing there smiling in her white bra and pink polka-dotted panties. "It's just us! Everyone's working, come on!"

I peered around at the trees for a moment, and then, like usual, I did what Cassidy wanted. I stripped down and piled my clothes neatly next to hers, and then chased her as she ran up the bank. We were lighthearted and breathless by the time we got to the waterfall. Holding hands, we stepped into the shallow edge and walked further in until we were treading water at least seven or eight feet deep.

As always, Cassidy's idea was exhilarating. We splashed each other, swimming and flipping under the water. We swam to the falls and let the water rush over our heads, joking about how this is where we should come for our morning showers. Then we floated on our backs until the sun was high in the mid-day sky.

"We should probably get back so Mom and Dad don't worry," I said after a long while.

Cassidy sighed and agreed. We climbed onto the stream bank and squeezed water from our hair. Cass's bra was lightly padded, so she bent over and squeezed it by hugging herself. Water gushed out of her cleavage and she chortled like a goof.

A rustling in the trees made us go still. I stared around us for a whole minute with my arms over my chest before shaking my head.

"The wind," I said, but now I was anxious to get dressed.

We walked back down the length of the stream toward

our clothes, shaking our limbs and feeling much more positive about our stay here now that we'd found this spot.

We'd been walking for a while before we both stopped, exchanging confused looks. I scanned up and down the marshy, bright green grass.

"Where are our clothes?" I asked.

"I don't think we were this far down the stream," Cassidy answered. "Look, the path is back there." We started walking back up. Our clothes were nowhere in sight. Foreboding filled me.

"Did we put them closer to the trees, up there maybe?" she asked.

I shook my head. "No, they were definitely here in the grass."

"Do you think an animal took them?"

"What kind of wild animal would take *all* of our clothes?"

"A smart and talented one?"

"Haha," I said.

"Well, it can't be a person because we would have noticed anyone walking around out here," Cass responded. "Or anything big, at least."

We both stopped and stared at one another, wide-eyed.

Anything *big*. Oh, crap.

"The Clourichaun!" we both said at the same time, and Cassidy threw her head back with hilarity at the possible practical joke.

"It's not funny," I said, which made her laugh even harder. I looked down at my satiny black bra and matching panties, which thankfully covered my whole bottom. But they clung to my every contour, and I really did not want to be seen like this. Cassidy darted around peeking behind tree trunks.

"Come out, come out, wherever you are!" she sang.

"Let's break up," I suggested. "You look upstream by the falls. I'll look around down here." She agreed and bounded away as if we were playing hide-and-seek.

I crossed my arms over my chest and walked into the trees, standing very still and listening for movement. After a full minute I heard the faintest sound of a high-pitched chuckle. I swung my head to the right where the sound came from. I saw nothing.

"I know you're there," I said, feeling foolish. "You may as well come out."

Another minute passed and then, like a blur, a foot-high man darted out of the trees toward the grass. I took off after him, sprinting. I don't think he expected the speed of my long strides because he grunted in surprise when I dove on my stomach and snatched him around his middle. I held him tight, careful not to squash him into my chest. I lifted him close to my face as I lay on my stomach, propping up on my elbows. He wiggled furiously like a worm and I recognized the brown curls.

"Rock, you little jerk! Where are our clothes?"

"Aargh! You're squeezing the life outta me bits and pieces!" he cried.

I did not loosen my hold.

"If you don't tell me where my clothes are I'm going to *crush* your tiny bits and pieces."

A sudden burst of magic caught me in the chest and violently forced my hands apart. I blinked, and found myself unsteady, sprawled on top of full-grown Rock, who lay back on the grass with his hands behind his head, giving me a lazy grin.

"What's that ye were saying about *tiny*?" he asked.

"Oh! You perv!" I struggled to roll off of him, but he grabbed me around the waist, chuckling. When I pushed him he grabbed my wrists instead.

So, funny guy wanted to wrestle, huh? No problem. All of my athletic skills surfaced and I twisted my arms hard toward his thumbs, breaking his hold on my wrists. We were sitting up now and I swiftly brought my legs up between us, giving him a kangaroo-kick to the chest that sent him backward before I swung my legs under myself and crouched, ready. Rock was still laughing in between spurts of coughing as he rolled around, clutching his chest.

"Blimey, what the blazes?" The voice came from the trees.

I glanced up and saw a flash of red hair. McKale stood there staring back and forth between the two of us. Oh, no. This probably looked bad.

Cassidy's soft footfalls came running up the bank. "You found him! And I found these." She held up our clothes, out of breath but happy, and then looked over where I kept glancing. "Oh, hey, McKale!"

He sputtered something incoherent and covered his eyes to shield against her near-nakedness.

"Rock stole our clothes when we were swimming!" I pointed to the rascal Clourichaun, who was still on the ground, enjoying the view. McKale lowered the hand from his eyes and glared hard at his friend.

"And aren't ye glad I did, Kale, m'boy?" Rock nodded his head toward me.

McKale's eyes traveled over to mine, and then slid slowly downward, landing with an abrupt halt on my boobs. He looked like a child who'd just accidentally discovered his Christmas gift. I allowed him two more seconds of gawking before crossing my arms and breaking the spell. I wanted to be flattered, but I was too busy being angry.

I stomped to Cassidy and began pulling my clothes on. She and Rock were making silly eyes at one another.

"Get your clothes on," I told her.

"Would you relax? It's the same as a bathing suit." She cocked her hip in defiance and Rock cocked an eyebrow.

"*Now*," I said to her. She sighed and begrudgingly began pulling on her clothes.

Without looking back at Cassidy and Rock, I headed toward the path where McKale stood. He took up silent residence beside me as I speed-walked. It took five minutes for me to slow down and relax.

"Sorry about Rock," McKale said. "Bit of a gobshite, that one."

"You don't have to apologize for him. He's annoying, but I know he's harmless."

"Eh, mostly. Yer sister should still take heed. Rock is like a brother to me, but he's unpredictable an' self-serving."

"Cass doesn't heed warnings very well. Not when she's got her mind made up about something."

"Perhaps they'll enjoy one another, then."

He glanced over at me as we walked, and I felt the warmth of him. I looked away, feeling self-conscious as I remembered his heated look at my chest earlier. We walked in silence for a few minutes.

"Do you have any brothers?" I asked. He didn't answer right away.

"Nay. I'm the only child from my father's binding to survive."

"Oh. I'm sorry. How about your mother? Is she here?" I knew the answer the moment the question left my mouth. If she were here, I obviously would have met her.

"They believe something tore internally during my birth and she bled for days before passing. I was too large for her."

"Oh, McKale," I said softly. Again with his size.

On impulse, I reached over and took his hand, twining our fingers together. The feel of it must have taken him by surprise because his steps faltered a second. From the corner of my eye I caught him peering down at our hands. My heart was beating way too fast. I'd never held hands with a boy.

I cleared my throat. "Are you on a break from work right now?"

"Aye. Mid-day meal. Leilah saw me and told me she'd sent ye to the falls."

We walked in silence, holding hands the rest of the way until the thick forest opened up into the bright clearing and we stopped.

"I must return to work," he said. I heard reluctance there, and it made me smile shyly. I watched his eyes explore my face. In the sunlight the hazel colors were a mix of sea green and light caramel.

Just then an obnoxious kissy noise sounded from behind us, followed by excessive girly cackling. McKale and I broke apart, turning to see Cassidy and Rock coming up the path.

"That was mean!" Cassidy gave Rock a shove. His dark curls bounced around his face and he started tickling her ribs.

As they carried on, McKale and I caught each other's eyes again.

"I guess I'll see you tonight," I told him.

He tilted his head down toward me and I melted a little when he replied, "'Til then."

EIGHT

I TOOK A LONG NAP back in our room while Cassidy found our parents and took them to the falls. I wondered if they'd had the pleasure of meeting Rock yet.

Doubtful.

Several hours later I dragged myself from the soft bed, still groggy. I'd been more tired than I thought. Sounds of people talking and moving came from outside, so it must have been near the end of the workday.

I brushed my hair and teeth. Using the makeshift restroom was not the most enjoyable experience of my life. There were just some things about village life I didn't think I'd ever get used to.

Cheers sounded from the field as I left my room. I walked out to find a friendly game of what appeared to be soccer. *Yes!* I looked around for McKale, but he hadn't come down from work. Joy filled me as I found my family and stood with them, watching the game. The ball was well-crafted brown leather that had been stuffed and stitched firm.

Unlike the version of soccer I knew, they were allowed to touch the ball if it was in the air—a swipe of the hand to knock it down and keep it in play. But it still involved dribbling the ball by foot, passing, and kicking it into a goal, which was made of rock pillars. I was itching to get in on the action, so when the players broke for water, Cassidy and I approached the leader. He was young, like McKale, with only a small bit of blond facial hair.

"Excuse me, sir?"

He looked up, wiping his brow with a cloth.

"Robyn, isn't it? The name's Keefe. What can I do for ye?"

"Hi, Keefe. Um, my sister and I were wondering if we might be able to play?"

His eyebrows went up in surprise and he didn't answer.

"I mean, unless you think we're at an unfair advantage because of our height," I added.

He chuckled, clearly amused and further surprised. "Please don't take offense, miss, but 'tis not your height that worries me. I fear *ye* are the one at a disadvantage because yer…"

He waved his hands up and down at me.

Huh? I'm what?

"A lass!" he sputtered.

What the crap? Okay, this gender thing was getting old. Cass planted both hands on her hips and gave me the stink eye as if to say, "Are you going to let him get away with that?"

I kept my face calm, while petting the hackles on my inner-feminist. She'd actually been a good sport about everything up until that moment. Now all I wanted was a chance to make him eat those words. Cassidy and I shared a conspiratorial smile.

"Where we come from girls play, too," I told him. "Many of the girls are as good as the men."

"Or better," Cass added.

Keefe was plainly trying to hold back a condescending smile. A small crowd of sweaty players gathered around us.

"Just for fun, give us a chance. Please," I begged. "We promise not to be upset by the outcome. We can be on different teams to make it fair. You just have to make us one promise."

"Oh, yeah?" Keefe asked, setting his hands on his hips. "And wha's that?"

"Not to go easy on us because we're girls." I grinned and the whole group of little guys cracked up laughing. Keefe grabbed his waist, apparently getting a stitch in his side.

"Alright, then, misses. If ye insist."

Cassidy and I gave each other a high five, and took our shoes off since everyone else was playing barefoot. I was sure Keefe was only letting us play because he didn't want to offend Brogan's guests and McKale's betrothed, but the reason didn't matter to me. I simply wanted to stretch my muscles and play something I knew I could win.

We took our places, opposing teams facing each other. One of the guys on the sideline whistled and we were off. The players ran slower than me because of their shorter legs, but they were a very rough and physical group, grabbing and pushing. There was no ref throwing penalty flags out here, that's for sure.

It didn't take long to figure out that my team wasn't going to pass the ball my direction, even though I was open. Nobody bothered covering me. Cassidy stood on the other end of the playing field and lifted her arms in frustration, also not being allowed to play. We were going to have to take this game into our own hands.

Cassidy's team had a strong offensive scorer named Mick who could get through our defenders too easily. No problem. I could do offense or defense. I hung back near the goal since we had no goalies, and the next time Mick broke through our defense, I was there.

I watched his feet dribble for a second to figure out his pattern, and then I ghosted in and stole it away.

"Hey, now!" I heard him shout, and people watching from the sidelines laughed. I turned back to Mick.

"You want it back?" I taunted with a grin. "Come get it."

He came at me and I feinted to the left, dribbling around him on the right. I took off amid cheers, making my way through the other team with too much ease. They wouldn't get physical with me like they would with one another. Instead of shooting I passed it to my teammate who ran parallel to me on the other side of the field. It was a perfect set-up, and he kicked a clean shot into the goal.

It might be cliché to say, "the crowd went wild," but they did. Especially the women. They acted like they'd never been so entertained. I jogged to the middle of the field where the players were converging.

"You guys let me through too easily," I scolded the other team. "Just treat me like you treat each other. You're not gonna hurt me. I'm a big girl."

Some smiled and chuckled, but a few still looked uneasy. Cassidy gave me an overdramatized wink that made me snort.

Her team started this time, and low and behold, somebody actually passed it to her. She and I went head-to-head all the time at home, and I could almost always take her, but she was fiercer when she had an audience. The fact that there were no rules and we were both competitive did not bode well. We became locked in a battle for the ball, which included scratching, elbowing, and cussing on Cassidy's part. There would be cuts on our shins from each other's toenails, and major bruising. At one point I had the ball and when I turned to dribble away she tripped me, and then we were at it again. The crowd was clapping in sync and chanting, "Ma-son Girls! Ma-son Girls!"

Distracted momentarily by the chant, Cassidy's attention wavered and I tugged the ball from between her feet with my heel. I passed it to one of my teammates who shot a beautiful long-distance goal. After throwing my arms up and cheering, I collapsed in a heap on the ground with Cass next to me, both of us laughing.

"You need to cut your toenails!" I complained.

"You're one to talk, bigfoot!" We slapped at each other for another few seconds before it was time to get up and reconvene with our teammates.

After another few exhausting rounds, my team won. Everyone had picked up on my and Cassidy's high-fiving; they were happening everywhere I turned, including among the spectators. Mom and Dad were *wooting* on the sideline.

I found McKale watching from the end of a table where he leaned back with a wooden cup in his hand. He was just about the only person not standing. He watched me with an expression I couldn't discern, but I wanted to figure out. Once I zoned in on him, everything else faded and my feet brought me to his side. I sat down, keeping a little distance between us in case I stank. He sipped his drink.

"Water," he said. "Ye thirsty?" I smiled at how he pronounced it as "tirsty." I liked that he was offering to share a cup.

"Please," I said. He handed me the cup and I sipped, trying not to drink all of it.

"Go on then, finish it," he told me.

"Thanks." I drank it and set the cup down.

He opened his mouth to speak again just as a hot sizzle of magic blasted us from the nearby long grasses. A collective gasp rose up, followed by silence while we all stared at the field. All the water I'd just drank threatened to come back up. McKale had gone still and pale as he eyed the air with apparent fascination and dread.

A full minute passed and the portal didn't open. Two of the little men from the game ran out into the field to check it over. Nobody moved or spoke until the guys shook their heads and shrugged, coming back to the clearing.

"What was that?" I whispered.

McKale turned back around, stiff. "It happens sometimes. False alarms. Perhaps the Fae guard of the realm got too close to the portal."

"Oh," I breathed. My heart rate was still too fast.

We sat in awkward silence and I wondered if he was thinking of Khalistah like I was. Hoping she'd never return even though she'd been so "nice" to him growing up. McKale, more relaxed now, pointed to where we'd played the game and said, "Ye're good."

My nerves finally began to settle as I trusted that nobody was coming out of that portal. "Thanks. I played a similar game at home. Do you ever play?"

"On occasion. With the Clour lads."

Ah. Maybe Cassidy had been right with her "reindeer games" analogy.

"We should play sometime. You, the Clour, Cass, and me. It'd be fun."

A sudden glint lit up in his eyes. "Aye. If yer up for it. Tho' the lads are rough."

"You'd be surprised what we can handle," I said.

He didn't say anything for a minute, and I wondered if he'd been turned off watching his future mate fight for the ball like a boy. I hoped not, because I wasn't willing to change that particular part of myself.

"This evening," he stated.

I must have looked confused, because he clarified.

"After supper, if ye'd still like to play we can go to Clour land." His voice was questioning and hesitant. Nervous.

"Sure." I tried to tone down my overly-eager grin. "That'd be great."

Cassidy would be beyond thrilled.

McKale peered down at his feet and smiled to himself.

NINE

CASSIDY HAD BROUGHT HER pink soccer ball from home. She tossed it from one hand to the other as McKale led us through the shallow part of the stream and into the patch of trees on the other side. Cass sent me an excited glance. We were entering Clour land.

As soon as we cleared the trees I could hear them. We walked into an open glade that slanted downward at the edge. A rundown cottage was barely visible through the trees below. Then I saw them—all twelve of them—at the bottom of the hill, on their knees watching something in the grass and cheering.

"Hopper racing," McKale said.

As we got closer I could make out the barrier of rocks lining the "racetracks" and a dozen frogs hopping every which way inside. Rock reached in to nudge his frog and one of the other guys bopped the back of his head.

"Hands off, ya cheatin' bugger!"

Rock grimaced at his dormant green racer and mumbled, "Bollocks." His frown turned to a giant smile when he looked up and saw the three of us standing there.

He threw his hands out. "'Ey!"

106

That quickly, the frogs were forgotten and we were surrounded by the curious Clour. Eight of them were full sized and four were little men. None of them were bearded, but half of them did have facial hair of some sort, ranging from all-around scruff to hair along the jawline like McKale, only not as well groomed. They were grimy and their clothes were threadbare, but they were undoubtedly cute guys. Just a little… untamed. And thin.

They pushed McKale out of the way to get a closer look at Cassidy and me. Rock threw his arm around Cass's shoulder as if claiming her. The playful smile she gave him showed she didn't mind. His claim didn't stop the boys, though. They were brazen in their introductions, shoving one another to move forward and take our hands, touching our arms.

"All right," McKale said, forcing his way back to my side. "Let the lasses breathe, then."

A guy with roughly chopped brunette hair leaned close to my face, his mouth near mine, and sniffed me. I had to lean away to avoid an accidental kiss. I didn't feel threatened, only amused, but the attention was kind of overwhelming. They had no physical boundaries.

Others took the brunette's lead, reaching their faces toward Cassidy and me and breathing deeply. A little guy pressed his nose against Cass's hip and smelled her shorts, making her laugh. Then his hand ran down the curve of her bottom and Cass jumped, saying, "Hey now!" He ran off, getting his hair rumpled by the other Clour who seemed proud of his boldness.

A dark haired guy came up behind me and sniffed my hair, his nose tickling my neck. "She smells so bleedin' good."

McKale gave him a shove. "'Specially compared to you lot, aye?"

They laughed, but I noted the way McKale sidled right up next to me, his arm heating mine.

"Will you introduce us?" I asked him.

He gave a nod and pointed to the brunette guy who'd been in my face. "This 'ere is Ardan. The bouncy twins there are Carrig and Connall." He pointed to two blonds with hair as curly as Rock and bright blue eyes. They waved in sync. "The four wees are Davin, Fancy Francis, Tyke, and Jax." The little guys all grinned and nodded, different shades of brown hair flopping. "This here's Blackie." Blackie was the tallest of them, the same height as McKale, with olive skin and black hair that reached his shoulders. He'd been the one to sniff my neck. With some meat on his bones and a brush through his hair, he was good looking enough to be major trouble.

Next McKale pointed at two redheads with freckled faces. "These are Finbar and Fergus, the carrot cousins." Their hair was much more orange than McKale's. "And the last Clour is Dashy. The quickest of the lot."

Dashy, standing at about five eight with sandy, strawberry blond hair, moved forward like a bolt of energy and grabbed both my hands in his before bringing them to his mouth for a kiss. "Please to meet ya." Then he moved to Cass and did the same.

"This is Robyn," McKale said, angling toward me. "And her sister, Cassidy."

"Ah!" said one of the blond twins, I think Carrig. "McKale's future shag mate! Here here!"

Holy…

Carrig punched the sky and the other boys did the same, shouting, "Here, here!"

Cassidy chortled and covered her mouth while my face turned red hot. Their laughter was lewd and devoid of regret.

McKale shook his head and scratched his cheek. "Do ya have to be a pack o' sods? The girls came to play a game o' ball wit' ya."

"Ooh! Is that the ball, then?" asked Dashy. "'Tis a strange ball indeed." They all leaned close, vying for position to get a good look at Cass's pink soccer ball. She held it out for their inspection.

I couldn't help but like them, even though they were what Mom would call "scoundrels and rascals." And I felt bad that they didn't have any kind of guidance, or the presence of females to keep their undomesticated natures in check. Being with them made the world feel off kilter and I wanted to balance it back.

Rock snatched the ball from Cass's hands and dribbled away, grinning over his shoulder when Cassidy yelled, "Hey!" and chased him.

Playing ball with the Clour was nothing like playing with the Chaun. It was a debacle. A hilarious debacle. It felt good to shed my proper exterior and play hard.

At one point in the game Cassidy screamed, "The next pair of grabby hands that touches my boobs or butt is getting a beatdown!" The guys were hands-on in every way. They would tackle one another, giving wedgies or yanking down each others' pants. Anything to distract and get the ball. Some of them would even use their magic to shrink small when they were about to be tackled, and then pop back into full form after the aforementioned tackler fell on his face. This was a no rules arena, and we were all panting with merriment, wrestling and cheering when the ball sailed through a goal.

I liked watching McKale handle the ball. He had great control, which was a major turn on for me.

It was the most I'd seen McKale smile. He'd been careful not to be touchy the first part of the game, but as time went on and everyone started getting carried away, he became bolder. During the team choosing, McKale and I were put on opposing teams. I was disappointed at first. I'd wanted us to work together, but it turns out that competition could be a good thing.

When one of the twins jumped on Dashy's back, I took the opportunity to steal the ball away. I only had it for three seconds before I felt an arm around my waist. In a blink I was yanked down and squashed under a long body. McKale and I were both breathing hard and smiling as he looked down at me. And then two little guys, Jax and Tyke, who'd been barreling forward at top speed, tripped over us and we all grunted. McKale stood and held out a hand. He pulled me up, but before we had a chance to wipe off the dirt, the ball was flying our direction, arching through the sky.

McKale and I jumped for it at the same time, but I grabbed his shoulders to lift myself higher and did a perfect header, sending the ball soaring off my forehead into the goal. The other team groaned while mine cheered. As I came down I brought my arms around McKale for an excited hug. We held each other, caught up in the moment, chests heaving with our rapid breaths, until one of the carrot cousins smacked my butt and said, "He ain't on yer team!"

And then someone pantsed McKale.

His eyes widened and I covered my eyes with a scream

of laughter. When I looked again McKale had his pants back up and was wrestling Blackie, who laughed so hard he could hardly defend himself from the nipple twister McKale gave him through his shirt. Blackie hollered and McKale fell to his back to catch his breath.

All around us the guys were tiring as the sun dipped low behind the forest. Cass came to my side.

"We should probably head back," I said with reluctance.

Cass stuck out her lower lip. Rock came up behind her and slipped his hands around her waist. He leaned down and rested his chin on her shoulder.

"Will ye return?" asked Blackie, sitting up and resting his elbows on his knees.

"Sure," I said.

"Look how dirty you are." Cassidy pointed at me.

"You're one to talk!" I countered. We were both filthy with leaves and grass in our hair.

"Aye, Cassie-lassie, ya need a good cleanin'!" said Rock. And with that he moved swiftly around Cass and threw her over his shoulder. "To the water wit' ye!"

"Uh-oh," I said, watching Rock run off while Cassidy screamed in glee. The rest of the Clour gave chase, pushing one another as they went.

McKale and I stood there as their voices trailed off.

"Are they always this wild?" I asked.

"Nay. They're usually much worse."

Ha. Together we ambled through the trees toward the waterfall. I felt comfortable at his side. It'd been awesome to see him let loose and have fun.

We got in the water and I waded out to my knees, bending to splash mud off my arms and legs. The others were further down the stream, hollering. McKale went farther into the water and dove, fully clothed. He wiped his face when he came up, and moved toward me. We shared shy smiles. My heart rate jacked up as he got closer, but at the last second he seemed to get nervous, veering toward the shore instead. He sat on the mossy bank, arms draped over his raised knees. I pushed aside my disappointment. What was I expecting? Him to ravish me?

The very thought made my cheeks warm. I walked out of the cool water to the shore and sat beside him. He was cute with his hair darkened from wetness and his clothes clinging to him. I tried not to stare, but when I stole a peek he was looking at my legs. He cleared his throat and stared down between his knees when he noticed me watching.

Dusk was darkening the sky, and shadows fell around us. We were thoughtful for a moment until inspiration hit and my nerves kicked on.

"So," I started. "Where I'm from we have this thing called 'dating.'" My voice quavered a little. "It's when two people are, um, interested in each other, so they spend time together one-on-one, getting to know one another. Would you… like to do that? Go on a date with me, tomorrow night, maybe?"

I felt nervous as he listened, still with that steady expression. He gave none of his thoughts away.

"I mean, it's not that big of a deal," I rambled. "We could just, like, go on a walk together after dinner. Supper. Whatever it's called. Or we don't have to if you don't want to." Oh, man. I needed to shut up. I stared down at my brutalized shins and bare feet.

"Ye talk so fast," he said.

My face heated and I felt stupid. "Sorry."

"No, I don't mind it. I like how ye talk."

My face heated further and I was glad it was getting dark out. "Okay."

"What's the word ya used? Dating?"

I nodded, biting my lip.

"I think 'tis a fine idea," he said.

I couldn't help but smile at his answer, and the way he said "tink" instead of "think."

"In that case," I said. "I have something I want to give you on our date. A present."

His eyes lit up, but there was something underlying, sort of a fearful edge to his excitement.

"It's nothing big. My mom told me that your clan values gifts," I explained. "So I sort of brought something."

Or a lot of things, but he didn't need to know that yet.

"Aye. Gifts are…" He scratched his cheek, searching for the right words. "We don't give or receive gifts lightly. To give a gift, no matter how small, tis like giving a piece of yerself. Accepting a gift means you're taking a part of them. 'Tis an honor."

"Oh." Based on that heavy explanation, I decided to take it easy. I would choose one gift for tomorrow night and hope he would accept it. Bringing the whole bin of gifts would probably freak him out. Like I was handing over the pink slip to my soul or something.

"Okay, well, where should we go?" I asked.

He thought about it. "There's a place I go to be alone." Again he spoke to me in the bashful tone that reminded me he wasn't accustomed to sharing anything about himself. It made me feel all mushy in a special way. I tried to concentrate on his directions. "If ye follow the edge of the east forest ye'll come to a hill with a single tree—" He scratched his chin. "I suppose 'tis better if we walk there together so's ye don't get lost."

"We could meet at the edge of the forest," I suggested.

"Aye. That'll do. After supper when night falls and most everyone's off to bunk. The moon should be light enough."

"Sounds perfect. It's a date."

"A date," he repeated. He emphasized the "t" sound and I giggled, which made him smile and shift self-consciously. I touched his hand on the ground beside me and his finger lifted to catch my pinky. He held it for a moment and gave me a warm look. My knees felt shaky when we both stood and began walking downstream toward the others.

Cassidy was on Rock's back as he swam. The others were throwing each other around and playing rough. I had no idea where they got their energy. When one of the little guys came up out of the water he had dripping cloth in his hand, which he threw ashore. The others laughed and followed suit.

"Is that…?" I began.

McKale nodded. "The britches are comin' off."

That was my cue to leave. "All right, Cass. Let's go. It's getting dark." *And the Clour are getting naked.*

She gave the whine like a little kid, trudging out of the water toward us.

"Bye everyone," I said, waving. "It was nice to meet you guys."

A pair of wet pants splatted at my feet and they all roared with amusement.

"Can we get a hug?" Blackie shouted, starting to stand.

I held a palm out to block the sight of him and keep him

at bay. "Maybe next time. Y'all just stay where you are. We'll see you later." I smiled and waved good-bye as the boys blew kisses and other nonsense.

"Til the morrow, Cassie-lassie," Rock said from the water. He threw his soaked pants at Cass, but she dodged them with a squeal and waved sweetly.

"Til then!" She spun and took my hand, whispering under her breath, "Oh my gosh, the Clour are so cute. We need to, like, bring all our friends here!"

I grinned at the thought, and we followed McKale into the darkened path of trees, happy.

Ten

THERE WAS NOTHING QUITE like sitting in a little tub with a single, thin stream of water to use for a shower. It took about a million years to wash my hair.

"Are you coming to dinner?" Cassidy called through the cloth drape.

"I don't think so," I hollered. "I'm going on a date with McKale tonight and I have to get ready. Will you tell Mom and Dad for me?"

"Ooh-la-la, a date. Wowee. Are you going to eat anything? Besides McKale's luscious little Leprechaun lips?"

I laughed through a nervous shiver. "I don't think I'll have time to eat." Plus, I was sort of running on adrenaline.

"All right. Well, I want every detail when you get in tonight. And don't use up all the water."

"Yeah, yeah."

I pushed the little valve to shut off the stream and squeezed out my hair. Then I maneuvered myself to the edge of the tub so I could shave using the water that was already in there. Man, that was some nasty looking water. How'd I get so dirty? It was mostly my feet. I was once again thankful not to be the person in charge of waste management.

It felt good to be clean and to dry off with a towel from my suitcase. There wasn't much I could do to my hair other than brush it and scrunch it with some light gel. I didn't bother with make-up, except a swipe of color high across my cheekbones and some sparkly lip-gloss. I put on my khaki skirt and a purple tank top with pink lace around the edges. I felt like being feminine tonight.

After slipping on my flip-flops I opened the door to peek out. The sun began to set in soft colors, and people were already filtering away from the eating area. Closing the door, I pulled out McKale's bin from the corner of the room and opened it, taking out the black and white soccer ball.

A little one-on-one match with him sounded fun. I smiled, pacing the room with the ball on my hip. This was boring. I couldn't wait any longer. I wanted to get there first anyway.

I walked a large arc around the clearing so nobody would see me, passing through the field of grass the Clour had come through. It was also the home of the Fae portal, which gave me the creeps, even though it was invisible. Jogging the rest of the way, I made quick time to the east edge of the forest without anyone noticing me. I walked into the woods, sitting against a tree far enough so I could see out, but nobody would see me in the darkness.

My legs stung like they were on fire. First from the marks that Cassidy had given me during the game, and second from the slap of sharp blades of grass as I'd run though the field. I blew on the front of my calves, feeling tingly. The tingle increased, moving to my chest, and I became still. Someone was using magic. I scanned the field and all around me, but didn't see anything. Maybe one of the Clourichaun were playing around in the near vicinity, changing size or something. I shook off the chill.

Ten or fifteen minutes passed before I saw a tall figure stride into the grasses. I sucked in my bottom lip and sat up straight to watch him. He hadn't noticed me in the trees. When he got to the middle of the field, another low-grade fizzle of magic touched me. McKale stopped and I knew he'd felt it, too.

The next few seconds was like something from a horror flick—one made personally for me. A stronger burn blew across my skin. Ten feet away from McKale a tiny shimmer of black cracked the air and Khalistah, AKA Freaky Fae Girl, climbed out like a mystical flower blooming from the air. My entire body stilled with fear. McKale peered over his shoulder, back toward the village, looking for me or any witnesses, I realized. But when she glided toward him, platinum hair dragging the grass behind her, gown flowing like a storybook cover, his concern seemed to drift away and he was lost to everything but her.

She was breathtaking, yes, and I loathed her to the core of my being. The FFG linked her frail arm through the crook of his strong one, causing him to seize up and breathe heavier. She smiled and motioned toward the forest. The two of them walked into the trees, not fifteen feet away from me. I was too horrified to move. They spoke openly, and I could hear them from where I sat.

"I was hoping you would pass through tonight, McKale of the Chaun. Are you heading to your tree on the hill? Shall I escort you there?"

"Eh, no. Just… an evening stroll but I should head back soon. 'Tis been a long day. We can speak here for a moment if it suits you."

"The view here suits me fine." Her silky voice turned my stomach. When she reached up and ran her tiny hand along the side of his face, I heard him inhale. She tilted her head to the side and gazed up at him. He leaned into her hand with a slight moan from his chest.

I clamped my teeth together, feeling way more than pissed. I was livid on several accounts. First, the fact that she had to sneak over to "slum" it with the guy her people had chosen for me. Second, the fact that he was so affected by her charms. And third, the cruelty of chance that I'd have to sit here and watch it.

She removed her hand from his face and he shuddered before standing tall again, blinking as if waking from a dream. He shot a glance toward the field then back at the Fae girl.

"Khalistah," McKale said in a soft voice. "We... we cannot do this. Ye must realize as I do that this cannot work. It has never been our fate. Especially now."

"Why ever not? Because of your *betrothed*?" Her last word snaked out like a whip. "You've never before seemed bothered by our differences. Have you grown to care for her so quickly?"

"She is kind." He turned his face away from her when he said it, but she took his far cheek and slowly turned it back to face herself, jolting him. He seemed to melt closer to her.

"Do not forget the one who has been kind to you all your life."

She ran her thumb across his lips and it took all my will-power not to stand and yell—to force her hands off him. My mother's words about the wrath of a Fae rang through me.

"Aye, ye have been good to me," McKale whispered, and

his hands slipped around her waist. "But my… my clan…" His hands began to roam up and down her sides and he closed the gap between them. The corner of FFG's lips turned up. McKale's face lowered to her cheek and he brushed his lips across her jaw. He moaned, forgetting what he'd been saying. She continued the conversation while his lips played across her magical skin.

"We can make this work, McKale of the Chaun."

"Aye," he murmured.

"We will find a way to ensure your clan's survival. Do not give yourself to the human yet. She could never dream of understanding you as I do. She—"

Another zap of magic buzzed through the air. Khalistah broke from McKale and looked toward the portal. It appeared as empty air to me.

"The Gatekeeper sends warning. I must return. Until then, please accept this token."

She pulled something shiny from her bodice—a golden talisman on a chain. McKale stared at her offering, dazed, making no move to take it.

"My love?" she said, her words stabbing my gut.

"Wait, I…" He blinked rapidly. "It is too much."

Don't take it! I silently begged.

She grasped his wrist and dropped the gift into his hand, curling his fingers around it. He closed his eyes.

"To remember me when we are not together."

He nodded once, almost imperceptibly, and then she ghosted into the field, disappearing into nothingness.

McKale leaned back against a tree, appearing dazed for a minute, and then he walked to the edge of the woods and peered again at the village. Looking for me? When he didn't see anything, he opened his hand and stared down at the gift he'd accepted. He sat hard on the ground, leaning his head back on a tree and shutting his eyes. I couldn't move, and it hurt to watch as he let his head roll forward. He propped his elbows on his knees and scrubbed his hands up and down his face, letting out a sound of frustration.

I wanted to go to him. But when I got there I wasn't sure if I'd want to comfort him or kick him in the head. I couldn't get the tender images from my mind.

I didn't want to hang out in the dark forest all night. Who knew how long he'd sit there waiting for me. I wasn't in the mood anymore after witnessing that sultry-eyed encounter. All I wanted now was to be alone. I stood up, tall and straight, holding the ball against my stomach with both hands draped over it. Then I walked out of the trees into the field.

"Robyn?" McKale called out, sounding unsure and confused. "Bloody 'ell." I heard him shuffle to his feet, and I walked even faster.

"Robyn wait!"

I did not want to look back. But I did.

He was standing stiff, appearing stricken as he realized I must've seen the whole thing. He started to make his way to me, but I shook my head.

"Don't." My voice was thick. "Please, McKale. I can't talk right now."

He stopped abruptly, as if I'd kicked him in the stomach. Facing forward again, I jogged the rest of the way back to my room.

ELEVEN

THANKFULLY CASSIDY WAS NOT in the room when I came storming in. I didn't want to talk. I was afraid I might cry, and that, above all, irritated the hell out of me. It was hard to see the positive in this situation. Even if he did like me, they had a history and she obviously had her mind set on him. All she had to do was touch him and he forgot me and everything else.

This dangerous little game was not a fair match. More like David and Goliath, only in this case Goliath was a small girl with big magic that could definitely kick my butt. Did I have anything in my faintly-magical human arsenal to use as a pebble and slingshot against her?

The only thing that came to mind was the fact that I could give him babies and she couldn't, but I would never use that. I wanted him to want *me*, as a person, not just my Leprechaun-growing hotel.

I lit the gas lamp. Then I tore open the lid to McKale's bin and shoved the soccer ball inside, slamming the lid shut again. *Do not forget the one who has been kind to you all your life.* Well, I'd dedicated my whole life to him too, and I hadn't even known him! I kicked the bin of proof. I was the person her people had hand-picked to bind with him. Why was she interfering?

I changed into pajamas and threw my clothes as hard as I could around the room. It was immature, but it felt good.

By the time I climbed into bed and settled down, I was ready to talk to Cassidy, but she still hadn't come back. I waited for her, running through the scene over and over in my mind. The way McKale touched her with tender familiarity and succumbed so easily to her will. Her words—telling him to stay away from me.

Geez, where was Cassidy?

I shut off the lamp. Darkness fit the mood. I must have waited for my sister a very long time because I fell asleep. I was startled awake by a shuffle and thump, followed by a loud whisper of, "*Shitballs!*" I sat up and fumbled for the gas lamp, finding and lighting it.

Whoa. Cassidy was a hot mess. Her clothes appeared damp and wrinkled. A lumpy pony-bun sat askew on top of her head.

"What are your clothes doing everywhere?" she asked. "I tripped over them."

"The Freaky Fae Girl came out of the portal and ruined my date."

"Shut up! What happened?" She came over and sank into the bed at my side while I told her everything.

After she'd called the FFG every bad name in the book, and then some creative names she'd made up on the fly, I felt the tiniest measure better.

"Why don't you just give him the presents and show him the video so he'll know how you really feel?"

My insides seized up at the idea of making myself

vulnerable in that way. She may as well have asked why I didn't dance a naked jig for him on one of the tables. Sure, he might like it, but then again he might think I'm a desperate fool.

When McKale explained his clan's feelings on the importance of gifts, he had really nailed how I felt about the bin. Giving him those presents was going to be like giving him a piece of myself. I wouldn't force my gifts on him like the FFG had done to him tonight. And I couldn't handle it if we weren't both honored in full by the giving and receiving of each heartfelt item.

"I can't," I told her. "Not right now."

"Yeah, you're right. He doesn't deserve it after kissing the enemy."

"He can't help it. She makes him lose his mind."

"Then why are you mad at him?"

"I don't know." I was shaking. "I guess I just want him to be strong enough that she won't affect him, but I know that's not fair. I've never felt this… this…" I searched for the right word.

"Vulnerable? Threatened?"

"Yes…" But I was feeling so much more than those two words.

"What else?" she asked. She scratched my back and I tried to relax.

"I don't know. I just, I'm starting to care about him, you know?"

"Are you scared he's gonna break your heart?"

"Maybe. I mean, I don't think he would on purpose, but if she keeps coming after him…"

We hadn't even kissed, and seeing him touch another girl

tonight, regardless of the circumstances, burned me up inside with hurt and jealousy. On top of that I was scared for my family. I felt powerless.

"Let's just take it day by day, 'kay?" Cass asked.

I almost grinned at her wisdom, but my face was not up for it. Instead I whispered, "Okay."

I almost asked Cassidy what in the world she was doing out so late, but then decided I didn't want to know. At least not tonight.

She hugged me, smelling like fresh mud and other stream life.

"You can have first dibs on the bathtub tomorrow, chickadee," I told her.

"You sayin' I stink?"

"To high Heaven."

She stood up and dropped her shorts on the floor with mine then climbed into her bed with the smelly shirt still on.

"Oh well," she said. "Night."

She sounded a little sad, but she was probably just tired and worried about me. I wished her goodnight and blew out the flame.

That evening I dreamed the FFG was luring McKale into the portal. I was running through the high grass, trying to get to him, but my movements were slow. Too slow. He followed her in, and the portal hung open, gaping. The two of them stood in the black hole, like a set of jaws ready to devour. I could see him, falling to his knees at her service. I screamed his name over and over, but he would not look away from her. She, however, looked right at me. And smiled.

The next week was awful and the weather didn't help. It rained almost every day.

Mornings were spent with Leilah and Rachelle doing chore duties. If it wasn't raining too hard Cassidy joined us. I'd really gotten the hang of it all, and some of the older women now acknowledged me and spoke to me in the kitchens. One even made an apron my size.

My favorite job was collecting eggs early in the morning. It was neat to stick my hand into the beds of straw in the hen house, wondering if my fingers would encounter a smooth shell.

McKale and I hadn't spoken. Not really. When my parents invited him to eat meals with us I greeted him and kept my face expressionless. I had to look at him, otherwise my parents would get suspicious, but the moment his eyes began to plead with mine, I looked away. I was torn between being wary of getting closer to him, and wishing he would seek me out and bare his soul. This inner turmoil made me grumpy.

My parents weren't dumb, and they knew me too well. No matter how hard I tried, I couldn't hide my mood. They planned picnics and walks for us as a family, attempting to cheer me or make me talk. Even when it was raining.

On the fifth day while thick clouds hovered above, we had a picnic dinner in a small flowery glen. Dad began walking around and pointing out different plants and herbs. He kept breaking off leaves and rubbing them between his fingers for us to smell. The fragrances were strong, spicy, and sweet. He peeled open a root of one and walked over to where I sat on the damp blanket. When he held it under my nose, an image of McKale's shy smile came to mind. I closed my eyes.

"Licorice root," Dad said. "You chew on it to extract the flavor. It's too tough to eat." Using a knife to cut off the outer layer, he handed me the bit of root like a candy stick. So this was what McKale often nibbled. When Dad turned around I tossed the thing away.

"It's wonderful in tea," Mom said, stretching out next to me.

"How do you know all of this?" Cassidy asked Dad.

"McKale's been teaching me."

My head snapped up. "He has? When?"

Dad plopped down next to me in the grass, not caring that it was wet. "We've taken a few walks together. He's a smart boy. Has an eye for botany."

It kind of warmed my heart that he'd been spending time with Dad. I pushed aside that nice thought and told myself not to care.

"I think it's a shame that he sits all alone at meals," Mom said. "Nobody pays him any mind."

"Yes, it's a shame," Dad agreed. "I think bad habits have formed over the years, and it doesn't help that McKale's introverted. Somewhere along the line he closed himself off to relationships with the others, so he's partially to blame for having no friends."

"He does have a friend," Cass said.

"Who? That Clourichaun boy?" Mom asked. "I imagine it's not the same as having a close friend in his own clan, though. The Clour don't share the same work ethic as the Chaun."

"The Clour have responsibilities in their clan," Cassidy said. "I mean, I assume they do, because otherwise how could they live. You know?"

"Doing the bare minimum to get by is a little different than having a hard-working, productive society," Dad told her. "It may seem sexist the way the Chaun have rigid responsibilities for the men and women, but each individual's role is important. Everyone benefits from one another's hard work."

Cassidy didn't contradict or say anything else.

"You know you can talk to us, Robyn." Mom reached out and took my hand.

"I know," I told her. "Thank you."

Inside, I was a bundle of confusion. I wanted them to like McKale and I was afraid if I told them what happened with the FFG, they would get upset all over again. I didn't want to incite "Protective Dad Mode" and I wasn't sure how much we needed to worry at this point.

Eventually the sky darkened and the rain started again, so we gathered our things and began walking back to the village. Mom and Dad took the lead, swinging their linked hands back and forth. None of us were bothered by the soft sprinkles. We'd gotten used to being rained on.

"Good job playing hard to get with McKale," Cassidy whispered as we walked.

"That's not really what I'm trying to do."

"Well, it's working. He just stares when you play soccer

and when you dance at the festivals."

"Maybe he's staring because he can't believe he's betrothed to an Amazon woman."

"Oh, please." Cassidy laughed. "If you saw the way he was looking, it's more like he's caught between whether or not to punch something or eat you up."

"Whatever." I really did not want to get my hopes up.

"It's not his fault the FFG's stalking him."

"I know, but…" But what? "You didn't see them together."

"His body has an auto-response to her magic, Robyn. You should be pulling him closer not pushing him away."

I grunted. The fact of the matter was that the FFG was a problem, and she wasn't going away. I couldn't seem to stop my instinct of self-preservation.

"Let's find the guys and hang out with them tonight!" Cassidy hopped a little as she walked by my side.

"No, Cass. I'm tired and it's raining. I just want to go to bed."

She exhaled dramatically and flopped her arms down at her side. "Are you, like, depressed or something?"

I bristled. I didn't want to be depressed, but maybe I was. And at the moment Cassidy's pushiness made me feel unreasonably annoyed.

"I'm honestly tired," I said. "I get up early and work all day, while some people get to sleep in because they stayed out all night playing."

"Hey, I help out sometimes. And you don't have to bite my head off, geez. I'm just surprised by how you're acting. I mean, if you want to give up so easily, that's your prerogative."

"I'm not giving up. But I'm also not getting involved in whatever game McKale and the FFG are playing. He hasn't even tried to talk to me. I don't expect you to understand. You're in a pressure-free relationship with a guy who doesn't have a life-sized murderous Barbie telling him to stay away from you."

Up ahead, Mom turned to glance at us and we smiled automatically, lowering our voices.

"Well, if it was me, I'd fight for him. That's all I'm saying."

"How do you fight a Fae, Cass? You can't! Even if I somehow make him really want me, I can't make *her* stop wanting *him*!"

"I was only trying to talk, sheesh. Calm down and take a Midol," she grumbled, quickening her footsteps until she was alongside our parents.

I sighed and crossed my arms, walking alone. I hated these ugly feelings and I knew I was taking it out on the people I loved. This was not me. Something had to give. Soon.

☘

On the tenth morning after the date that didn't happen, I smiled to myself and placed a warm brown egg into the basket on my arm. It was the first dry morning, which lifted my spirits. Preparing to reach into the straw and feel for another, I caught sight of something moving on the other side of the fence that was bigger than any farm animal. I stood abruptly, banging my head on the top of the hen house and making a chicken squawk and flap her wings.

"Ow. Sorry," I said to the hen. Then I stooped to set down my basket. Through the slats in the wood I spied McKale's profile and my stomach flipped. The hen stared up at me like she was wondering what I was waiting for. I took a deep breath and ducked out of the hen house to face him.

I looked at him openly, hoping he would see that I was glad for his visit. And insanely relieved that he'd sought me out.

He stood there shifting his feet, his arms behind his back. His sideburns stuck out more than usual, like he hadn't bothered to trim them. I took no satisfaction knowing this situation was affecting his grooming. But maybe if he let himself go long enough the FFG would lose interest. Ha.

"Are you on your way to work?" I asked.

"Aye," he whispered, more gruff than usual.

In a slow movement, he pulled his hands from behind his back and held out a tiny woven basket brimming with plump strawberries and blackberries. "I brought ye something, Robyn."

My heart sputtered.

He held the berries out to me in the palm of his long hand. I reached out and took his offering, pulling it gently against my chest.

I'd never seen any berries in the kitchens. There were mostly breads and proteins in there. Fruits and veggies were picked outside and eaten at will, like snacks. I noted the slight way McKale's hand shook, and the look of anticipation in his eyes as he watched me, waiting. It was then that it hit me.

This was a gift.

"Thank you," I whispered, feeling everything that had

hardened inside of me softening again, that easily. Guilt for avoiding him punched me from the inside and I felt horrible for the wall I'd built around myself.

A relieved huff of air blew from his lips and he put his hands on his hips, hanging his head.

"I'd best be on my way," he said.

"Wait." I stepped forward, but I had no idea what to do or say. *What happens now?* Movies and books always made it seem so easy to open up and talk to someone you liked. But in real life it was so, so hard.

"Have you seen her again since that night?" Of all the questions I could have asked him, this was the one I didn't even want to know the answer to. Why was I torturing myself? It was bad enough that I'd lie in bed every night imagining her sneaking through the portal and slipping into his room.

McKale's forehead tightened at the question and he hesitantly met my eyes. "No."

"You know you can't have us both," I whispered, feeling courageous.

I almost told him that he couldn't have his cake and eat it too, but he probably wouldn't understand the old adage. It was a stupid saying anyway.

McKale looked tense enough to bolt at any second, but I was all geared up now, so I kept going with nothing to lose.

"I need you to know, McKale, that I want this to work. I like you—"

"*Robyn…*" The tone of his voice was laced with layer upon layer of "I don't believe you," and it frustrated me.

"Why is that so hard to believe?"

He stared downward, running a hand over his face while

I questioned him.

"When you were growing up, didn't you ever wonder about me? About what I'd be like? Didn't you ever get excited that it could be *good*?"

I knew he was way out of his comfort zone, but I didn't care. He opened his mouth and paused a second before blurting, "Aye, Robyn, I wondered. And I assumed you would dread the arrangement as much as I. No female had ever shown interest in me until…"

I closed my eyes and held up my free palm like a stop sign. "Until her." Familiar envy churned, but I forged ahead. "You might have been dreading our binding, but that doesn't mean I was. Some day I'll make you believe me. I'll prove it to you."

"You needn't prove anything. Ye've already surpassed my every expectation."

"Only because your expectations were so low."

He winced.

The morning chores weren't complete, however I needed to take advantage of this moment while I was feeling brave.

"Come with me," I told him. Still clutching the basket of berries to my chest, I headed toward my hut with McKale following, silent.

"Wait right here," I said when I got to my room and he nodded. "I'll be right back."

Cassidy sat up groggily in her bed.

"Whatcha doin'?" she asked.

I bent down to the bin, opening it and taking out the soccer ball. I felt a rush of excitement mixed with nerves. Cassidy's eyes got huge and she perked up.

"You're giving it to him?"

"Yep. Get dressed and come help me with the animals in a little bit. I'll tell you everything."

She fell back on the bed, kicking and punching the air. "Yes! Yes! Finally!"

I left the room smiling. When I saw McKale leaning against the wall of our hut it was my turn to feel shy and uncertain. He eyed the ball with curiosity as he came to stand in front of me.

"I guess you haven't heard of the World Cup, have you?" He shook his head, so I briefly explained how it worked. As I held his interest and attention it hit me all at once how much I'd missed him. He crossed his arms and listened as I told him about the game we'd attended.

As he stared down at the ball in my hands, his arms uncrossed and fell to his sides. It was hard to breathe, I was so nervous. When he finally looked at me I had to grit my teeth against a wave of emotion. He wasn't crying, but his eyes were definitely shining, and his face wore an emotion of awe and disbelief.

"It's for you, McKale." I held out my offering, just as he'd done. I was awarded with an adorably boyish grin.

"Truly?"

"Yes. It's been yours for a long time. And if you accept it, I want you to use it. Have fun with it."

He reached out and placed a hand on each side of the ball, but didn't take it yet.

"I'm honored to accept this gift from ye, Robyn." His eyes were bright and the walls around my heart were smashed to pieces.

"I'm honored that you will accept it." I swallowed hard as he took the ball from me. "And maybe we can play together?"

"I'd like that very much," he said.

"Have a good day at work," I whispered.

I clasped my hands behind my back. He gave me a small bow and ambled away, absorbed in every detail of the ball. But when he got to the corner he stopped to glance back. I stood still, soaking in the look of him. That brief glimpse of gratitude spoke volumes to my heart. Come what may, I would not be avoiding him again.

TWELVE

IN THE HOURS BEFORE supper, I sat in a quiet corner of the open field to paint my nails. I leaned back against a tree at the edge of the forest, admiring my view of the village. It was interesting and sweet to see a few of the younger males helping the women folk do their chores, mostly the heavy lifting. They had flat carts, resembling wheelbarrows, which they used to move buckets of waste to a far area of the lands where they made compost.

Laughter sounded in the forest behind me. Rock chased Cass down the nearby path, and when he caught her, he pinned her to the tree and kissed her with a passion that surprised me. I had to look away and keep myself from yelling when he started getting handsy. I'd been so preoccupied with my own drama and emotional overload that I hadn't taken time to ask what was up with those two.

Cassidy didn't have the best track record when it came to guys. She couldn't have a romantic fling without becoming emotionally involved. Rock posed a huge dilemma—too many factors stood in the way of them being together. His history being the biggest. Second being no way of having a long distanced relationship. Rock didn't exactly have WIFI out here.

Cassidy came bursting out of the trail, running right past me.

"Hey," I called. She spun, looking breathless and flushed, and smiled when she saw me.

"Hey." She came over and sat down at my side. "Ooh, paint my nails?"

"Sure. You look happy."

"Yeah." She placed her hand on my knee and zoned out, visiting la-la land while I painted. I waited until I was on her second hand to talk.

"So… what's up with you and Rock?"

She was silent as I swiped the polish twice over her pinky nail. I was afraid to look up.

"I've never met anyone like him. Ronan's amazing."

Ronan. Yeah, she had it bad.

"Amazing, huh?" I looked at her now, at the dazzled glint in her eyes.

"What would you say if I told you I'm thinking about… you know…?"

Uh, what the what? I cleared my throat and I fought to stay calm as I answered. I didn't want her doing anything she'd regret.

"I would say I think it's a very bad idea."

Her face tightened. "Why?"

She really had to ask?

"Cass, why would you give your virginity to a miscreant cousin of the Leprechaun who you'll probably never see again?"

It came out meaner than I'd meant, like a major bash against her overall judgment, not to mention the guy she liked. She yanked her hand away from me.

"Oh, did I say *thinking* about it?" she snapped. "I meant I already have."

"What?" I leapt to my feet, standing over her. "No. You're lying."

She shrugged nonchalantly, the challenge leaving her.

I needed to stay calm, but my voice rose despite my efforts. "When?!"

She looked away from me. "The night we first went to the waterfall."

Oh, my goodness. She was serious. I thought back to that night. "When he stole our clothes? That was, like, our second day here!"

"Yeah, I guess I'm just fast like that." Her eyes filled with hurt.

"No, that's not what I said, Cass. I just meant… that was a long time ago. Why didn't you tell me?"

Reigning in my emotion, I sat back down across from her. Cassidy had never withheld anything from me. I knew every detail of how far she'd gone with all of her past boyfriends. We told each other everything.

"Because I knew you'd react like this." She crossed her arms, then uncrossed them and checked to see if she'd messed up her nails. "And because you were busy. And sad. I didn't want to upset you more."

While I'd been wallowing in self-pity about the stupid FFG, my baby sister had lost her virginity and had nobody to talk to.

"I wish you would have told me," I whispered.

"I'm sorry, Sissy."

She hadn't called me Sissy in years. Cassidy's eyes

scrunched up and she covered her face as all the emotion she'd kept hidden came to the surface.

"Oh, Cass." I sat down and held her close, letting her lean on my shoulder. "I'm the one who's sorry. I should have been there for you."

I was pretty sure Cassidy had never kept anything secret for two weeks.

"This whole trip I've been so emotional," she sniffed. "I cry almost every time I'm alone. I don't know what's wrong with me."

I did. In a way, she was losing her big sister. We only had a couple more months together. There was also the fact that she couldn't help me against the FFG. Things weren't working out the way we'd hoped. And then there was Rock: a fun distraction to help her escape it all.

"This whole thing has been overwhelming for both of us," I told her. "But no matter what, don't ever feel like you can't talk to me. No matter how crazy things are."

She sat up, nodding.

"Here comes McKale," she whispered, wiping her eyes.

I followed her gaze. He'd finished work a little earlier than normal. Cassidy stood.

"You don't have to leave," I told her.

"It's okay. I'm gonna go shower."

"All right. I'll see you at dinner."

She left me, giving McKale a little wave as they passed one another.

I wished I had a more cheerful greeting for him when he sat down.

"Are ye all right, then?" he asked.

"I don't know." I felt myself clamming up.

Things had been more comfortable between McKale and I the last few days, but with each hour that passed I wondered if he'd been visited again. Constant fear nagged the back of my conscience. I hated it. And now there was this strange sense of loss that settled over me for Cass.

Needing to keep my hands busy, I opened the red polish and began to paint my toes. I'd already removed the cracked old polish. I felt McKale watching me.

"Has she come to see you again?" I made myself ask.

My stomach knotted up, and I felt him stiffen next to me.

"Nay," he answered.

I kept painting. "Will you tell me if she does?"

"Do ye wish me to?" His voice remained quiet and solemn.

"Yes."

"Aye. Then I will."

I gave a curt nod and tried to push the topic from my mind.

One foot was done. I dunked the brush back into the little jar and McKale stilled me, placing his hand on mine.

"Might I try?" he asked.

I let him take the bottle of nail polish from me. He dunked the brush several times. When he brought it to his nose he jerked his head back and coughed.

"Yeah, the fumes are really strong. I should have warned you not to sniff it."

He blinked his hazel eyes rapidly. Once his head cleared and he'd finished examining the bottle, he moved himself into position in front of me. I forced back a smile and pushed my foot closer to him. Just as he was about to touch the brush to my big toe, he pulled away.

"What if I bung it up?"

"I have this magic stuff here called nail polish remover here to fix any mistakes." I held up the plastic bottle.

McKale looked apprehensive, but decided to take my word for it. He got to work, his tongue peeking out from the corner of his mouth as he concentrated. It was one of the most adorable things I'd ever seen. He was accurate, with an eye for small detail. We both peered down and admired my foot when he was finished. He lifted the brush to put it back in the jar, and his eyes got big.

"Oi! Bollocks. It's on me!" We both looked down at his ankle, where he'd accidentally touched the brush. He tried to wipe it, but it smeared and he rubbed it frantically. I laughed and grabbed the polish remover, soaking a cotton ball.

"This is really strong, too," I warned him. "Try not to breathe it in."

I ran the cool cotton ball over the inside of his ankle, swirling it around until the red polish was gone. He ran a finger over the spot, marveling as if it really were magic.

"McKale?" I said.

"Hm?"

I didn't want to ruin this nice moment, but I craved complete honesty between us.

"What's going to happen?" I asked him. "She told you to stay away from me, and I'm pretty sure she wasn't joking."

He watched as I positioned my feet in the grass with care.

"I was no' expecting a reaction such as that from her," he said quietly. "I meant to be firm when I told her t'would not work, and then she laid hands on me… and my mind…"

I didn't like the way his voice trailed off when he remembered her touch.

"Yeah, I know. I saw," I reminded him. "You were… *dazzled.*"

His forehead knit together in misunderstood frustration.

"Aye, but it cannot be helped e'en when I fight it. A simple touch of Fae buggers the mind. Only the body can react."

Lovely.

"Have you kissed her?" I asked. My heart kicked with jealousy at the thought.

He hesitated. "Nay… not properly."

"What does that mean—not properly?" I asked.

He got shy again. "Just a touch of the lips, not like I've seen others snog."

They'd pecked. How sweet. I wanted to kill her.

Someone called my name from a distance. McKale and I looked up. Mom was walking toward us, so we got up to meet her. She was worried, crossing her arms.

"Hi, McKale," she said before focusing on me. "Did you have a fight with Cass?"

"Wha—no. I mean, we talked, but it wasn't a fight." Not exactly.

"I just went to get her for supper and it looks like she's been crying. I don't know what to do. She won't talk to me. *You* won't talk to me. What is going on with you girls?"

Oh, shoot, she was about to cry. Her eyes watered and she uncrossed her arms, running hands through her hair and then smacking them down at her sides with a shaky, loud sigh. I looked at McKale, who peered back at me with discomfort.

I nodded and touched his arm, signaling that he could leave us.

Mom sniffled and shook her head. "I'm sorry," she said. "I didn't mean to chase him off."

"It's okay, Mom. Come on, walk with me."

We grabbed hands and strolled to the edge of the clearing, away from where the supper crowd was filtering in.

"Is it that boy, Rock?" she asked me.

"Partly. And part me. You know Cass. It's hard for her to be cooped up here, knowing when it's time to leave I won't be coming home."

"She's going to have a hard time without you."

I looked down at the damp dirt under the tree canopy where we walked. "I know. She's probably going to drive you and Dad nuts."

"No more than usual. Okay, maybe slightly more than usual, but we can handle it." She smiled and dabbed remnants of moisture away from her eyes with her fingers. "Are you sure that's the only thing going on? She's been so edgy."

I carefully responded. "She's just growing up."

The simple answer seemed to pacify her. We walked in silence a few moments until she stopped and pulled my arm to turn us face-to-face. "Tell me what's going on with you. Why have you been so sad? It looks like you and McKale are getting along. Am I wrong?"

I opened my mouth, prepared to feed her more generic falsehoods. When I looked into those loving eyes, what tumbled out instead was the truth.

"The Fae girl came back once after our first night here. She won't keep her hands off McKale and I think she's jealous that he seems to like me." Terror flashed in Mom's eyes and she stopped walking. "I don't know, Mom. Please don't say anything to Brogan. *Please*. We're trying to work through it. McKale is trying to break ties with her, but you know. It's a delicate situation."

"Oh, dear heavens. Have mercy." She closed her eyes.

"I don't want you to lay awake at night worrying," I told her. "I'm sure everything is going to be fine. I'm not getting involved—I'll stay far away from her. McKale will deal with her and fix this."

I hoped.

"It's my job to worry about you, Robyn! Och, you've been holding this inside yourself this whole time? Do you have any idea how that grieves me so? I'm going to worry no matter what, so you may as well be open. Sometimes you have to rely on others for help. It's not just about you and McKale. Your father and I, and Brogan, too, we all need to work together. If the Fae comes again—if there's another altercation, no matter how small, come to us. *Immediately*. Swear it."

I nodded. "I will. I swear." Her grip tightened on my hand. She pulled me into a firm hug, mumbling something Irishy in her motherly way. Her accent had returned with a flourish since we'd been in Ireland.

As we turned to walk up for dinner together, the burden on my soul felt much lighter having confided in someone I trusted. When we got to the table, Dad was already there, sitting with Cassidy and McKale. Mom gave Dad a meaningful look and he nodded. They'd talk later.

♣

Days passed with no visits or "altercations" as Mom called it. McKale was sweet to me, and I felt a rush each time I caught him gazing my way.

I tried to keep Cassidy busy and spend as much time with her as I could. I felt guilty for how self-centered I'd been and I wanted to make up for lost time. McKale showed my sister and me where we could find wild berries growing. We spent afternoons gorging on sun-sweetened strawberries and blackberries until our fingers were stained deep red and violet. Her spirits lifted, but with each passing day mine grew heavier with thoughts of my family leaving me and wondering when the FFG would show her perfect face again.

McKale and I went to the waterfall with Cassidy and Rock one week before my birthday. The weather was hazy and warm that afternoon. I spread out a blanket, but McKale and I ended up scouting the forest floor for different edible mushrooms while Cass and Rock swam. The two of them were a loud pair, screaming with laughter and splashing. At least she wore a bathing suit this time. I had mine on under my sundress, but didn't feel like swimming.

We made our way back to the blanket with handfuls of morel and oyster mushrooms.

"We'll give them to Leilah," McKale said, sitting next to me. "She does this thing with venison and butter and 'shrooms. 'Tis amazing."

I crossed my ankles in front of me and smiled at him. Maybe I'd learn to cook some things with Leilah's help. So far

I'd avoided the kitchen as much as possible, intimidated by the lack of a microwave and easy-to-use stovetop. But I was beginning to feel comfortable enough to give things a try.

Cassidy and Rock walked up from the stream, shaking off excess water before lying on the blanket next to us. Rock tickled the underside of Cass's knee and she laughed, curling into him until they were kissing. They embraced and rolled, bumping me.

"Uh, guys, I don't think there's enough room on the blanket for that," I said, staring intently at the pile of mushrooms between McKale and myself. Rock looked up at me with a lazy grin, not moving away from my sister in the slightest.

"Always room for a bit o' snoggin'. Perhaps the two of ye should give it a go."

He bent his head to kiss her again and my face flamed.

"Rock!" Cassidy chastised, pushing him back a little. "Don't embarrass them."

"They could use a bit of proddin', is all. McKale's ne'er properly been—"

"Rock…" McKale's low voice oozed warning. I wondered if Rock knew about the peck with FFG.

Cassidy's head sprung up and she turned to look at McKale sitting at the edge of the blanket. "You've never kissed anyone? Awww! That is so cute!"

I cringed and he shifted, glaring daggers straight at his friend.

"Don't worry, McKale," Cassidy said. "Robyn has a little experience. She'll teach ya."

I frowned down at her. "Not cool."

"What?" She shrugged and laughed, so I gave her a hard shove with my foot.

Rock exclaimed, "Oho! An experienced lassie, eh?" His eyebrows danced at me.

Before I could respond, McKale asked, "Have ye been with another bloke?" His serious voice made us all shut up and look at him. His eyes were a cloudy blaze on me and I flushed with heat at his jealous tone.

"What? No! I haven't..." I stuttered. "There were two kisses, but I'm not, like, *experienced*. If anything, I wish I could erase both those from my memory." I pulled my knees up and wrapped my arms around them, refusing to look at him now. I shot Cass a glare.

My first kiss had been during a game of truth or dare in seventh grade. I did it because I hadn't wanted everyone at that party thinking I was chicken. The second happened last year, and I blamed Cassidy for that one. Mostly. Brad had a crush on me, and Cassidy talked me into letting him kiss me. Her reasoning? She said I needed the practice so McKale wouldn't think I was a bad kisser.

Well, Brad hadn't exactly been "good practice" with his overly eager tongue that treated my mouth like an extreme sports arena. I shuddered thinking about that choke-worthy incident.

And was McKale jealous? I wanted to tell him not to worry, that neither of those guys had "dazzled" me, but it was too humiliating.

Cassidy sat up next to me, reaching out and touching my shoulder in apology. "We're just messin' around." I ignored her.

A rustling noise and voices sounded from across the

stream. Dashy of the Clourichaun and one of the carrot cousins came out of the trees, their strawberry blond and red hair sticking out from their heads like straw. They were as thin and grungy looking as ever. Dashy's face lit up when he saw us.

"Mason girls! When are ye comin' back to play a bit o' ball again?"

"Hey, Dashy," I said with a smile. "We do need to come back soon."

"Oy, there Rock!" cried the redhead, sounding grumpy. "'Tis your turn to cook the meal and clean the kitchen. Get on wit' ye! We'll no' do it for ye again!"

"We're hungry," Dashy said.

"Shite," Rock groaned.

I was struck dumb by the thought of Rock cooking anything. They were like a bunch of overgrown orphans. I couldn't help but feel concern for their health and well-being over there all alone.

"Do you want some help?" I asked Rock.

His head spun toward me, a look of wide-eyed panic on his face. "Nay! 'Tis no' fit fer company. I'll return on the morrow."

"Rock," McKale called. He scooped up the pile of mushrooms and held them out. Rock's face lit up as he pulled out the bottom of his thin shirt, making a carrier for the fungi.

"Much obliged, Kale, m'boy."

He clambered to his feet, patting down the wet curls on his head with his free hand. Sparing a wave and a brief backward glance at Cassidy, he waded through the stream to the other Clour boys. They immediately began jabbing at one another, grabbing ears and grunting as they disappeared into the woods.

"Do you think they're okay over there?" Cassidy asked. She and I both looked at McKale.

"Aye, they get by."

McKale and I sat close that night at supper, across the table from the rest of my family. Mom smiled at the two of us with nurturing warmth, willing us to be strong, come what may.

"Will there be music and dancing tonight?" Dad asked McKale.

"Oh, I believe so, Mr. Mason, aye."

"Are you gonna bust a move, Daddy?" Cassidy asked.

"Well, I have been practicing." He puffed out his chest and Mom giggled like a girl. You'd think the two of them would be sick of each other after being cooped up in this village, but they acted like it was a second honeymoon or something.

After dinner, my parents went for a walk before festivities began. The three of us sat there in silence. Cassidy stared at the fields.

"I wish we could do some *real* dancing." She zoned out for a second, and then her eyes cleared and she bolted up straight. Her eyes twinkled and her telltale mischievous smile appeared. *Uh-oh*. Cassidy had an idea. She whispered, leaning over the table toward us with a zealous look in her eyes.

"Let's leave the village tonight!"

"What?" I asked. "We can't. You're crazy."

She reached across the table and grabbed my hand, trying to get me to share her vision.

"Yes, we can! Oh, my gosh! I'll get Rock, and the four of us can take the car. We'll be back before the morning. Nobody will ever know!"

Dreams played out across her face as she bounced up and down on the wooden bench. A sliver of her excitement sneaked into me, cool and tingly, and I looked up at McKale.

"I'm no' certain," he said, wearing the tense-forehead look.

"Have you ever left here?" Cassidy asked. He shook his head and her eyes grew big.

"Never? Come on, guys! Let's do it! It'll be so much fun, I promise."

"Where will we go?" I asked, always having to play the devil's advocate, even though I already knew without a doubt that Cassidy would win. Her enthusiasm had infected me and I could feel it pumping through my veins. "What if we get lost?"

"There aren't exactly many roads to get us lost. We'll go to the nearest town."

"Okay, but, maybe we don't have to be sneaky," I said. "We could just ask Dad. He'd probably let us go, and even give us directions—"

"Uh-uh! No way!" Cassidy shook her head. "What if he decides to be all over-protective and say no? Or, even if Dad agrees, he'll want to tell Brogan, and *he* might say no. We can't take the chance. I *need* to get out of here. Come on, Robyn. Please?"

Aw, not the little sister doe eyes. She knew I was softening because she bobbed her eyebrows up and down.

She then pinched my leg under the table with her crazy monkey toes and I laughed, kicking her toes away and squirming on the bench. Giddy glee bubbled inside me, and I welcomed the presence of happiness after weeks of tension.

McKale and I shared a smile, and it sent a hot shiver down my back. The thought of getting far away from that evil portal was glorious. Cassidy was a fun-loving genius. Suddenly I didn't even care if we got in trouble. It would be worth it.

"Okay, fine."

Cass gave a little squeal and clapped her hands.

"Has she gone mad?" McKale asked me.

"She does this kind of thing all the time," I assured him. "Curing boredom is sort of her specialty."

Cass beamed at us with crazy eyes.

"What will it be like?" McKale asked. "Out there?" It was nearly impossible to imagine never having been off this land. His timidity made him look younger, and he was so cute I wanted to kiss him. The thought of kissing him caused me to suck in a breath. I looked at his mouth. His bottom lip was fuller than the top one; it looked soft and inviting. I had to blink and force my eyes back up to his. What had he asked me? Oh, yeah.

"It's a lot different out there, McKale. *A lot.* It might be weird at first, but it'll be fine. We'll be together."

He nodded, and this time it was his turn to look down at my mouth. I held my breath and savored his absorbed interest. When my lips felt suddenly dry, I gave them the smallest lick, and he jolted in his seat.

"Aww, look at you two," Cassidy said. She fluttered her eyes at us and sighed, laying her chin on interlaced fingers.

McKale scratched his cheek.

"Right, then. I'll fetch Rock," he said, standing. My sister and I watched him retreat into the trees, then we grinned at one another like a pair of exalted deviants.

Oh, yes. Tonight, we were taking McKale and getting the heck out of this place. I could hardly wait.

Take *that*, FFG.

THIRTEEN

I THOUGHT CASSIDY WAS going to give us away with her erratic behavior all night during the Leprechaun festivities. She strummed her fingers on the table and shifted nonstop, staring at the sunset and glowering at the partying Chaun. Our family sat together at a table while the music played and people danced.

"You're sure hyper all of a sudden," Mom said to her.

"She wants to dance," I blurted. "But... nobody's asked her." I sent Cass a warning glare that I hoped would make her chill.

"I'll dance with you, chickadee." Dad stood up and held out his hand, which she accepted, and she seemed relieved to be doing something.

Mom and I watched them for a bit. Then she got up from her side of the table and came over to sit close next to me. She ran a hand over my hair, then the backs of her fingers down my cheek—all the while gazing at me like I was some kind of miracle. I didn't mind. It was one of those mom things I loved, although at the moment it made me feel guilty since we'd hatched our secret plan of momentary escape.

"Do you need more time before the binding, Robyn? Because I'll tell Brogan myself, if you do."

Ah, so that's what was on her mind.

"I don't know." I chewed on my bottom lip. "Maybe ask again in a few days?"

She smiled. "Okay. Is there anything you want to know? About what to expect… after the binding?"

My face warmed and I peeked around to make sure nobody was listening. "I don't think so, Mom. You've already explained everything."

"Well, the science of it, yes, but there's so much more, love."

There were a lot of things I wondered, but I didn't know how to articulate them. Right now, the thought of binding and sex and all of that made me feel like I was taking the drop on a roller coaster. I was too nervous. I wasn't ready.

She wound my hair behind my ear and her eyes shone. "I'm always here if you need me. Your father and I will visit every year. I promise. And I'm certain Cass won't be able to stay away either."

Now she was making me feel a little weepy. I hated thinking about being here without my family. Especially while things weren't one hundred percent stable. But would things here ever be stable with the FFG lurking? Would continue to interfere even after we were bound? Angry discomfort reared inside of me. Each time I started to feel normal and happy, I remembered her and all cheerful thoughts vanished.

Mom gave my cheek one last pat, and we turned to watch the party together. Mom kept an eye on her man, and I watched McKale. He sat on the stump again while the other musicians stood. I had a feeling he didn't like to stand tall in the midst of the other Chaun if he could help it. He tapped a foot and moved the bow at hyper-speed as the song reached its crescendo, the volume rising to meet demands of an exuberant, stomping crowd. He caught my eye and winked.

It was my first McKale wink. I leaned my chin against my palm and smiled into my hand.

That night seemed to last extra long, but the moon was finally high and the crowd began to thin. Mom and Dad called the party quits, kissing us girls and then strolling to their room arm-in-arm. Soon the band was packing up. Cassidy and I went to McKale.

"Let's go back to our rooms to get ready," I told him. "We'll come knock on your door to get you when it's time." Half of his mouth went up in a grin, like he was still unsure but humoring us. He agreed, and we went our separate ways.

Cassidy and I were on a sheer adrenaline high. We ran to our room, tearing through our clothes as quietly as we could and putting on the best outfits we'd brought—black pants and shiny tank-tops. We took our tiny purses with as much money as we could stuff in them, plus lip-glosses and IDs. Cassidy had snuck into our parent's room during dinner for the car key. Time to go.

Opening the door a crack, we found that the coast was clear and tiptoed out of our bungalow, holding our heeled shoes in our hands. I led us to McKale's room, since of course I'd stalked my binding mate to find out where he slept. And I didn't even feel like a creeper for doing it. After all, it was my future room, too. I placed a hand on my stomach, feeling flutters.

I tapped on his wooden door, and he opened it, stepping

out with care to stay quiet. He stopped and took in the full sight of me, paying special attention to the fitted pants. At first I feared that he thought I looked funny, but his stance and appreciative gaze assured me otherwise. He was being the tiniest bit bolder toward me lately, and I liked it.

The three of us shared rebellious expressions before ghosting our way around the bungalows, passing the big Shoe House, and rounding the corner. Rock was already there, sprawled across the hood of the car. Cass ran to him for a hug, and he spun her around. They kept silent, which amazed me.

She then climbed into the driver's seat just as we'd planned, leaving the door open a crack, so no one would hear the "click." She put the car in neutral and steered it while the boys and I pushed. The initial hill was killer, despite how compact the vehicle might have been, but we were so pumped on adrenaline there was no stopping us. It took ten minutes to get over the hills and to the edge of the forest with the driving path. It was far enough away that nobody should have been able to hear the engine start, but just in case, we pushed it into the trees before the three of us hopped inside.

Rock sat in front with Cassidy. I'd agreed to drive us home if she drove there.

"It's so weird to drive on this side of the car," Cassidy murmured.

My heart jumped when she started the engine. It sounded so loud.

"Go!" I whispered from the back seat. She took off, kicking up a little foliage, and by the time she got to the boulder, the four of us were laughing, exuberant.

"Japers!" Rock exclaimed. "Bloody brilliant!"

"I can't believe we're doin' this," McKale said, turning to look through the back windshield.

"Are you nervous about being caught?" I wondered aloud.

"Nay, not that. 'Tis just I've ne'er been farther than the end of Rainbow Lane."

"Rainbow Lane?" I asked. Cassidy turned past the boulder, putting us on the main road.

"Aye." McKale pointed back over his shoulder. "The lane through the trees. Long ago visitors named it Rainbow Lane. They say each time they came through the forest they'd find a rainbow over the village."

Cassidy cast me a smile over her shoulder. McKale sat behind her since she was able to pull up her seat to give him more leg room.

"You don't guard a giant pot of gold, by any chance, do you?" she asked.

"Gold?" McKale shook his head. "We've no use for it. Jewels are far more worthy. Only thing we guard is the portal."

His mention of the portal gave me the heebie-jeebies. I couldn't wait to be far, far away from that thing for one night.

"So, a giant pot of jewels, then?" Cassidy asked. I wondered if the guys could pick up on her underlying merriment as easily as I could.

"Wha's with the pots 'o shiny things?" Rock asked. His arm rested over the back of her seat.

"There are lots of old fables about Leprechauns," she told him. "People all around the world have heard of you guys."

"Truly?" asked McKale. "What sort o' tales?"

Cassidy and I spent the first half hour of the trip telling them all of the different Leprechaun legends. Rock was offended that tales of the Clourichaun were not as well known, and that the Chaun actually received some of the credit for Clour history.

Rock seemed at ease and treated our outing as the adventure it was, but when we quieted McKale sat stiff in his seat peering out of the windows with apprehension. I placed a hand on his warm forearm.

"Are you okay?" I whispered.

He relaxed under my touch.

"Aye," he whispered back. "'Tis strange, is all."

Before I could respond, Cassidy's loud, excited voice filled the car.

"Do me a favor," she said to Rock. "Say *'They're always trying to steal me Lucky Charms.'*"

Oh my freakin' gosh…

Rock and McKale shared a confused, amused look. Then Rock shrugged and said the line with true Irish gusto.

We were all quiet for half a second before I snorted. I'm not sure how Cassidy managed to stay on the road because she and I went into a state of hysterical laughter. Her warble of giggling was so infectious even the guys began to chuckle.

"Wha's so funny, then?" McKale asked. "Ye all right, Robyn?" I tried to nod, because talking was impossible.

"That's how she laughs!" Cassidy sputtered. "No sound comes out—she just gasps!"

I was totally self-conscious of my laugh, but some things just couldn't be helped. And now that McKale knew I was okay, he let himself laugh as well, and patted my back.

When we finally began to calm, Rock said the line again

with a big smile, and Cassidy and I went into another fit. I thought I'd pass out from lack of breath. And it didn't help when Cass sang, *"They're magically delicious!"* Her laugh was loud and adorable. I practically made no noise except sucking air as I doubled over, smacking the door rest and shaking my head.

Cassidy tried to explain to them about the cereal commercial, but she wasn't making much sense through her laughter. Besides, the terminology completely confounded them. Television. Marshmallows.

"Never mind," I said, able to breathe again at last. "We'll get you a box of it someday."

Cassidy turned on the radio, but static filled the reception. After a few minutes of trying, she found a station playing folk music. McKale sat up straighter.

"How'd ye do that? Where's it coming from?"

We explained radio signals as best as we could, and spent the next half hour showing the guys different gadgets on the car and telling them about the different technologies available. Although they asked a lot of questions, I didn't think they really believed such things were possible—human magic. The irony was not lost on me, given that they were magical Leprechauns who most humans didn't believe in.

My face and abs were hurting from smiling and laughing so much. Without thinking, I found McKale's hand resting on his knee. I let my hand lay on his a second before taking it back. He watched my hand move back to my lap and then reached for it, twining our fingers together and looking at me. A mingling of hope and excitement surged through my body.

Cass and Rock chatted in front of us. McKale leaned down and his warm cheek brushed against mine on his way to whisper in my ear, "Is this a date then?"

"Yes." I motioned toward the two in the front seats and told him, "It's a double date."

I squeezed his hand and felt his thumb move back and forth over my hand and wrist. That single, small movement did big things to me. I snuggled closer to his side, and unlike my family's trip to the village, this time I was happy to be in a compact car.

The drive into town seemed infinitely faster than it had taken to get to the Chaun land on the first day. It was really late when we found ourselves in the busiest part of Sligo, but plenty of people still milled about. We passed a pub with a live band playing, but it wasn't what Cassidy wanted. She found a spot and parked the car before flinging her purse across her shoulder.

"I'm guessing there aren't any stores open, so sit tight. I'll be right back," she told us.

"Don't go where I can't see you," I said.

"Yes, Mommy." She got out and walked up to three men standing on the nearby corner.

"Wha's she doing, then?" McKale asked.

"Working her magic," I answered.

"Blazes, would you look what those blokes are wearin'?" Rock pointed at the men talking to Cass. They wore jeans with sandals. One had on a plaid button-up shirt and the others wore collared polo shirts. They looked completely normal.

Within minutes those guys were stripping off pieces of their clothing and being rewarded with laughter and kisses on the cheeks from Cassidy. She skipped back to the car, getting in and tossing a shirt and pair of shoes to both of the guys.

"Sorry, they wouldn't part with their pants, but this is better than nothing. You can glamour if you want to."

Rock stared at the plaid shirt in horror. McKale lucked out with a navy blue polo.

"If I had me way I'd magic meself small and ride in yer shirt," Rock said.

"Not happening," I told him before Cassidy had time to consider it. "That shirt is fine, I promise. You'll fit right in. Where we going, Cass?"

"They told me there's a dance club at the next corner. Get dressed and let's go!"

She clapped her hands and the guys pulled off their shirts. I planned to play it cool with McKale being half-naked, but I accidentally opted to stare. He'd ogled my boobs that day at the waterfall, so it was only fair.

McKale's appearance in clothes was misleading. I'd expected him to be too thin underneath, but he wasn't. I mean, he was definitely lean, but there was small definition around those muscles, especially his arms from the tanning crank. And a very small patch of red hair right in the middle of his chest. And—

"Stare a little harder, why don'tcha," Cassidy said from the front seat as she watched me.

"Wha…? Shut-up." I reached across and punched her shoulder, but she was already laughing. She deserved a strangling. McKale slung the shirt over his head and ruffled his hair. The collar was up on one side and down on the other. I straightened it for him while he fixed me with a staredown that made me hot all the way to my feet.

"Let's go!" Cassidy yelled, jumping out of the car.

I climbed out, stretching my legs. The boys slid their feet

into the shoes Cassidy presented. McKale made a face and Rock grunted.

"Ye can't expect me to walk with somethin' crammed between me toes!"

"You'll get used to it." Cass's voice held no trace of sympathy, although she did stretch up to peck his lips, which momentarily stopped his complaints. She took off in the direction of the club, and we followed. The guys looked funny in their highwater cloth pants, but oh well.

McKale stared around, his head swiveling back and forth with quick movements to take in every strange sight. He and Rock kept trying to stop and examine things like neon lights and pubs with overhead speakers that filtered live music to the street. We tugged them along, promising we'd plan a day trip soon.

McKale and Rock's pants earned them a couple of odd looks from people on the street so we made them glamour, and we got into the club without a hitch. A clock above the bar told us it was one o'clock in the morning. Earlier than I thought. I didn't recognize the song blaring overhead, however some things in life were universally understood. Like a techno beat.

"Let's dance!" Cassidy grabbed Rock's hand and tried to pull him, but he was planted in that spot like a stone. Both guys peered around the darkened room with their jaws dangling in fascination.

"Let's get a table and have a drink first," I suggested.

We found a table with people preparing to leave and made ourselves at home, ordering three pints and a soda for me.

I leaned close to McKale. "Is this okay?"

"Aye, yes. It's just… everyone is so…"

"Tall?" I guessed. He nodded, seeming almost frightened. I tapped his glass with mine. "Cheers."

He let out a stress-relieving lungful of air and lifted his glass to mine. The four of us clinked our glasses together and drank. It was easy to fall into the carefree atmosphere of the small club. We talked for a while, until Cassidy began to stare longingly at the sunken dance floor, crowded with gyrating bodies.

"Are you guys ready to dance yet?" she asked. The guys looked at the dance floor, then at each other. They weren't budging.

"'Tis no' proper dancing," McKale said. "Not one of 'em are doing the same steps."

"There aren't any steps," Cass explained. "That's the fun of it! You just move your body to the beat of the music."

"Ye're sayin' there's no way to bung it up, then?" Rock asked.

Cass and I shrugged at each other. We'd definitely seen some bad dancing in our time. But that was the least of our concerns tonight.

"How about this," she said. "You two have another drink, loosen up, and watch while Robyn and I dance. And then if you want to come down, you can come. No pressure."

They agreed, and before I had a chance to take one last sip of my drink, Cass yanked me from the stool and dragged me to the dance floor. The moment we were nestled in the midst of moving bodies, we let go, arms in the air. It felt awesome.

As the song changed to something grittier, Cass put her face close to mine, shouting to be heard.

"McKale has been watching you the *whole* time!" I tried not to smile. I didn't look over at him, afraid I'd ruin the moment by tripping and going down like someone on a treadmill who'd lost their concentration.

After a few minutes Cassidy signaled to Rock, curling her finger to lure him. She bit her bottom lip and then turned back to me, never losing the beat.

"They're coming!" she said.

My heart sped up. "Both of them?" I hollered.

She nodded, cool and nonchalant.

Suddenly I was nervous. McKale, my sweet fiddle player, was making an effort even though he was way out of his comfort zone. What if he ended up hating this whole dance experience? What if it was just awkward?

My pulse went into rocket-launch mode when Rock's curly head found Cassidy, and she turned to him, bouncing. And then I felt McKale behind me, timid. He was being bumped into me, and his chest touched my back. I turned my head just enough to show him an easy smile as I reached back for his hands and led them to my hips. His touch was gentle. I kept my hands pressed over top of his until his grip became firmer. I was so nervous. I wanted this nearness, and I didn't want to screw it up.

More people joined the already crowded dance floor, forcing everyone closer. It was now or never. Time to be bold. I leaned back into him, just as a hip-hop song began, bass thumping. His reaction surprised me. With the slightest hesitance, he pulled my hips until our bodies matched up, aligned.

My breathing became jagged as I reached back, putting my hands on his hips. I started moving mine to the tempo of the music, slowly at first. He met me move for move, so I deepened the pace until we were both dancing. *Really* dancing. Cassidy took a moment from her groping session with Rock to look over and mouth dramatically, "*Oh, my gah!*" when she saw us. I just smiled.

My Leprechaun had rhythm. And it was hot in a way that made me dizzy. I let myself lean back hard against him, raising my arms to the air and moving my hips. I could feel his breath on my hair, against my ear and neck. His hands roamed, but not too far. Just over my waist and hips, down the top of my thighs. Arms still lifted, I bent my elbows and brought my hands behind me to his head, sliding my fingers into his hair. He nuzzled my neck and I was suddenly on fire.

Killer moths attacked my abdomen as I turned, wrapping my arms around his neck and fitting my curves to him, still dancing. His hands found my lower back. I was about to ask him what he thought of the club when the look in his eyes silenced me.

He watched my mouth, slowly leaning in, and I forgot about everything around us.

Oh, my... was he about to...?

The first touch of his lips was measured and timid—the perfect picture of the McKale I'd met on our first day. We breathed against each other's parted lips until I dared to let my tongue touch the soft fullness I'd admired the night before. That action was like a lit match to a firecracker.

Moving quickly with masculine instinct, one of his hands stayed on my lower back, pressing our hips together, while his other hand found the back of my neck and tugged me to him, hard, in a gesture of possession that had me moaning when his mouth opened mine with his own. Unlike my previous failed kisses, this one was the perfect combination of lips and tongues and hands. There was nothing shy about it. I was meeting this McKale for the first time. This was a McKale I wanted to get to know much better.

I loved the way he smelled and tasted. Hops and barley on the surface from his drinks, but something sweeter underneath: the licorice root he liked to chew. As we kissed, I ran a hand over his cheek, feeling where his smooth skin met the rougher line of hair along his jaw. Every contour amazed me.

I tried to reign in my self-control since I found myself practically climbing him for more, but he didn't seem to mind. In fact, he seemed just as hungry for more of me.

I knew part of my desperation stemmed from the fact that someone very powerful wanted to keep us apart, but I wouldn't allow thoughts of her to surface. I let myself breathe him in. We had this moment, right now, and nobody could take it away.

We finally broke the kiss, followed-up with several more slow little smooches until we were ready to look at each other. He was half-grinning as if he couldn't hold it back. Leaning into my ear, he said, "I fancy yer form of dance."

I laughed. With my arms still around his neck, I pulled him down and put my lips to his ear.

"I fancy *you*, Kale." I don't know what made me shorten his name but he didn't seem to mind.

He slid his lips to my ear again. "Do ye, now?"

I bit my bottom lip to hold back a giant smile, and murmured, "Yeah." We were *flirting*!

A new song started. Techno again. McKale began moving first, and it was my turn to match him. Cassidy and

Rock pushed their way closer beside us, and together the four of us danced. Cass found my hand and squeezed it.

It was a night to trump all others: Cassidy's best idea ever. The guys made us laugh the entire time. Especially Rock with his exaggerated dancing as he tried to imitate how other men at the club moved.

This night was more than a simple act of rebellion born of boredom. It was even more than getting away from the portal. It was about getting McKale to see me—*really* see me, and to see the possibility of what we could have together. I wanted us to have something worth fighting for.

Cassidy must have recognized the wheels of thought churning in my expression because she shook her head at me and bumped my hip.

"Not tonight, Robyn," she shouted in my ear. "Just dance!"

Yes, I thought, finding McKale behind me once again. *Tonight we dance.*

FOURTEEN

THE SUN WAS PREPARING to rise when we got back to the village and glided the car into its original spot. I'd woken the others to help me. I guess Cassidy and Rock got tired of being yelled at to quit making lip-smacking noises in the backseat, and they'd fallen asleep halfway home.

Knowing dawn would break at any moment, we made our way to the bungalows. My hand tingled, remembering how McKale held it the whole way home except the few times I needed both hands on the wheel. The memory of how he'd kissed me on the dance floor, then watched me while I drove had me sighing with contentment as my brilliant sister and I slipped into the room and collapsed onto our beds.

Falling asleep would be a bad idea. Even though today was not a workday for the Shoe House, I still needed to get up and care for the animals this morning. I allowed myself a few minutes of remembrance before I trudged out of bed to change.

"What're you doing?" Cassidy mumbled. I thought she'd be asleep already.

"I'm gonna do my morning chores early and then I'll

come back and go to bed. We can't sleep too long though 'cause Mom and Dad will get suspicious."

She grunted, falling asleep before I made it out the door.

The sky was brightening and birds were chirping as I walked up the worn path. Weariness overtook me and I couldn't wait to get back to the room and sleep. At the corner of the fence, I picked up my basket and the small bucket used to scoop meal from the barrel. Something moved by the hen house and I looked up, heart accelerating.

McKale was leaning there with his arms crossed, waiting for me. My body reacted to the sight, heating and buzzing. I got my act together, gathering my things and moving toward him.

"Hey," I said, feeling shy and self-conscious about the potato-sack apron that covered my shorts and t-shirt. "Is everything okay?"

He stared at me warmly for a minute without replying, and then he ran a hand through his red locks.

"Aye, all is well. I needed to see ye once more before I took to bed."

"Oh," I breathed. His voice sounded different. More confident and serious. The heat that began when I saw him now completely took over my body. Unlike when we'd first met, he didn't try to avert his eyes from me. He was openly drinking me in with an inquisitive newness, unperturbed by my less-than-attractive clothing ensemble in the morning light. I set my basket on the thick fencepost.

We moved forward at the same time, not stopping until we were kissing again, his hands wrapping around my waist to pull me close while my fingers found his hair. It was just as passionate as our kiss on the dance floor, only this time we could hear one another's shortened breaths and satisfying little sounds. A low moan rose up from his throat. Knowing I caused that pleasure from deep inside him gave me a strange taste of power.

A sudden snap from the path startled me and I pushed away from him. He kept a hand on my waist, protectively.

"'Tis alright," he whispered.

Leilah and Rachelle stood at the opening of the path in their aprons and bonnets with baskets in their hands and astounded looks on their faces. McKale lifted a hand to them in greeting. The girls simultaneously broke into giggles and turned, running down the path away from us. I let out a laugh and McKale grinned.

"I'd best leave ye to yer work. Unless, er, perhaps ye'd like a hand since I frightened away the help?"

I smiled at his offer. I appreciated that he was willing to jeopardize his man card to help me, but I was perfectly capable of doing it on my own.

"It won't take me long, McKale," I told him. "You go get some sleep. I'll see you this afternoon, right?"

He pulled me to him again and laid his lips gently against mine.

"I fancied it when ye called me Kale."

A shiver slid down my back and I sighed. Who was this guy? Was this who'd been hiding under that shell all along? Because I liked him. A lot. He made me feel like a new and improved version of myself.

"Another date today, aye?" he said against my lips. "The two of us."

"Okay," I whispered. One more cute grin, and then he was walking away, down the path, standing taller than I'd ever seen him. I couldn't bring myself to move until every trace of red hair disappeared into the village.

Mom came to our room and woke us with two plates of food at midday. We took the plates with slow, guilty movements.

"You girls must have stayed up too late last night." She was sitting cross-legged on the woven throw rug while Cassidy and I sat on our beds. We nodded at her and chewed our food.

"So, where exactly did you take the car for six hours?"

The bite I'd just swallowed halted in my esophagus, and Cass turned as green as a pixie. For a moment I wondered if Mom was talented enough to give us both the Heimlich at the same time. She gave a halfhearted grin at our choking silence.

"You girls know I'm a light sleeper when I'm not exhausted. And I've been on my guard with everything going on lately. We would have let you go if you had asked, you know. You could have left sooner and had more time away." She shifted her pointed gaze back and forth between the two of us. "Ah, well. What a shame."

Cassidy and I looked at each other.

"Mom…," I began. As the "mature and responsible" older sister, I felt the sting of blame from within. Saying sorry seemed so measly.

She put us out of our misery by shrugging and standing, brushing off her bottom and leaving us.

"Shitballs," Cass said, around the mouthful of bread she'd yet to swallow. I nodded my head in agreement. Mom tried not to show it, but I knew she was hurt that we'd run off behind her back. I set my fork on the plate, not hungry anymore.

I couldn't restrain the snark. "Told you we should have just asked."

"Oh, shut up. You were having the time of your life, all, *kiss me Leprechaun!* Don't act like you regret it."

I whacked her head with a feather pillow and she whined. "I regret hurting Mom," I clarified. "We need to go apologize."

"And beg forgiveness," Cass added, sounding grumpy. She threw the pillow back to my bed. "At least you can't be grounded anymore. I might not have a life for the beginning of my senior year now."

We crawled out of bed and got ready to face the day. Cassidy grabbed my arm.

"Please tell me it was worth it," she said.

I looked in her pretty brown eyes. "It was *so* worth it," I admitted.

She grinned. "Is he a good kisser?"

I felt embarrassed and tried not to smile, which made her poke me in the side.

"Tell me!" she said, tickling my waist.

"All right, yes!" I laughed. "Oh, my gosh. Just… *yes.*"

She stilled and eyed me with loving affection. I knew all of her expressions so well. She was happy for me, and sort of proud. But it was the kind of pride laced with sadness, like a parent whose child was growing up and preparing to leave them.

"Come on," I whispered, afraid to get emotional.

Cassidy and I walked down to the clearing where people ate and played various games.

McKale sat with my parents. He looked pale when he saw us.

"Ah, girls!" Dad said. "McKale was just telling us all about the dance club."

Oy. My stomach tightened. McKale gave us apologetic looks as we sat down in our usual places, slumping.

"Mom and Dad," I said. "I'm sorry we took the car without asking." My voice was somber, but the words still sounded lame.

"Yeah, we're sorry." Cassidy looked like she might cry again. The girl had an endless supply of tears at her disposal.

"If something had happened to you all..." Mom let the thought taper away as she closed her eyes and shook her head, imagining the worst.

We hung our heads in shame.

"You girls aren't children anymore. We're prepared to give you more freedoms if you act responsibly. Your mother and I are reasonable people, aren't we?"

Cass and I nodded at him, barely raising our chins.

Dad exhaled a heavy sigh and went on. "You're old enough now that we should be able to talk through things. Let's just put last evening behind us for now and try to enjoy the rest of the summer. We can plan another trip out of the village at some point before we go, okay?" Again we nodded. "Alrighty then. What's on your agendas for today?"

We were all quiet for a second, and then I decided to throw out some positive vibes.

"McKale and I are going on a date today. Right now if that's okay."

My parents perked up.

"Of course," Mom cooed, taking Dad's hand and smiling at us. I watched as McKale's eyes took in my parent's affectionate interaction with one another.

"Yeah. I think it's time for the video and the bin."

Cassidy gasped and Mom covered her heart.

"Oh, honey, I think that's a wonderful idea."

"Thanks," I said, relieved that the worst of the tension had passed from the table. I looked at McKale again, whose face now showed obvious confusion. "I'm probably going to need your help carrying something," I told him. "I thought we could go to your favorite place today."

"Erm… aye, of course." He stood after I did and we reached for each others' hands.

When I turned to say good-bye to my family, both my mom and sister had tears streaming, and I swear my dad's eyes glistened as well. Ah, my family. Sweet cry babies. My heart was full, and I said the only thing worth saying.

"Love you guys."

McKale gave me a what-the-heck-is-going-on? look, so I gently tugged his hand and led him to my room. He stood in the doorway like a gentleman. He looked happy when he saw the tiny berry basket he'd given me on the table next to my bed. I'd started picking flowers to put in it every morning after chores.

"So, I have an idea," I told him. "We're going to be out for a long time today, if that's all right. Probably past dinner."

"A long date?" He seemed to love using the foreign word. "Well, tha's just terrible, it is."

I laughed, charmed because he'd never really teased me before. I bent to pick up my backpack and put it on my shoulders. It had my laptop and a spare battery pack. To be on the safe side I shoved my compact umbrella inside, too. Then I leaned down and lifted the bin. It wasn't heavy, but it was bulky. McKale took it from me, looking down at the blue plastic container with interest.

"You'll see," I promised him. "Come on, let's go."

We stopped at the kitchen and grabbed a bundle of bread, dried meat, and a jar of mead. And then we were off, veering out from the village to make a wide arc around the portal. Neither of us made mention of the other realm or its freaky occupants. McKale led me through the grasses and underbrush, stopping once to pull a small licorice plant from the ground. We skirted the edge of the forest, which was lined with beautiful, tall flowers. McKale must have seen me admiring them.

"Hollyhock," he said, nodding his head toward the flowers and then looking straight ahead as he carried the bin with ease. His ears seemed to redden. My eyes went back to the flowers growing along the border of the woods, and I was amazed. I reminded him of those? They had solid stalks where they shot up from the earth, spiking upward into multiple stems with light green leaves and clusters of gorgeous blooms. There were hundreds of the flowers lining this path, in soft violets and rich maroons. Looking at them made me feel beautiful and strong.

"'Tis here," McKale whispered. We came to a hill with an oak tree sitting at the top. I relished the slight burn in my legs as we climbed until we were shaded under the oak's thick canopy. It smelled earthy, like moss and mushrooms. McKale set the bin down amid the soft grass and clover as I spread a blanket, motioning for him to sit next to me. My whole body was alight with anticipation.

"I'm going to start at the beginning," I explained, cracking the bin just enough to pull out the paddle and ball. My hands were shaking. "This is a toy. It goes like this." I tried to show him and he chuckled as I fumbled. A perfect example of why I didn't play hand sports. I held the toy out and told him to give it a try. After a few failed attempts, he totally had it going, just like the seven-year-old-me knew he would. He was so cute concentrating with his tongue poking out again.

"Kale?"

"Hm?" He continued bouncing the ball on the paddle, almost losing it but recovering with a slight tilt.

"I got that for you when I was seven. Will you do me the honor of accepting this gift?"

He brought it down to his lap. "Seven? Ye were but a wee child…"

I nodded. "And I was thinking about you."

He was motionless, and I could sense thoughts circulating in his mind, trying to process the idea.

"Aye, Robyn. I would be honored to accept this gift from ye."

"Yay!" I laughed at my own girly exclamation.

And so the fun began. One by one, I pulled out each gift in chronological order, explaining and asking him to accept it. My inner child rejoiced with each acceptance, and as the gifts piled up around him, I felt something lifting in each of us, shifting us closer. When we got to the first gift that I'd talked about on video, I set up the laptop and watched McKale's eyes pop.

He wanted to push the buttons and know what they each

did, so I gave him a brief tutorial before pushing play. My nearly fourteen-year-old face filled the screen.

He laughed and pointed. "Blazes, 'tis you Robyn!"

I laughed, too, mostly out of embarrassment about my badly chopped bangs in the video. And, oh geez, was that a pimple on my chin? Would it have killed me to wear some make-up?

"Almost four years ago," I said.

We watched for several hours, cracking up laughing about some of the silliness, especially things that Cassidy said whenever she'd video bomb. I'd forgotten about a lot of it. But the best part about the video was watching McKale's reaction. He stared, riveted, leaning toward the screen. Sometimes he would nod in response to the on-screen me, or say something under his breath. He was oblivious to anything else.

In retrospect I can say it was during those hours of video-watching under the tree that I fell in love with McKale. As he watched me transform from an awkward new teen to a young woman on the screen, I watched him change from a jaded young man to a man who realized he'd been wanted all along.

I watched him heal, and I knew he finally saw the truth—finally saw *me*.

It was dusk when the video ended. He sat with his knees up, looking around at the gifts, understandably overwhelmed. He shook his head and ruffled his hair.

"I don' know what to say, Robyn. I…"

"It's okay. You don't have to say anything."

"But I do." He spread his arms at the display of things around us. "I never thought… If I'd had any notion…"

"I know. I just wish I could have written you or *something*. And I didn't expect you to do anything like this." I motioned toward the gifts. "I know bindings are for the bloodlines, but it's hard to spend every day growing up with parents like mine and not hope for that kind of happiness."

He turned to face me where we sat, placing us closer with our legs touching.

His voice was quiet and hesitant. "Do ye think ye could find that happiness with me, Robyn?"

I held his hazel eyes. My feelings for him had grown exponentially in the past few days. I cared for him now. We still had a long way to go, and obvious obstacles to overcome, but I was filled with hope.

"I think I could," I whispered. "But it'll only work if we both want it."

He didn't answer, and his face was so serious. In the next breath McKale bridged the space between us, his warm mouth on mine. His hands held each side of my face. I reached up and held his forearms until he pulled away just enough to see my eyes. We sat there, reading each other and savoring our prospects.

"I've found more happiness since ye came along than e'er before in my life. For the first time I look forward to the future. I still can't believe me own luck."

Luck of the Irish. I let out a rattled laugh of emotion, but McKale frowned at me.

"Are ye sad?" He swiped the back of his fingers up my cheeks.

"No. I'm happy." My chin trembled as I said it and I realized I was crying. I'd never cried happy tears in all my life. I never understood how joy could make someone cry. It was unnatural, like the way the sun sometimes shone through the clouds while it rained. Apparently I required profound, blissful relief in order to trigger a tearful response. And clover kisses.

A light pattering of rain began to tinker around us. We hurriedly packed up my laptop and returned all of the gifts to the bin. Instead of leaving right away, we opened the umbrella and sat under it together, eating. And kissing.

Now I knew why romantics listened to love songs and gushed about stories with happy endings. There was exhilaration in such sweetness. Feeling like this made me see the world differently.

It was after sundown as we jogged the long way around the portal back to the village. We slowed our pace once we heard music playing in the distance and saw light from bonfires in the clearing.

"Will you dance with me tonight?" I asked him.

He answered with a shy grin. "Aye."

I was eager to get to the party. A twinge of magic zapped me in the torso. McKale and I stopped mid-step. My eyes scanned the darkened field with dread as mist wet our faces and hair. My heart pounded so hard I was certain McKale could hear it next to me. I couldn't see anything out there. The portal was still invisible.

"Nothing there," he whispered, still staring out into the blackness. "Perhaps someone shifted." But he sounded unsure and his Adam's apple dipped and rose when swallowed. I stepped a little closer to him, wishing he didn't have to carry the bin so we could hold hands.

"Let's get out of here," I whispered.

The twinge of magic had been an unwelcome reminder

of the girl from another realm, lying in wait. I didn't fool myself into believing she'd be a gracious loser when she found out about McKale and me. But the question was, what would she do about it? I stared in the general direction of where the portal was as we passed it, feeling with each step that we were dodging bullets and jumping land mines.

Maybe it was time to search for a four-leaf clover. Or a whole field of them. I was going to need all the luck I could get.

FIFTEEN

IT WAS STRANGE TO part ways with McKale and watch him carry the bin away. The blue container had been a constant part of my life for so long, and now it was going home where it belonged.

I went back to my room and was surprised to see Cassidy in bed. She stirred when I came in, rolling over and shoving something under the covers.

"Still tired?" I asked her.

She nodded and rubbed her eyes. "What time is it?"

"As if I know." I laughed. "What were you looking at?"

She sat up and shrugged.

"Show me."

"It's nothing," she insisted, pulling out a small item I recognized as her pocket calendar. "I've been keeping track of the date. Do you know your birthday's only six days away?"

"Yeah, I know." My insides leapt with nervous energy at the reminder. I plopped myself down next to her and we both laid back.

"You okay, Cass?"

"I don't know."

I took her hand and we continued to stare up at the low thatched rafters.

"What are you thinking about?" I asked.

"A lot of things."

"Please don't be sad. Especially about me. I think everything's going to be okay."

She waved it off and cleared her throat. "How did it go when you gave him the gifts?"

I rolled toward her, curling up and smiling into her shoulder.

"It was amazing," I whispered.

"Really?" I could hear the happiness in her voice. "Finally."

"Everyone outside is dancing and stuff. Will you come with me?"

She shrugged and said, "I guess."

"I wish Rock could come," I whispered.

"You do?"

"Yes. He's fun, and he makes you happy." I touched the tip of her nose. "I do want you to be happy, even if I worry. Now, come on."

We struggled out of her bed and got ready, pulling our hair back in ponytails. We walked out to the open area where a light rain still fell, finding McKale sitting with our parents. He stood when he saw me, and his face lit up.

"Whoa," Cassidy whispered as we approached them. "Must have been a *really* good date."

When we got to the table I stretched up to kiss McKale on the cheek before taking his hand. My family appeared ready to burst into a round of applause. Instead, Dad stood and announced he would get us all a round of mead. Cassidy made a face, sticking out her tongue.

"I'm sick of that stuff. I'd kill for a soda."

"Sorry, chickadee. I'll get you some water." Dad walked off with a grin.

"Ready to dance?" I asked McKale.

He kicked a small tuft of grass. "I'm no' the best o' line-dancers."

"We'll get through it together. Come on."

I tugged his hand toward the dance formation. It was the middle of a song and the dancers were holding hands in a circle, moving back as they lowered their arms, and moving in as they lifted joined hands to the sky. When we stepped into the circle of dancers, a few people started clapping, and soon the entire clearing of Chaun broke into cheers. McKale's grip tightened on my hand. They were cheering for *us*.

It was mine and McKale's first time dancing in front of the Chaun as a couple. Our first true appearance together. Seeing their expressions of relief and joy made me realize they'd been worried that McKale and I weren't hitting it off. So much was riding on our union. Seeing us hand-in-hand brought the clan's hopes to the surface.

Emotion swelled inside me as McKale and I took our places among them. Every person who wasn't dancing circled around us, clapping in sync.

Brogan stood with my family, and even from a distance I could see firelight reflecting the moisture in his eyes. This was the confirmation they'd all been waiting for, and I was glad to give it. Maybe I was biased, but as I linked hands with my betrothed and we stepped in tune to the music, I was certain it was the happiest dance ever performed. Despite his worries, he moved lithely, full of grace. And the way he captured my eyes… there was no way anyone watching could doubt what had grown between us. Especially as the dance ended and he tilted his head down for a kiss, which was met with a round of hooting from the clan.

Leilah and Rachelle came running over afterward, and I embraced them.

"By glory!" Leilah whispered in my ear. "I've never seen our McKale so sure of himself! A lucky lad, he is."

Brogan climbed atop a table and belted out, "Well, Leprechauns! It looks as though we're going to have ourselves a binding!"

Raucous cheers bellowed and I smiled up at McKale as that roller-coaster sensation wooshed through my body.

"Leon Mason!" Brogan shouted. "As the father of the binding female, you shall name the date."

Daddy looked at me. I nodded, though nervous energy ratcheted under my skin.

"Six days from now!" Dad announced in a loud, clear voice.

"Six days it is!" Brogan lifted his glass and the clan raised theirs with him. "Here, here!"

"Here, here!" the clan chanted.

Oh, wow. Oh, gosh. Oh, shitballs. *Six days.*

One by one, Chaun members and village women approached us, kissing our hands and hugging us. In that moment, I admitted to myself I'd been harboring mild negative feelings toward the majority of McKale's people. It bothered me how McKale was treated, and how they seemed to think women were lesser in many ways. But with each well-wish received, hurtful emotions shed away into forgiveness, leaving behind fresh, new sentiments.

My family was the last to embrace us. Dad held me close and kissed my head.

"You'll always be my baby girl," he whispered. I swallowed hard and squeezed him in return.

Mom and Cassidy cried. Shocking, I know. But I understood their happy tears now. I knew love was bursting inside their hearts for McKale and I, and it made me adore them more than ever.

Heavy, celebratory drinking ensued that night. Even after I headed off to the bungalows with Cassidy, we could still hear slurred singing drifting up the path.

"Somebody's in love," Cass teased. "Two somebodies, actually."

I wanted to respond that there'd been no L-word action, but something in her voice was off. Her smile felt forced, and none of her usual amusement filled her words. She seemed fragile. We entered our room and closed the door, lighting the gas lamp. I needed to be gentle with her.

"What's going on, Cass? Talk to me."

She swallowed hard and blinked. Her hair was matted to her head from the rain earlier in the night. I'm sure I looked just as pleasant.

"I'm just tired." She concentrated on changing out of her damp clothes.

"It's something more than that."

She didn't answer me, choosing instead to climb into bed.

"No, I'm seriously so tired. I'm just going to sleep, and when I wake up, everything is going to be okay."

Before I could attempt to get to the bottom of the issue, a weird buzzing and flapping noise came from outside our door.

"What the hell is that?" Cassidy sat up in bed with wide eyes. We stared at the door.

It continued, and we both jumped to our feet.

"Sounds like… a bird or something," I said. A really *large* bird. Cracking the door, I peeked out into the darkness with Cassidy looking over my shoulder. I reeled when I heard the flapping again, but it was further away now. We opened the door enough to step out and look around. A small, hazy green form disappeared into the dark trees. Faint, high-pitched cackling sounded from within the nearby forest. I stared out, frozen, but Cassidy grabbed my wrist and tugged me back into the room, slamming the door behind us. We both leaned against it, breathing hard.

"That was one of those creepy little pixie things, wasn't it?" Cassidy asked.

"No way." I had no idea why I was denying it when we both knew that's exactly what it had been.

"Freaky Fae Girl has a spy," she said.

My stomach churned, threatening to send up all the mead inside.

"I hate her," I whispered.

"I do, too. Let's kick her ass. Two against one."

"Don't even joke," I said, feeling queasy.

"You're scared of her." The realization seemed to shock Cassidy, and she grabbed my hand.

I'd never admitted fear, but I couldn't deny it. We both

knew that the FFG could take away everything I loved and royally screw up our lives if she had the notion. I was glad Cass didn't say anything trite about how it would all be okay and there was nothing to fear.

"McKale loves you."

Those cozy words made me close my eyes. I wanted him to love me. My heart was definitely headed in that direction, and I didn't want to go alone. "Maybe," I whispered.

"He hasn't said it?"

"No."

"Well, it was all over his face tonight. I'm happy for you, Robyn. So happy."

Again with the sad voice, despite her sweet words. Something was off, but I was afraid to push her anymore tonight. She would likely clam up and get mad.

I lay my head on her shoulder and she leaned her head against mine. We stayed like that until it was clear the pixie wasn't coming back, and then we climbed into our beds. Cassidy hadn't been lying about being tired. She fell right to sleep.

She didn't even wake when a gust of wind blew our door open. We must not have shut it all the way. I leapt from the bed with my heart in my throat, groping in the dark for the swinging door. I closed it hard and pushed my heavy suitcase in front of it. While I tossed and turned all night, afraid of monsters outside, Cassidy slept hard, even snoring at times.

I hoped she was okay. My world felt off kilter when Cass wasn't well.

At some point that night my body's exhaustion overrode my mind's fears. I woke in the morning to the sound of Cassidy whispered cussing in our bathroom. She shuffled out and sat on her bed, leafing through her mini-calendar again.

"Hey, chickadee."

She jumped at the sound of my sleepy voice.

"What are you doing?" I asked.

Cass let out a derisive laugh and rubbed her temples. "I don't know. I think… maybe… *ugh*! Never mind."

"You think what? Tell me." I sat up and took out my hairband, smoothing my hair back into another ponytail. She dropped her hands and looked right at me.

"The Clourichaun can't, like, reproduce or whatever, right?"

A sickening dread filled me and the world seemed to stop.

"No. Why? Is your period late?"

"Yeah," she whispered. "Four days."

We stared at each other. Cassidy and I were never late. We were like the clockwork sisters.

"I'll be right back," I said, jumping up.

"Where are you going? Don't tell Mom and Dad!"

"I'm not. I'm getting McKale."

I ran from the room in my pajamas and bare feet with my heart threatening to beat out of my chest. I only saw one other person, so it must have been super early. Crap, I had to feed the animals! I sprinted and almost tackled Leilah and

Rachelle as they came around the corner. I panted, leaning down with my hands on my knees.

"I'm going to be a little late on my chores." I felt light headed. They eyed me like I was a scary sight.

"Don' worry, miss Robyn. We'll take care of the lot this mornin'. Ye just relax now." Leilah patted my arm and they ambled off to work.

"Thank you," I called.

I made it to McKale's room and knocked on his door. He answered after a minute, shirtless with half his hair sticking up. He attempted to flatten out the mess of red when he saw that I was his visitor.

"Wha' happened?"

"Can you come with me?" I whispered, wishing I didn't sound so frantic. "I can't talk about it out here." He nodded and left the door open while he flew around his room, throwing on a shirt and scooping a handful of water to tame his hair. I waited outside the door with my arms crossed.

Cassidy couldn't be pregnant. She was under a lot of stress with this trip: being in a strange place, knowing she'd soon be without her sister, getting involved in a serious whirlwind romance with someone she'd met a month ago. That stuff could have thrown off her body. I did the dates in my head. She would have conceived during one of their first times, if not the very first. What were the chances?

McKale came out, closing the door, and we rushed to my room where Cassidy waited. Once we were in with the door closed, the three of us stood close so we could keep our voices low. We each crossed our arms over our chests, which might have been comical under different circumstances.

"The Clour cannot have children, right?" I asked.

"Tha's correct." He looked back and forth between the two of us with a crease in his brow, then his gaze stopped on Cassidy and his forehead smoothed. "Ah."

"Please tell me they can't get women pregnant," I whispered.

McKale paused, too long.

"Aye, they can." He sounded respectfully sorry. "But it does no' last beyond the early months."

Cassidy whimpered, covering her mouth, and angry fire raged through me.

"McKale," I said through gritted teeth. "Please find Rock and bring him here."

He pushed a hand through his dampened hair and nodded at me, looking pained.

"Wait!" Cassidy's hand shot out and grabbed his arm as he turned to go. "You're not gonna tell him, are you?"

He looked down on her with sad eyes. "Nay. If I did, he'd no' come."

She watched him leave with her mouth agape. "He would still come." She sounded childlike.

"Cass—"

"No!" She pulled away when I tried to touch her and went to her bed, sitting down and pulling up her knees. "McKale's wrong. It's not like that. Ronan loves me."

I curled my hands into tight fists. My sister could be pregnant with a baby that had no chance of survival. And I had a terrible feeling the only person Rock loved was Rock.

We waited in silence. She stayed in bed and zoned out while I paced. It felt like forever before the guys came. Rock's hair looked particularly big this morning and he wore a good-humored expression.

"Wha's the secret, then? Are we off on another grand adventure today, lasses?"

"Oh, it's grand alright," I said.

"Robyn, stop!" Cassidy jumped out of bed and went to Rock. He draped an arm over her shoulder and they gazed at one another.

"Sorry," she said to him. "It's just that…"

She looked down, not able to say it, and Rock absorbed the silence. He noted our serious faces, and lost the stupid grin on his own. His hand dropped from Cassidy's shoulder. When he took a step away and her chin quivered, I trembled with anger.

"Och. Ye should have warned her," McKale told him.

"It's okay," Cassidy said. "I'm not mad at you, Ronan." She moved toward him, but he looked afraid.

"I thought ye knew it was possible," he said, eyes darting toward the exit, which was blocked by both McKale and myself.

"Well, you thought wrong." I worked hard to thaw the ice from my voice. "So, now's the part where you comfort her and tell her you'll be there for her."

Cassidy sent me a furious look. Rock reached out with uncertainty and laid a hand on Cassidy's shoulder. When she leaned on him and began to cry into his chest, he put his arms awkwardly around her.

"Och, shiteballs," he said.

Cassidy laughed at his funny-sounding use of her word before her tears tapered off and she wiped her eyes with the back of her hands.

"Will ye be tellin' yer folks?" he asked, seeming terrified at the prospect.

"No way. If I told my mom she would tell my dad and he'd probably kill you."

His expression of terror expanded, and Cass managed a small giggle. "I won't tell them, but I'm not good at keeping secrets. Maybe I'll tell Mom when we're back home."

Rock didn't look reassured. He'd obviously had bad luck with fathers in the past. Imagine that.

"Everything is okay," she told him. "It'll be okay."

Why was she comforting him? It was *not* okay.

"Aye, Cassie-lassie." His smile was nervous, but she beamed back at him anyway. I was shocked. She *hated* being called Cassie. She once chased me and gave me a wedgie when I said it.

At least Rock seemed to be making an effort now, even though he appeared unaccustomed to doing so.

"Um, so, Robyn and McKale are having their binding ceremony in five days," she told him.

"Truly?" He grinned, but not as wide as usual.

"Perhaps I'll see if me father can make an exception and allow the Clour to attend," McKale said.

"Aye, if ye can get the stubborn old man to agree, I'll be there."

"Right." McKale cleared his throat. "Well, we should get ye out of here before anyone sees ya."

Tension still filled the air when the boys got ready to leave. Cassidy kissed Rock, and he was out the door, out of sight, quicker than a pixie.

McKale looked at my sister who stood there rubbing her arms. "Cass, if ye'd like I can have one of the women folk speak with ye. There's several in the village who can advise ye what to expect. They'll be discreet."

She swallowed and shook her head. My heart tightened at what she'd soon be going through.

"No thanks," she whispered. "I'm gonna take a bath now."

She left us, and I took McKale's hand, leading him outside of the bungalow door.

"Thank you," I told him.

He nodded. I didn't let go of his hand. In fact I tightened my grip when he started to leave. "Wait, Kale." My stomach turned as I thought about the previous night. "Nobody came to visit you last night, did they?" He didn't have to ask whom I meant.

"Nay. Why? What's the matter?"

"There was a pixie outside our room last night."

His jaw tensed and he stared out into the trees. "When she comes again, I will speak with her, and surely she'll see reason."

I didn't know about that. I loathed the idea of them speaking, but what more could we do? He bent and kissed my lips, too briefly. But he kept his face close to mine and I admired his light eyes.

"Five days until our binding." He spoke in a husky whisper.

A thrill tore through me and I reached out to grip the doorframe. The way he said it sounded much more like a sexy promise than a mere statement. Anxious excitement pinged around inside me.

"Five days," I repeated.

The moment he walked away my happiness evaporated as I entered my room and remembered what unnecessary heartache we now had to deal with.

I paced the small room with my arms crossed. I knew I should have crushed Rock's bits and pieces when I had the chance.

I was so engrossed in my dark thoughts about my little sister's predicament that I didn't notice the round-bellied green creature crouched on the bedside table until it freaking waved at me, grinning evilly. I stumbled, biting back a scream and tripping over a suitcase. The pixie flew up in the air, laughing with that unnerving high-pitched cackle as I dove for the door and flung it open.

"Robyn?" Cassidy called from the bathroom.

"One second!" I managed to say as the thing flew for the doorway, kicking me on the side of the head on its way out. *Ow.* I'd have given anything for a can of Raid at that moment. I slammed the door and sat in front of it, leaning my head back.

It was a spy. It had to be. No doubt, the pixie was going straight to his mistress to tell her everything he'd learned here this morning. *Crap!* How long had he been in our room and how'd he get in? And then I remembered the door bursting open during the night. Sneaky little bastard. He'd stayed still and quiet the whole time, hidden. The FFG would be proud of her little pet. I kicked the suitcase hard.

"What is going on?" Cassidy shouted, annoyed now.

"Oh, nothing much. Just found our freaky little pixie friend in our room."

Frantic splashing sounds came from the tub. "Ohmigawd, nuh-uh!"

"Don't worry, it's gone now."

She stilled. "Are you sure? Come in here."

I stood and went to her, pulling the curtain aside and squatting on a small stool next to the tub. She was sitting up with a washcloth over her chest, and her knees pulled up in the cloudy water.

I told her what happened and Cassidy proceeded to once again call the FFG every bad name in the book. She knew it gave me great joy when she did that.

Cassidy ended her tirade, saying, "She needs to get a life and leave you alone."

We were both thoughtful for a few minutes until she broke the silence.

"You know, McKale's kind of cool."

"Yeah?" I grinned. "He needed to warm up, I guess."

"I'm glad he's being good to you. I wish…"

"I know, Cass." She wished a lot of things, and so did I. We reached out for each other and rested our joined hands on the edge of the tub. She laid her cheek on her knees.

"I'm scared." Her voice hitched and a tear fell, sliding down her leg.

"Sweet girl," I whispered as my heart shattered. "I'm here. I'll do anything I can."

"I keep thinking," she said. "The Clour usually get humans pregnant, right? But I have magical blood. What if, you know, that makes it different? Maybe it'll cancel out the curse and I won't lose the baby."

I stared at her. I didn't believe for a second that her having magical blood would somehow reverse the curse against Rock's people. Entertaining such thoughts would only make it harder. Plus, the idea of Cassidy as a teen mom was frightening.

"Don't get your hopes up, chickadee, okay?"

She nodded and closed her eyes, pressing out more tears. "I love you, Robyn."

SIXTEEN

BROGAN DECLARED IT A week of celebration in the village. The Shoe House was closed for business. Because of the feasting and constant excited bustle of the men, the women ironically worked overtime. They didn't seem to mind, seeing how all of their men were in such fine spirits. There was an abundance of winking going on, and no female's backside was safe from an onslaught of pinches, including mine. By the end of the first day I was certain a wager was going around to see which wee man could make me squeal the loudest.

It wasn't viewed as an act of disrespect. Even McKale thought it was funny. I think he enjoyed how each pinch caused my face to redden. I was unsure how to react to the jolly men's attentions.

"If someone back home pinched my butt they'd get slapped," I explained to McKale.

"Well, yer bum is very near their faces. The lads can't help themselves."

"Ha-ha," I dead-panned.

Despite the festivity of the villagers, I couldn't bring myself to share in the cheer.

My mood was further dampened by several twinges of

magic in the air throughout the day, though nobody in the village seemed to notice or care. Maybe they were used to it, but I didn't think I ever would be.

The surrounding busyness did keep my mind occupied for long stretches. While my parents and sister agreed to partake in some games, I helped in the kitchen. The women taught me to make fruit pastries from fresh wild berries. And as much as they loved the men, they'd smack any hands that reached for food before it was ready to serve.

From the corner of my eye I saw a brown head poke around the doorframe. I looked up at Cassidy, who frantically waved me to her. She grabbed me by the wrist and pulled me around the corner where we were alone.

"I got my period!" she said, beaming. She threw her arms around my neck and I hugged her around the waist. My lungs released the world's largest and happiest exhale. Ah, sweet friggin' relief! Finally, something went right.

Without letting go of me, Cass said, "I'm sorry that I even told you I was late. I've been so out of whack, but I shouldn't have worried you. This is your time and you have so much going on."

I held her tighter. "No, I'm glad you told me. Please don't ever feel like you can't come to me. I might… freak out a little because I worry, but I love you no matter what."

We released each other and Cass cast her eyes downward.

"I'm going to find Rock tonight and tell him," she said.

I wanted to tell her to stay away from him, but they would have been wasted words. So instead I lamely said, "Okay, just… be careful."

"I will." With a newfound lightness she left me, returning to the festivities. I shook my head and went back to the kitchens. I wished I could inject a dose of caution into that girl's veins.

When the last rack of pastries was cooling, the ladies eyed one another as they removed their smocks.

Leilah smiled at me. "We've got something for ye, Robyn."

"You do?" My mouth lifted in return, wondering what they were up to.

"Aye, we do. All of us women folk, that is. Let me fetch yer sister and mum. Then we'll show ya."

I washed berry juice from my hands and patted flour from my shirt until Leilah returned with Cassidy and Mom, both grinning. So, they were in on it, too. Hm. The group of women led me down into the female cottages. Other women saw us going, and joined along the way. Leilah and Rachelle went into one of the rooms and came back out, gingerly holding a long swath of lavender silk across their arms. I sucked in a breath and grabbed my mother's hand.

The village women motioned to Cassidy, who took the gown and held it up for me to see.

"We loaned them your sundress to use for measurements," Mom said. "It's a binding gown."

The dress was unlike anything I would have chosen for myself, and yet, it was perfection. I examined each detail. The neck was a deep scoop, which rounded up over the shoulders with dainty short sleeves. It had an empire waist that flowed to the ground. My favorite part was the coloring. They'd specially dyed it so the top was lavender, and it gradually darkened as it lowered, becoming a deep purple at the bottom. The colors reminded me of a Hollyhock. I wanted nothing more than to have McKale see me in this dress.

"You made this?" I asked, getting choked up as I looked around at the twenty or so expectant faces.

"Aye. We hope ye will not mind that it's not entirely traditional," Leilah explained, appearing worried. "Customarily the sleeves are longer, but we were inspired by the style of a few pieces the two of ye gals often wear."

"I love it," I said, reaching out to touch the fabric. It was as soft as it looked. I gathered it in my hands and held it up to myself. There were murmurs and affirmative nods. Mom and Cass moved together to get a good view.

"Och, the coloring is spot on, just as I told ye lasses," boasted the oldest woman, the one who'd made me the apron. I leaned down and kissed her cheek. Before I could straighten again she grasped my face and kissed one of my cheeks, and then the other.

"Bless ye, child," she said.

Handing the dress back to a tearful Cassidy, I went around and thanked each woman, giving hugs and receiving kisses, ending with Mom, then my sister who opted to give me a bear hug. The women clapped as Cass and I rocked back and forth, laughing. I liked to think that it helped Cassidy and Mom as much as it helped me, knowing I'd been accepted by the women of the clan. It was one less thing they had to worry about when it was time to leave me.

Early dusk was upon us by the time we brought my lovely gown to my room and headed for the clearing. Our large group of females made quite an entrance. You would have thought we were celebrities the way the men hooted and carried on as we walked down. Some of the women curtsied or twirled and we all laughed, feeling punchy.

McKale approached me, fiddle in hand.

"I fancy playing a few songs, if ye don't mind."

Good gosh, was the boy asking my permission? I reached up and kissed him, not letting his lips go until I heard people cheering.

"Of course I don't mind. I love hearing you play. I'll come sit near you."

He gave a bashful grin at the compliment and took my hand, leading me to the table nearest the musicians. My family followed and sat with me. We clapped to the tempo as the music began, and though all seemed well on the surface I couldn't fully let loose and rejoice. The closer I grew to McKale, and the nearer our binding date came, the more I felt a looming threat from the FFG.

The first song ended, and a murmur went through the crowd. I sat up straighter, on alert. I felt my family do the same. Drawn-out voices sounded from down in the field. I stood to look, heart sprinting. Movement caught my eye as a row of men exited the trees, all in a line with their arms draped around one another's shoulders. It was the Clourichaun boys, singing in sloshy voices, stumbling in a zig-zag line through the tall grass—eight regular sized boys and four little men ambling along. They seemed so young. I didn't think the Clour lived lifestyles that allowed them to reach ripe old ages.

McKale had gained special permission for them to attend the binding ceremony, but Brogan did not look happy about seeing them so soon. He crossed his arms over his beard and shook his head, mumbling about how he'd boot the lot of 'em if they didn't behave themselves. Brogan then ordered the musicians to take up their instruments. A song promptly began.

I glanced at Cassidy who was craning her neck for a view of Rock. McKale watched me, fiddle to his chin. His hands moved over the strings, but his eyes questioned if everything was all right. I nodded.

The Clour boys made it to the clearing and broke away from one another. They must have been holding each other up before that because they all went sprawling and rolling when they let go and kicking their feet in the air.

Women clucked their tongues or giggled. Some of the Chaun boys laughed and greeted the Clour, helping them to their feet while the older men harrumphed with disapproval.

Cassidy's eyes were bright. I knew she was dying to give Rock the happy news. "I'm just gonna go say hi," Cassidy said to our parents. Mom pursed her lips together.

"I don't think that's such a good idea," Dad told her.

I knew she would go no matter what, and I didn't want a scene.

"I'll go with her," I said, taking her hand. "We'll come right back."

Dad glared in Rock's direction, and I could see why.

Rock could barely stand. His ankles kept bending under his weight. Cassidy and I stood and moved closer, watching as Keefe, the soccer guy, greeted Rock, pulling back his hand and flapping it in front of his nose.

"Och, Rock! Ye stink of Farmer Teague's wife, ye do! Was she boiling another batch of her death-by-roses perfume, then?"

You've got to be kidding me.

Laughter ensued, and Rock half-grinned. Other guys leaned in to take whiffs and make faces. Cassidy's steps faltered and her clammy hand tightened on mine. I felt her eyes stray to me but I couldn't take mine off Rock. We were close to them now. I prayed the guys were only joking. But as we pulled up to the edge of the group an unmistakable, strong flowered perfume scented the air.

My blood pressure rose.

"Bloody fool," one of the Chaun boys said, slugging Rock in the arm and nearly knocking him over. "Ye'll never learn."

Rock spotted Cassidy and I through bleary, half-closed eyes. "Cassie-lassiiieeee!" He shoved through the other guys and draped his arms around her, bumping me away.

"Ronan, stop," Cass said, wiggling out of his grasp and staring at him with wide eyes. Her next words were hissed in a dangerously low whisper that only the three of us could hear. "Did you just sleep with some woman? Someone's *wife?*" Her eyes begged him to deny it. He could feed her a lie right then, and she would eat it up.

"Tell her the truth," I warned him. He stank; there was no denying that.

Rock looked at me through a mop of long curls. He stood a touch taller at that moment and looked as serious as I'd ever seen him. There was a message for me in his eyes. I didn't like it, but I understood it. Rock was about to sever ties with my sister. He looked back at Cassidy, who'd wrapped her arms around herself.

Before Rock could say anything, Blackie came up and clapped him on the back, giving us a devilishly handsome wink.

"Old man Teague should know better than to leave 'is young bride so long while he tends to trade matters, 'eh? Somebody has to take care of business at home!" He slapped Rock's back again, running off and leaving us to digest his words.

Cassidy closed her eyes and pressed her fingertips to her pink lips.

"No," she whispered through her fingers. "Tell me it's not true."

"Cassie…," Rock said, tilting to the side and then righting himself.

The regret in his tone was evident, but it wasn't enough.

"Don't call me that," she snapped. "I can't believe you would do that to me. I *love* you!"

Her words seemed to punch breath from his lungs. Rock's sorrowful eyes were haunting as he stepped back, distancing himself.

"This is no place for the likes of ye, Cassie." He still used her nickname, defiant. "And I'll no' be tied down to a lass. Ever."

"Why are you doing this?" She sucked in a shuddering breath and her eyes filled with tears. I watched her face turn hard as her words turned spiteful. "Whatever. I just came over here to tell you I'm not pregnant. Not that you cared. Not that you were worried about me. I can't believe I was so stupid."

She tried to leave but he grabbed her upper arm.

"I ne'er meant to hurt ye," he said.

"Then why did you?" she whispered.

Beyond Rock's shoulder I saw a shift in the crowd as people moved out of someone's way. Someone big.

"Go," I told Rock. "Our dad's coming. You need to get out of here, *now.*"

Cassidy and Rock both looked to see I was telling the truth. My parents and Brogan were making a straight line for us.

Rock gave Cass one last heart-shattering look of apology before staggering three steps backward. The other Clour must have been keeping an eye out for Rock, because they all followed his lead back into the grass, pushing and shoving one another as they hurried away. They'd come with a purpose, and it had been achieved.

Cassidy cried silent tears now, one hand over her mouth. I looked for my parents. Dad's eyes were on the field where Rock had disappeared. Mom's eyes, of course, were on Cassidy, no doubt reading the heartbreak there. She began moving through the crowd toward us with Dad behind her. Mom wore the same fierce expression she had when she caught us watching Cinderella as kids—she hated anything that depicted Faeries in a positive light, fictional or not.

As they got closer, Dad scrutinized Cassidy's tear-stained face. He stopped, hesitating only a moment before stalking toward the field, slow at first, then breaking into a sprint. The three of us girls watched him, astonished. I'd never seen him move so fast.

"Leon!" Mom shouted. The three of us ran after him, and others followed.

Dad caught up to the boys just before they got to the

trees. He grabbed the back of Rock's shirt and spun him around, pulling him so they were face-to-face. Dad's biceps flexed with restrained fury. I had no idea his muscles were so big.

"Daddy, please!" Cassidy cried.

He gave the Clour a hard shake. "What did you do to my daughter?"

Rock's mouth hung open, no noise escaping.

I chimed in, afraid for Rock. "They just broke up, Dad… they broke things off."

Dad, keeping a tight hold on the boy, looked to Cassidy who nodded. Mom placed a hand on his shoulder. "Let him go, love."

He snarled down at Rock, pulling his face a touch closer and whispered through clenched teeth. "You stay away from her. Do you hear me? Don't come around here again until the summer is over and we're half a world away."

"Daddy!" Cassidy cried.

Rock swallowed and nodded, croaking, "Aye, sir. I'll no' bother her again."

"Good." Dad shoved him away.

Brogan stood next to him now, glowering at the Clourichaun who were rushing into the trees. A large group of villagers stood behind us, watching. McKale came to my side and took my hand.

We all looked at Cassidy. She let out a muffled choking sound and turned, pushing through the crowd, running back to the village.

Dad exhaled and rubbed his face. "I'm sorry about that, Brogan."

"'Tis fine, sir. I cannot blame ye fer going after the

bugger. We'll see to it they don't come back."

"Thank you."

Brogan looked hard at McKale. "I'm takin' back the invitation I extended to 'em for the binding ceremony. Understand?"

"Aye, Father."

We walked back up to the field in silence, and McKale never let go of my hand. People dispersed into the clearing, whispering amongst themselves.

"I think I'll call it an early night," Dad said.

"I'll be along," Mom said. "I'm going to check on Cass first."

He nodded. "Tell her... tell her I love her and I'm sorry. I didn't mean to lose my temper, but I think there's more to this story. Stuff I don't even want to know."

I dropped my gaze to the ground as Dad walked away. My heart thudded when Mom turned to face McKale and me.

"Robyn, what have your sister and that boy been up to?"

McKale looked away. I swallowed and whispered, "I..." I dropped my eyes.

She pressed fingertips to her temples, appearing even more anguished than she'd been when she broke the news to me about McKale's heritage. "Never mind. I don't need to hear it."

"Oh, Cassidy Renee," she whispered into the air. Her eyes watered. "Why must you learn everything the hard way?"

I squeezed McKale's hand and released it. "You can go. I'll see you in the morning."

He left us.

I walked to my room with Mom at my side. Stress reverberated off her. Cassidy's sobs were audible long before we got there. I was scared about what Mom planned to do. Would she yell at her and lecture her? Would she tell her what a foolish girl she was and how disappointed she was?

Nope. My parents were full of surprises tonight. Mom climbed straight into my sister's bed and curled around Cassidy's balled form. She whispered and smoothed her hair back from her face. Over and over she did this until Cass quieted, hiccupping for air every minute or so. I climbed into my own bed, but couldn't relax as the minutes ticked by. Mom didn't return to her own room until Cassidy was hard asleep.

I woke the next morning to the gentle shake of a hand on my shoulder.

"Robyn," Cass whispered.

I sat straight up, slurring, "What's wrong?"

"I woke up early and I can't fall back asleep. I feel like I need to talk to Ronan about last night—"

"Cass!" I felt much more awake now. "Don't you remember what he did?"

"Well, yeah." She frowned. "But I think he was just trying to push me away because he knows I have to leave. I think he's scared."

I looked at the ceiling, gathering my thoughts. "Maybe he is, chickadee, but then again maybe he's just a big, selfish jerk."

"I don't think so," she said quietly. "He was drunk last night. I need to talk to him while he's sober."

The bad thing about romantics was they put themselves out there for heartbreak. I wished she'd guard her heart better, but it was hard to fault her trusting, loving nature.

"I'll have McKale get a message to Rock today, okay? After last night I think it'd be bad for you to go after him."

She sucked her bottom lip into her mouth. "Okay. But you have to find out from McKale exactly what Rock says and tell me."

I let out another deep sigh. "Alright."

She smiled and hopped up, digging through her bag for the day's outfit as if yesterday hadn't been the worst day of her life—as if Dad hadn't gone ballistic on the guy she loved.

"Mom was really worried about you last night," I said.

"Oh... yeah." That stole a little of the hop from her step. "Do you think I'm in trouble?"

"No. I think now Mom's stressed for both you *and* me."

"I'll go talk to her." She bit her lip. "Maybe I can help you with the animals first?"

I admired her procrastination technique. "Sure."

SEVENTEEN

MCKALE HELD MY HAND as we walked down the path toward the waterfall that evening. The clan was still partying it up, but the Masons had been a subdued bunch all day. I accepted with gratitude when McKale asked me on an early evening "date."

When we reached the gurgling stream the first thing I did was look around for mini-men. I'd come prepared with a bathing suit, but I wasn't opposed to breaking out a few more wrestling skills if someone dared to mess with us today.

We walked up the mossy, damp bank to where the stream thickened at the base of the falls. As we stopped and looked at each other, a shyness overcame us and we laughed.

"I guess you don't own any swim trunks, huh?" I asked him. I motioned to my shorts.

"Nay. The lads and I swim without clothing."

"Oh." Heat prickled my skin and I cleared my throat.

"I'll wear me pants today."

I nodded, looking down at a spongy patch of earth that my toes were squishing around in.

"Okay. I have a swimsuit on under this. It was made for swimming. In case you couldn't tell from the name."

Ugh, go away embarrassing babble!

We looked at each other before reaching for our shirts and pulling them over our heads. He dropped his tunic and rubbed his hands over his flat stomach, taking in the sight of my fuchsia tankini. My heart was beating ridiculously fast as I bent to slide my shorts down. My heart never had a chance to relax because his hot hazel eyes never looked away. It was hard to breathe and I didn't know what to do with my hands. He lifted his eyes to my face.

"Are ye all right, then?"

"I'm… nervous."

"Aye. All is well."

His voice soothed me. Geez, if I was this nervous about swimming with him, I'd be a complete wreck three nights from now. I needed to calm down. Little nerves were natural, but I was feeling faint here.

"I've ne'er seen material such as that. May I?"

I nodded and he reached out, feeling the edge of the tankini top where it met my mid-section. The back of his fingertips brushed against my stomach and the prickly heat flared up again. He used both hands now, pulling at the fabric to see how it stretched. I could see the cobbler in him, fascinated by this creation and wondering how it might be used on the feet of Fae.

When he was done examining my suit, I held out my hand and he took it. Together we waded into the water near the falls. It was cooler than I remembered, probably from all the recent rain. I hissed and walked on my tip-toes. McKale let go of my hand and dove straight into the water's depths, coming back up in the middle of the pool with a giant smile. He gave his wet head a shake, slinging water to the side.

When he motioned me to him, I let my chest go under. *Cold*! There was no way I was diving like he had. After a few steps the water was too deep and I had to swim the rest of the way. He took my hands and pulled me to him. Close. When his lips covered mine and his tender tongue sought my own, I almost forgot to kick my feet to stay above water. He wrapped his arm around my waist and pulled me to a spot where we could touch bottom.

And then he kissed my breath away.

My hands slid over his body in the crisp water. I loved the hardness of lean muscle under his skin. I ran my hands across his chest and around to his back, feeling him from the line of his pants up to his shoulders. Unlike me, he kept his hands in one place, around my back. But he groaned with pleasure at my touch and kissed me harder. The water no longer felt so cold.

McKale's mouth left mine and he pulled me to his chest to hug me. His cheek rubbed the side of my head.

"I can't get enough of ye, Robyn. I didn't know it could feel this way."

I leaned back enough to look at him. "I'm full of surprises."

He chuckled. "Careful now. Ye aren't the only one who can give a surprise."

I lifted an eyebrow, wondering what he meant, but he must have taken it as a challenge because he jumped up and dunked me under the water. I came up gasping, wiping water from my eyes.

"Not nice!" I rushed for him and we wrestled, laughing with sudden playfulness. It was an enjoyable release after the past twenty-four hours.

"'Tis not right for a lass to be so rough!" He laughed as I struggled my way out of his hold.

"That's me. Take it or leave it." We'd moved close to the shore now. I yanked the back of his knee forward with my heel so he'd lose his balance. As he fell forward he grabbed my waist and twisted us around so that I would fall on top of him. He grasped my wrists and pulled me down to him. Our upper bodies were on the dirt, but our legs were still in water.

"I'll take ye, I will."

McKale lifted his head to try and kiss me, but I dodged to the side. Instead I kissed his cheek before moving further to nibble his earlobe. He tensed underneath me and I could feel *everything.* Instead of making me nervous, his apparent arousal spurred me on. I kissed his neck and he held his breath. My mouth was hot in comparison to his cool skin. He sucked in air when I ran my tongue over his lightly freckled shoulder, down to his collarbone. I'd never done such a thing, and the way he reacted made me experience another delicious surge of power like I had when we kissed by the hen house.

"Aye, yer likely to drive me mad if ye keep that up."

"Just getting you back for driving me mad my first month here," I said against his chest.

I was only teasing, but he sat up and pulled me up with him, setting me at his side and taking my face in his palm.

"Robyn." His eyes pleaded with mine. "Ye did not deserve to be treated so. I was a fool boy and didn't know how to act. Fer awhile there I thought ye'd given up on me."

"No." I shook my head. "I was sad and scared, and maybe a little stubborn too, but I never gave up."

"Will ye forgive me?"

"I already have. And I'm sorry I was upset with you and

wouldn't talk to you." So much wasted time we could have been getting to know one another.

"Ye don't need to apologize to me fer anything."

He laid me back in the moss, one knee between my legs and a hand on my waist. McKale kissed me with such sweet tenderness I thought I'd come apart at the seams. My body was impatient for more of his touch, but he remained a perfect gentleman. I squirmed closer, arching my back, needing more.

"I think I'm ready to bind with you, like, right now." The words spilled out with abandon, spurred on by my greedy body. "I'm not even kidding."

He laughed heartily at my admission and I savored the sound of it.

More words surfaced and I let them tumble out bravely. "I'm falling in love with you, Kale." My heart pounded as I watched his laughter turn serious. "Do you believe me?"

"Aye," he whispered and touched our lips. "I believe ye, *Bláth mo chroí*."

"What?" I asked.

"'Tis the old language. Gaelic."

"What does it mean?"

He held me with his eyes. "Flower of me heart."

In that beautiful second, as he leaned to seal those words with a kiss, an itchy burn buzzed across my skin. I recognized the feel of being glamoured, but this was stronger than when I put a glamour around myself. It felt thick and unnatural around me.

McKale's eyes widened as he pulled back from me. "Khalis-!" Before he could finish saying her name, another burst of magic hit me and McKale was gone.

But not really. There was a tiny bit of weight still on me.

"Oh!" Mini-sized McKale was splayed across my belly. "Are you okay?" I asked, unsure if I should try to pick him up or something. My voice sounded strange in my ears and he seemed frightened of me. When I peered down at myself I almost puked. I looked like *her*, pale skin swaddled in white gossamer. McKale clambered off me, sliding down my waist and running a few feet away.

A giggle sounded from behind us and I sat up fast, turning my torso to see her.

"McKale shifts small when he's startled. But you wouldn't know that, would you, Robyn Mason? You hardly know him at all." Khalistah smiled pleasantly from the opening of the trees where she glowed. Her white-gold hair rested on her slim hips, glittering in the twilight. The green pixie was perched on her shoulder, its fat face like a pug, minus the cuteness factor.

She stepped out and I stood to face her. The glamour felt so strange—I couldn't see my own skin. This was a power show, and she had the upper hand. She'd stolen my identity and individuality, turning me into *her*.

Khalistah looked me up and down, amused. "I thought McKale might find your moment together more enjoyable if you appeared this way."

I bit back the obvious retort that he'd been enjoying himself just fine. I planted my feet a foot apart and squared my shoulders, refusing to cower, even though I couldn't help but be petrified on the inside.

I must have come off as aggressive because the stupid pixie came flying at me and grabbed a handful of my hair. He made little yipping sounds like a barking squirrel while I screamed and tried to slap him away. My head felt like it was on fire. Khalistah clapped her hands and he flew back to her shoulder. He flung his hands to try and rid his fingers of my loose hairs. I rubbed the tender spot from where the strands had been pulled.

Khalistah clucked her tongue and sighed. "Pixies are such beastly little things, aren't they? No manners whatsoever."

Another smaller burst of magic made me flinch, but it was just McKale. He stood now, normal-sized, but he gave himself distance from us both, creating a triangle. His tan pants were slung low from the weight of water, revealing a happy trail of red hair between the V-line of his hips, heading downward. I wasn't the only one to notice.

"Mmm." The FFG looked McKale up and down with fingertips fluttering above her throat.

Nobody was going to *Mmm* my guy but me. She needed to get those glacier eyeballs back in her head.

"Will you please unglamour me?" I asked through gritted teeth.

She slowly turned her eyes to me. "I have seen the way you look at me. In awe. Admiring the sort of beauty humans can only obtain in dreams. But if your pride is so great that you prefer the less attractive appearance, then so be it." She waved a finger and the glamour disappeared. I felt lighter.

"Khalistah," McKale said. I tried to ignore the way his voice softened and his eyes still held a small amount of awe as he looked at her. "I'm glad ye've come. I wish to speak with ye."

"How long were you going to wait to speak with me? Moments before your mockery of a binding, or afterward?"

"I… I'm…"

She glided toward him and pressed a finger to his lips. He flinched then shivered.

It took all my willpower not to snatch that finger and snap it.

"I'm not angry with you, precious one. You are not to blame. I know she has pursued you with persistent forwardness."

Give me a break.

He blinked and looked at me. I crossed my arms over my chest and he pulled his face back from her touch. I think he recognized he was turning to a pile of mush like he always did in her presence.

"I wish to speak with ye alone, Khalistah. Please allow Robyn to return to the village."

"I think not. I know what you wish to say. You are but a man and you have been led astray from the one thing you have always wanted. Does she know how you feel for me?"

McKale's forehead creased and his eyes flicked to me. The FFG never glanced my way as she moved forward and began petting his face like she'd done in the trees that night. This time she even placed her hands on his bare chest, where my own hands had been minutes before. His breathing went ragged, but I had to give him credit because he stayed very still and appeared otherwise unaffected, allowing her to touch him for that brief moment before closing his eyes and stepping back from her again.

I, on the other hand, was having a difficult time retaining my fury. McKale pushed his hands hard through his hair as a shudder tore through his body. He began to pace with his hands behind his head, putting more space between Khalistah and himself. The FFG stood firm and calm, fueled by confidence as she spoke to him.

"Does she know about the years when you yearned for my presence and followed at my heels with childlike devotion? I had never met a living thing like you. Brave enough to seek me, yet too shy to touch me. Such a refreshing change from the arrogance of Fae males. I am here now to tell you that your years of dedication have paid off, McKale of the Leprechaun."

"Khalistah." He closed his eyes to muster courage before facing her again. "I was but a boy. I was reckless to seek ye as I did. I'll always be grateful for yer years of kindness, but my future is here, in the village with my clan, bound to Robyn."

Her eyes flashed hard with anger before smoothing again.

"Will you discard me so easily? Your first love?"

I nearly gagged at her crooning voice.

"What we had was no' love." McKale said it with extreme gentleness but I froze as I awaited her response to those strong words. The FFG blinked twice, the only sign that her composure was not solid.

"I know this notion of *love* that humans search for and abuse. It is easy to speak of lifetime loyalty when your lives are so bitterly short. If you were Fae you would become bored with Robyn and come crawling to me in less than a thousand human years." Though she appeared unruffled, I had a bad feeling she was about to throw a major hissy fit.

"But I am not Fae," McKale said. "And I cannot pretend to be. Neither of our people would accept a union betwixt us. What would yer friends say in the courts? And yer father? The Summer King will no' be havin' it."

The Summer King? Excuse me? Holy crap! The FFG was a friggin' princess? I covered my mouth, afraid I might be sick as the weight of the situation crashed around me, dimming like the evening sky.

The FFG waved a hand, dismissing his words. "Fae take human consorts all the time—"

He stepped back, a small bit at a time. "But not for purposes of love, Khalistah."

Ugh, each time he pronounced her name so beautifully felt like a punch in my already upset stomach. She strode toward him, ever steady. As he lowered his head I saw his eyes dart from side to side, looking for the best escape route.

"There is no need for any of my fellow Fae to know what is truly between us. They will see you as a consort and nothing more. It will be our secret."

"That is no way to live!" His voice rose. "And what of my people? The bloodlines of my clan? The union was ordered by your father's own consort."

"It can still be. I have a plan that should please all."

Oh, no. She smiled up at him, running her fingers from his shoulders down the length of his arms until their fingers were together. He let her hold them for a second before pulling away and groaning with his hands behind his head again. A smile remained on her lips, but there was no warmth in it.

"Do not fear, McKale."

"I will not go to Faerie." His words were firm.

She lost her smile. "Oh, but you will."

My stomach twisted and I had to swallow. I'd never before experienced such extreme fear as I did while I waited to hear her grand scheme for our lives.

"In three days you will bind with Robyn as planned, but when evening falls you will accompany me into Faerie. Everyone must know that you do this of your own device. Once we are in Faerie, all thoughts of *her* will be erased." She glared at me before turning back to McKale. "You will live the life that other men can only dream; pleasure heaped upon pleasure will be yours, ours. Once a month I will allow you to leave Faerie to attend to your binding partner when she is fertile. She will be glamoured to appear as me, for that is the only way you will have her. In that way, you will bear children on her. And all will be well for your clan."

His face had turned a shade of pale green akin to the moss under his feet. I fought to remain standing as I clutched an arm around my ribs.

"But he has the ability to see through glamour." They were the first words I'd spoken in a while, and she turned her head to me. A wicked smile grew on her exquisite face.

"Once McKale gives himself to me, his magical abilities will dissipate. He will no longer need them."

In other words, he would be turned into a mindless zombie to do her bidding. His brain would not be able to process anything other than its obsession with her.

"Khalistah…" McKale's apologetic tone prepared us for his next words. "I'd never want to hurt ye or upset ye in any way. Please believe that. But I cannot go to Faerie with ye. I want more than simple… pleasure from life. I want to be a father to me children, and work as a man should. I will not go along with this plan."

The FFG let out a peeling laugh of disbelief and covered her mouth, surprised by her own outburst. The pixie, who'd been licking himself, raised his head to cackle as well.

"You do not mean that, McKale. Your mind is clouded from the physical intimacy you shared with one another. That was her intention. But that feeling is temporary and it will pass. I am simply speeding along the process to help you, so do not deny me again. I have your best interests at heart. I can assure that you will enjoy a life with me far more than a life with her. There will be no further discussion."

"Yer right. No more discussion, Khalistah. With all due respect, I choose Robyn. It's time fer ye to return to yer land while this all passes. I'm certain ye will find another male far more interestin' than me."

Khalistah turned toward me so quickly that the pixie squealed, flying off her shoulder to a nearby tree branch.

"What have you done to him?" Her icy blue eyes were terrifying in her anger, swirling like boiling silver. "You've poisoned his mind against me!"

Holy evil attention. This chick was crazy as hell.

"Khalistah, no," McKale said.

She ignored his attempt to gain her attention and came straight for me, a tiny force of nature. I cursed myself for taking a step back instead of standing my ground, but dude, she was scary. Even in her fury, her voice stayed even and sweet.

"In your petty, vile, human jealousy you have turned the one source of goodness in my life against me. You have hurt me, and now you will hurt as well. I shall take the one thing you cherish most." She paused for dramatic effect. "Cassidy is her name, yes? She will make a fine plaything for the Fae males. We already know she enjoys—"

"*No!*" I screamed. She'd gone too far. "I'll never let you take her! *Never!*" My hands were balled in fists and I was ready to throw down, Fae royalty or not.

She smiled at my explosion. I'd proven she'd chosen correctly the worst way to punish me. McKale stepped close, angling partway between us, facing the FFG.

"Don't do this, Khalistah. I beg you."

She wore the stubborn expression of a spoiled woman. "She stole something from me. It is only fair."

"I am surprised at ye, princess. I'd no idea ye could be so cruel."

"Cruelty is when a choice is not offered. I will not be cruel to you, McKale. You have a choice. Will you come? Or will you let this Cassidy go in your place?"

McKale and I stared in horror at the determination in her eyes. One way or another she would have her way. She would either get to have McKale, or the satisfaction of hurting me by taking my sister. And I had no doubt she could make either one of those scenarios happen. She could take them both if she wanted, and I'd be powerless to stop her. What we needed right now was time.

McKale looked like he was prepared to argue. He obviously still believed there was some goodness hiding in her if he could get her to see reason. But squabbling was only going to make her madder. We needed her to think she'd won so we could have time to figure something out.

"McKale," I said. "Please…"

Both sets of eyes were on me. McKale's mouth was open from the argument he'd been prepared to give. He closed his mouth and blinked away the pain on his face before looking away from me and nodding.

"I will go with you after the binding," he said to the FFG. "Take me."

My insides lurched.

She reached up and stroked his jaw line. "Someday you will thank me for this, McKale. You see how quickly she chooses another over you."

That wasn't what I'd meant at all, but his posture stiffened. He couldn't possibly know that I'd never throw either of them to the Fae! Oh, my gosh—what if we couldn't find a way to fix this? What if he really went? Hot tears stung my eyes and I wrapped both arms around my waist.

From the corner of my eye I saw a slight movement in the distance. FFG was too focused on McKale to notice the mass of brown curls peeking out stealthily from behind the trees.

Rock.

There was no sign of mirth in the Clourichaun as his eyes locked to mine. We shared a moment of joined, silent panic.

"Seal your promise to me with a kiss," Khalistah told McKale. My attention snapped back to them. No. *Don't kiss her!*

McKale hesitated while she waited, patient.

"Please allow Robyn to leave us now," he requested.

"She stays. I was forced to witness the two of you carrying on. Now she must do the same."

I was going to be sick.

McKale bent down and gave her a peck on the lips. She barely had time to close her eyes before he'd jerked his head away with the tiniest of moans.

"Kiss me like you kissed her," she demanded.

I closed my eyes. There's no way I could stay and watch this. Willing to take a chance on a magical beat down, I sprinted away from them toward the path. Fast pixie wings flapped behind me, screeching laughter, but the creature didn't follow for long. When I got to the edge of the forest my empty stomach convulsed and I bent over, retching with dry heaves. Salty tears rolled down to my lips.

Bonfires flickered in the clearing, and music rang out. The Chaun were continuing their celebrations of a binding that had been cursed—doomed to misery. I wiped my mouth with the back of my hand and ran for the clearing, straight to the only people who might be able to help: the people I knew I could always turn to. My family.

EIGHTEEN

"DADDY!" HE WAS IMPOSSIBLE to miss, holding hands with my mother in the line formation and towering over the other dancing folk. He turned his head toward the sound of my voice, smiling. I was still a ways off, running toward them, and when he took in the sight of me, he broke from the group with Mom right behind him. Cassidy jumped up from a nearby table. I was probably giving them heart attacks—me, the most modest person in our family, running in front of all these people in my bathing suit, looking a fright. The three of them met me at the entrance of the clearing. I collapsed into Dad's arms, trembling.

"What happened?" he asked. "Where's McKale?"

I sucked in some air and forced myself to articulate. "She's going to take him!"

Without question, Dad jumped into action, signaling Brogan to us. The song had stopped and everyone was watching. Over a hundred worried faces stared. Leilah stood with both hands on her mouth.

"We need to speak privately," my father told Brogan, who nodded.

Brogan waved to the musicians and forced a smile at his

people. They whispered in speculation, but did as they were told, continuing the music.

I looked out into the darkened field of grass, searching for any sign of McKale or the FFG.

Brogan began to lead us away, but I held out a hand. "Wait! What if she tries to take him tonight?" The very idea had me afraid I might hyperventilate.

"Who? McKale?" Brogan studied my face, aghast, as I nodded. "Is he with the Shoe Mistress now?"

"Yes. We were by the falls…"

Part of the crowd had shifted closer to our group, and Brogan held up a hand to quiet me so they wouldn't hear.

"Keefe!" he called over his shoulder. Keefe jogged over and Brogan spoke to him in hushed tones. "Watch this clearing for McKale. We'll be speaking in the guest quarters, and I want ye to alert me immediately if ye see him or the Shoe Mistress. Watch the portal closely."

"Aye. Of course, Brogan, sir."

Brogan turned and led us to the bungalows.

"Yer rooms are closer, so I hope ye don't mind speaking there."

"Not at all," Dad said.

When we got to my parents' room I inhaled a huge breath before telling them everything about the encounter with the FFG. Cassidy held my hand the whole time. It was therapeutic to let it all out, but it also made the nightmare more real. By the time I was done, every face in the room appeared ready to retch just as I had. For once, even Cassidy was speechless. Mom gathered her close, wrapping protective arms around her, but Cass kept her fingers linked with mine and wouldn't let go.

"What's our plan?" Mom asked.

"Please," I begged. "Can someone find McKale and get him away from her?"

"Aye. I'll send a handful of lads to flush him out. I'll return shortly."

"Wait!" I said. "Rock was there! He was watching from behind a tree. He'll know what happened after I left."

Cassidy gave a little squeak of worry and Brogan nodded.

He rushed from the room and my family stepped into a close huddle, shoulder-to-shoulder.

"What can we do?" Cassidy asked. Her voice was one notch away from frantic. "I don't want to go to Faerie, but I don't want McKale to go either!"

"We won't let that happen," Dad said. "We'll need a power play on our part, something that will take her by surprise. What are her weaknesses? Is there anything she fears?"

Cassidy laughed dryly. "If I were her I'd be afraid of her daddy!"

She said it as a joke, but the other three of us exchanged thoughtful stares.

"She *has* been sneaking out of the portal against her father's wishes," Mom stated.

I shrugged. "But we don't know for sure if he cares what she does. He doesn't want Fae coming out whenever they please, but maybe he makes an exception for his little princess."

I ran the earlier conversation through my mind again, specifically the things FFG had said about her people.

"She wants it to look like McKale is choosing to come on his own." I was thinking out loud. Dad had his arms crossed, rocking back on his heels as I rambled. "Because she's afraid of what the other Fae will think if they know she's developed feelings for a human. She said it has to look like he's just a consort."

"So we blow her cover, then?" Mom asked.

We all nodded. But how would we prove to her people that she wanted McKale?

A quick knock sounded on the door, and Brogan came in, huffing from the exertion.

"Still no sign of 'im, but the boys are on it."

"Brogan," Dad said. "Do you have means to contact the Fae? To get them to open the portal?"

Brogan opened his mouth and paused, unsure, until my father swore that the information would never leave this room. Brogan pulled a thin rope from around his neck. Hanging from it was a golden tube the size of my thumb. It was a whistle. We all leaned forward to look at it. There was indecipherable writing and a symbol.

"Hey, is that…?" Cass pointed at the image, crinkling her brow, and we leaned in further.

"You gotta be kidding me," Dad said.

"It's a picture of a pot of gold!" I grinned.

"Aye," Brogan tucked it back into his shirt. "I've never been certain of its meaning, except that the Fae believe their realm to be the ultimate treasure. Not another soul has seen this caller, 'cept the Keepers who passed it to me."

"How does it work?" Dad asked him.

"It makes no noise to the human ear, but the Fae who guards the gate will hear it and open the portal to attain the message. 'Tis rarely used."

"I'll bet." Dad rubbed his large, squared chin and looked

at me. "Robyn. You brought all of your video stuff? The camera and laptop?"

"Yeah…" Where was this going? He cleared his throat and began delegating responsibilities.

"Brogan, I'm going to need you to pass a message to the Summer King through the portal guard. Tell him that the long-awaited binding will take place two evenings from now and you'd be honored to have the King and his court present for the event."

Brogan nodded.

"What if they don't come?" Cassidy asked.

"Let's just try and stay hopeful, love," Mom told her.

"Cass." Dad looked at her pointedly. "You and I are going to leave the village tonight—"

"But—"

"We'll be back in time for the binding. We have to be quick. There are some electronics I need to get and I'm going to need help. Plus, I'd rather have you with me, away from here, considering."

She looked at me. "I don't want to leave Robyn."

"It'll be okay." I squeezed her hand.

"All right, listen up." Dad's voice sounded like a military commander and our postures straightened. "We don't have much time, so here's the plan."

I lay in bed next to Mom unable to sleep. By the time Dad and Cassidy left, McKale and Rock still hadn't been found. Keefe did witness the FFG return to her own realm, thank goodness. But it killed me to know McKale was out there somewhere feeling… however he was feeling. Did he think I'd let him go so easily, as the FFG said? Had she been able to influence him once I was no longer in their presence? And worst of all, did he kiss her? Or worse?

I couldn't stand the thought. I rolled over and pressed my face hard into my pillow until I could feel tiny feathers poking through the cloth, jabbing my face. I didn't care how they stung. Nothing could hurt worse than the thought of McKale losing himself in her touch.

I wondered if Rock stayed silent the whole time, or if something might have happened to cause him to interfere. He was reckless, but I didn't want him to be hurt.

At the sound of a knock, Mom and I bolted upright.

"Coming," she called. We helped each other stand and went to the door. Brogan and Keefe stood there together.

"We found McKale," Brogan said. "He and Rock both made their way to Clourichaun land. They're fine and safe fer now."

I let out a loud breath.

"Aye, fine if you count the bloody pixie tailing 'im," Keefe clarified.

That gave me goose bumps.

"It would seem the Shoe Mistress is keeping an eye on 'im by leaving her pet behind," Brogan explained. He sounded tired. Mom must have noticed, too.

"Thank you, Brogan. And Keefe. Please thank all the boys for us. I'm glad McKale's okay. Let's all get some rest so we can do everything that needs to be done tomorrow."

Brogan stroked his beard and nodded. "I've sent a message for McKale to stay over there until after dark tomorrow so the blasted pixie won't be able to see any of the goings on over here."

"Good idea," Mom said.

Sadness weighed heavy inside me. I wouldn't get to see him at all tomorrow? Mom rubbed a hand over my back and said good night to the men as they left.

We climbed back into her and Dad's bed and prepared for a long, fitful night of sleep.

I took extra time doing my morning chores. The animals had a calming effect. The chickens pecked at their feed and the goats nudged my hands without any idea that today was different from any other day.

Afterward I went down to the clearing and pretended to eat breakfast. I noticed Mom only took a few bites as well. Word traveled fast through the clan. They may not have known the details, but they knew there was a threat at hand. Gone was yesterday's playfulness. People gave me respectful nods to let me know they were there for us and I returned the gesture.

Mom and I spent the early part of the day pacing, accompanied by whispers and murmurs from the clan. I kept eyeing the sun, watching for it to get high in the sky. Dad and Cassidy were supposed to return mid-afternoon.

Leilah approached me in the middle of the clearing with a hot cup of honeyed tea. I took it and thanked her.

"Is it true then?" she asked. "About the Shoe Mistress claiming yer McKale for herself?"

Her words hurt my stomach, but I nodded. "It's true."

"Och! The brazen cow. Ye'll tell me if ye need anything from me, love?"

"Yes, Leilah. Thank you." I bent and we shared a hug before she left me standing in the middle of the clearing with my hands around the ceramic mug. I kept watching the tree line, half-expecting McKale to come walking through.

I was nearly finished with my tea when I heard the rumble of an engine over the hills. Everyone in the clearing stilled to listen. I set my mug on the table. Mom came running down from the huts. We grabbed hands and took off toward the side of the village with everyone following. Excitement rippled through the clan as a small van came barreling down the hill.

"Keep it down!" Brogan reminded everyone as the voices began to reach a crescendo. Everyone quieted.

Yes, we needed to stay low-key today and not gain the attention of the pixie on the other side of the forest.

Dad and Cassidy jumped out, coming first to give hugs to Mom and me. The four of us went around back of the van where Dad opened it to reveal a hodgepodge of techy equipment—everything from a generator and projector to a giant, white pull-down screen. Clan members jostled to get a view of the foreign objects.

"What is all that?" one of them asked.

Daddy smiled and answered loud enough for everyone to hear. "This is what I like to call human magic. Technology."

A line of helpers assembled, lifting and carrying the heavy items as a group. Everything was brought down to the bottom of the clearing where Dad calculated the best angle for the movie screen, based on where the late afternoon sun would be at the time of the binding. They set up and tested the equipment before the sun set. When Dad gave a sample run of the technology, eliciting gasps and delighted chatter, Brogan had to remind everyone to quiet down again.

It was all starting to come together. We had the technology. Now we needed four more main components to make this a success: McKale, the FFG, the Summer King, and other Fae witnesses. *Please let them come.* Brogan gave the official invitation last night. We could only hope they'd accept. And if they didn't, Dad alluded to the idea of going into Faerie to speak to the Summer King himself. I did *not* like that idea. None of us did.

Human workers only entered Faerie when they were summoned for purposes of giving their reports. They did not seek out the Fae. Humans who entered Faerie of their own accord were not guaranteed safe passage back to the earthly realm.

McKale would return this evening and be briefed on his part. When I asked how we'd talk to McKale with the pixie there, Brogan assured me that the Leprechauns had done their share of battling pixies in the past. He said they knew how to deal with the little bugger.

Kitchen workers brought out trays of cheese sandwiches with pickles and jugs of mild ale. It was starting to get dark as everyone sat down to eat. Cassidy held my hand through most of the meal, and we sat with our hips touching. I glanced down at the equipment, which had been covered with waterproof tarps in case it rained overnight. My eyes darted to the tree line. Nothing there but trees. I took a large gulp of ale to wash down the bite of bread that had lodged in my dry throat. Half a sandwich was all I could manage.

"Walk with me?" came a voice above me.

I looked up at my father's handsome face and glanced at Cassidy.

"I'll be okay," she told me. Mom leaned over from Cassidy's other side and smiled at me, patting my sister's leg. She wouldn't let Cass out of her sight. I stood and took the crook of Dad's arm, letting him lead me away from everyone.

When we were well out of hearing range he rubbed my hand.

"So… eighteen tomorrow, eh?"

"Yeah." I thought about saying something lighthearted, but didn't have it in me.

We ended up by the animal holdings. I sat down and leaned against a fence post, giggling when one of the young goats stuck his head through and nuzzled my neck.

"Quit it," I said, pushing him away.

"They like you." Dad squatted in front of me and admired the gaggle of goats that stood at my back.

"That's 'cause I feed them."

He smiled and watched the animals until the mood between us grew serious again.

"There are things I planned to tell you when you turned eighteen, even before all this happened. You know, whether it feels like it or not, you'll be doing a duty for the Fae by binding with McKale tomorrow. But after the fertile years you'll be expected to work for them in other ways."

"Like what?" My heart gave a bang. "Are you *finally* going to tell me what you do?"

He grinned at my unabashed tone. "That was the plan. It's nothing so mysterious as you might think. I'm just a Tracker. Do you know what that is?"

"Ah." I leaned back against the pole, staring at my father's thick jawline and seeing him a little bit differently. I tried to remember everything Leilah had mentioned about Trackers.

"You can make people forget when they meet Faeries?"

He took a seat beside me, leaning against the next fencepost.

"When Fae enter into our realm, I follow their magic. They leave traces when they glamour or sift from one place to another. I can feel a path of burn in the air, and I follow it. They can never sift too far. I usually find them. I can't stop them or approach them, but sometimes they address me and I'll respond. Otherwise, I just visit the people they've come into contact with. And, yes, I make them forget."

That gave me a chill. "What do you do? Like, get in their heads somehow?"

"No, I can't invade anyone's mind. I shroud them in magic and use the Gaelic phrase, *Ar oscailt intinn*, which roughly translates to *open your mind*. It's more like hypnotism. And then I tell them precisely what I want them to forget. It's important to be exact so you don't take too much or leave anything behind. When I pull the magic away, the memory is gone. It's painless."

"Wow." I didn't know what else to say. How weird to think of my dad doing that. "You work in the U.S.?"

He'd always traveled a lot. Sometimes he was gone for months at a time. But it didn't make much sense for him to live in the U.S. and work in Ireland.

"I work in the U.S., mostly. There's a portal there."

"Where? *In D.C.?*" The idea of it made me feel violated.

"No, no. It's in Vermont on the border with Canada."

"Oh. Well, at least it's not too close. So, what does Mom do?"

"She's an information gatherer. She informs us when strange reports are made. We check out anything that sounds like it could be Fae related. There are dozens of us in U.S. offices, including Mom and I."

I twisted blades of grass between my fingers, trying to process it.

"Do you work for the CIA, then?"

"Nope. Army. It's a paranormal division nobody's ever heard of. Except, of course, those in the military elite. And us." He grinned. "Scared yet?"

"A little," I admitted. "Does your voodoo magic work on Fae? Can we make them forget?"

"No. Faerie magic only works against their kind at the hands of another Fae, not a human. It's too weak."

"Darn." It would be nice to make the FFG forget she ever wanted McKale.

"Robyn." He touched my chin to make me look at him. "Everything's going to work out tomorrow, I'm sure of it. But... in the off chance that things don't go as we intend, Mom and I are willing to pack it all up and get you out of here. We'll have to live on the run, trying to evade the Fae, and we won't be able to use our magic anymore because they can track it. But—"

"No, Daddy." I scooted over and let him envelop me in his big embrace. "Thank you, but I'm staying here no matter what. Not because the Fae are demanding it, but for McKale and his clan."

I'd thought about this a lot the previous sleepless night. Even if McKale were forced to live in Faerie, I would be there for him. The thought of looking into his dead eyes and listening to him call me by her name was sickening, but I couldn't leave him—not if there was even the slightest chance that I could break that trance. I guess when it came down to it I was as much of a hopeless romantic as my sister. I tightened my grip around Dad's waist, wanting to make all frightening thoughts disappear.

Dad held me and kissed my head. "We'll see how it goes. All I'm saying is if you want out, we'll make it happen."

"Thank you," I whispered against his shoulder.

In return he murmured, "You have no idea how proud you make me, Robyn."

ΠΙΠΕΤΕΕΠ

AFTER MY WALK WITH Dad, McKale still hadn't returned to the village for the night. Cassidy and I retired to our room early. I scouted it for nasty little Fae spies, but the room was clean and we felt safe enough to get in bed. We'd hardly gotten any rest the past few days, and after a couple hours of lying there talking, sleepiness took its toll, pulling us both under.

With the feathery down surrounding my head, the first notes of distant music were almost indistinguishable. I lifted my heavy head from the pillow, listening. There it was again: a faint, woeful tune ringing like a soft wail from the strings of a violin.

I bolted out of the bed and ran from the room. The music beckoned me, its song of sorrow matching the song of my own heart this night. It was an audible version of all my emotions. As I chased the source of the invisible grieving, my feet took me straight toward McKale's bungalow where I halted.

The pixie was sitting on McKale's doorstep, hands behind his little head. Its wicked smile revealed tiny razor teeth when it caught sight of me. I stepped back, right into

Cassidy who was breathing hard. She grasped my upper arms and held me close to her. We stood there together saying nothing as the evil creature eyed us and the slow cry of low musical notes filled the air.

McKale's song had captured my heart, urging me to him, and yet, because of this creature I couldn't see him.

I looked up at a motion in my peripheral vision. It was Leilah, standing next to her boyfriend with a hand on her heart. A trickle of others began to join her, drawn to the power of the song. Mom was there, holding her robe closed with Dad at her side. As clan members drifted into the spaces between bungalows, I felt the power of their support. Our numbers were great in comparison to one small pixie. Revived, I lost all fear for the creature on McKale's doorstep. I stared at it and took a step forward.

"Be careful," Cassidy whispered, sensing my intentions, but she dropped her hands from my arms.

I went forward and stopped a few feet from its beady-eyed stare as it raised itself up to face me like a giant, fat, green bumblebee. "Let me pass."

I was prepared for his attack this time, so when he darted up I swatted, my hand connecting to its squishy belly. But only for a second before he disappeared with a *poof* and reappeared on my other side, yanking my ear with his claws. The clan was on him before I had a chance to feel pain from his scratches. It was too much for the unsuspecting pixie. He tried to sift away, only to be grasped, punched, kicked, and smacked by another person wherever he reappeared. Leprechauns cried out in urgent voices about the "gloves and cage," while little women screamed and skittered out of the way.

A bearded man ran out with crazy-looking gloves that appeared to be woven with thin metal. It took a moment before I realized it was Brogan without his hat. He was fearsome in his focused state, and he moved quicker than I thought possible. Behind him ran two of the Chaun holding a small, iron cage. One of the guys thunked the pixie hard from behind with his fist, dazing it. The pixie let out a hideous snarl when Brogan snatched it mid-air and the gloves wrapped around it. Brogan tossed the creature into the cage and someone slammed the door shut, locking it securely. We all cheered. Cassidy and I high-fived each other, laughing. Mom and Dad hugged us.

Brogan walked over, slightly out of breath. He pulled off the gloves and held them up for our inspection.

"Iron," he said. "Makes 'em ill—depletes the magic in their skin."

Brogan nodded toward the cage where the pixie now huddled, shivering and growling in the center. "We'll return the little sod to 'is people on the morrow." And with that, someone whisked it away.

Cassidy nudged me and nodded to the side with big eyes.

I followed her stare to find McKale standing in his doorway watching me, uncertain.

"Kale!" I ran, bumping people and knocking McKale back as I flung my arms around his neck. He was a rumpled mess from his time with the Clourichaun.

"Robyn," he whispered into my hair. His arms tightened around me.

"I didn't mean I was choosing for you to go," I said.

"I know it. I knew it then, but I couldn't let her think there was any way we'd let her have yer sister."

I pulled back enough to look at him. "Thank you. You bought us time."

He cupped my face in both his hands and examined my face with tender urgency. His eyes told me he hadn't given Khalistah the kind of kiss she desired. If he had, he would still be dazed and unable to focus on me in this way.

Someone cleared their throat, causing McKale and I to remember we had a full audience of worried people. We broke away and opted for holding hands as Brogan stepped forward.

"We found McKale coming back to the village," he explained to me. "He'd rid himself of the pixie fer a time while it ran after some grub, so we told 'im the plan."

McKale's thumb stroked the top of my hand. "I was coming yer way to see ya when the blasted pixie came back, so I went to me own room to be safe."

We were all quiet.

"Keefe," Brogan said, running a hand down his beard.

The young man stepped up and removed the beret from his head.

"I want someone watching the portal all night. Ye lads can take shifts. Tell 'em to keep the horn handy and sound it if the gate opens."

"Aye, Brogan." Keefe gave a small bow and ran to do his duty.

"Brogan, sir, if I may…" Leilah stepped forward and gave a timid curtsey.

"Aye, lassie?"

"'Tis no' the tradition, I know, but…" Even in the dark of night I sensed the flush of embarrassment on her features. She stared at the ground and Brogan urged her to continue.

Leilah lifted her head and asked, "Might McKale and Robyn bind this very evening? The official ceremony on the morrow could still take place fer show."

Murmurs rose around us.

McKale and I looked at each other. Brogan ran a hand down his beard, unsure.

Mom stepped forward. "It's a good idea. If they want to, I say let them bind. Let them have this night."

She didn't have to say "just in case" because we were all thinking it. The thought of what might happen tomorrow if our plan failed made my stomach seize. This could be our last night together: our only night. Brogan looked at my father, who nodded his agreement. I smiled at McKale as a fluttery nervousness settle inside.

"Aye?" he whispered to me.

"Yes," I whispered back.

He gave me a half-grin and nodded before turning to Brogan.

"We wish to bind this night, Father."

"Aye. Well, then." Brogan nodded to Leilah. "Fetch the bindings. McKale, straighten yer room, son. 'Tis no' fit fer a female in that state of disaster."

My cheeks flamed. Everyone cheered as Leilah ran off and a group of older women descended upon McKale's room, bustling past him and clucking about the mess. He gave them a sheepish shrug and grin as the oldest woman swatted his backside then shut the door on us.

A sudden thought hit me and I thought aloud, "What about my dress?" My current outfit was a t-shirt and cotton shorts. I wasn't even wearing a bra! I crossed my arms.

"You'll wear the dress tomorrow for the fake binding,"

Cassidy said. "You don't need it tonight." She dug an elbow into my ribs and I met her glinting eye.

Oh my goodness… I'm gonna pass out. I couldn't even look at my parents, even though I knew they hadn't heard Cass's remark.

Cass giggled and wrapped an arm around my waist. "It'll be fine," she whispered.

Leilah returned with a woven basket full of colorful silken scraps. I pressed my free hand to my nervous stomach as the women began to untangle the mass of material.

Mom sidled close to my side. "Are you okay with this?"

I nodded. Dad cleared his throat behind us.

"Nothing like an impromptu wedding," he said under his breath. I turned to see him rubbing his neck.

Mom wrapped her arms around his waist and laid her head on his chest. "Our babies are growing up, Leon." They both gazed at me, eyes full of sentiment, and Cass squeezed my hand.

Things got a little crazy when McKale and the women emerged from his hut. It didn't take long to realize this was a "hands-on" kind of ceremony. McKale and I were pushed by excited hands to the middle of the group where a small opening had been made. Mom and Cassidy followed us while Dad hung back with the other men. A fiddler and flautist had retrieved their instruments and began to play soft, sweet music. Love ballads.

There was no big announcement. No gown or flowers. Just McKale and I in our pajamas with messy hair. We were moved into position, facing one another. Led by Leilah, my mom and sister took a long strand of purple cloth and wrapped it around our waists, forcing our abdomens together as they tied a tight knot. I giggled up at McKale's wistful face when the oldest woman insisted, *"Tighter!"* I'd always thought the term "binding" was metaphorical.

One by one, women of the clan stepped up to take part. Strip after colored strip was tied around us, from our hips to our chests, pressing us together. Knowing what this symbolized, it was hard not to be embarrassed. But that feeling fled when I looked at my betrothed. My Kale, who'd turned out to be even more than I'd hoped. His eyes glistened with happiness in the moonlight.

When it came time for the father part, Mom waved to Dad, who followed Brogan's lead. Dad cleared his throat several times, evidently not at ease with the marital mummification of his daughter, but he played along.

Dad and Brogan each had two white strips of cloth. Brogan bent down and moved our feet so that our ankles were side-by-side. There was a bad moment where I thought we might topple over, but each time we tilted the crowd would push us back into place, saying "Whoa!" in unison and laughing with merriment. Dad and Brogan tied our ankles, and then stood up and tied our wrists. I watched McKale's stoic face the whole time. When they finished I pressed my cheek to McKale's and tried to breathe evenly. My parents stepped back. Cassidy stood in my sights and winked.

The song ended and the area quieted with anticipation.

Brogan spoke with hearty volume. "We come together this eve to bind the lives and bodies of our Leprechaun, McKale, with Robyn of the Masons!"

"Here, here!" shouted the crowd. The reverence and excitement in the air gave me chills.

"We wish them blessings and fertility," Brogan said.

"*Here, here!*"

Brogan then spoke something beautiful in Gaelic and the people responded in kind. It sounded magical and I experienced another set of goose bumps.

"We're gettin' the short version," McKale whispered in my ear.

The Leprechauns and women chanted lines in Gaelic, and it produced the sort of mesmerizing sound that was probably meant to stir my ovaries into action or something. And then an ominous silence fell.

"Brace yerself," McKale whispered.

"To the lodgings!" Brogan shouted, punching his little round fist in the air.

"*To the lodgings!*"

I yelped with surprise as we were swept off our feet sideways with a falling sensation and carried by dozens of hands into McKale's room amid shouts and cheers. We were both laughing as they rolled us onto his bed and bowed low before leaving. We lay there in a literal tangle with me on top of him, listening to their happy chants get quieter and quieter until everyone was gone.

"Um, wow," I said. "So…" Now what? My pulse danced wildly.

They'd wrapped our torsos and legs, but left our arms free except the wrists. My breath caught as McKale brought the wrists of one set of our hands up to his mouth. The gas lamp in his room was lit on low, and I watched in wonder as he bit the end of the neat bow with his teeth and pulled it until our hands were free. He did the same with the other wrists. Then he captured both of my wrists and kissed them.

I sighed, too overcome and nervous to say anything.

"Thank ye fer coming to me tonight," he said in a low voice.

"How could I not? That song... They beat up the pixie for me! Did you see that?" Okay, I was feeling a little nervous, and I think McKale could tell because he chuckled and looked at me like he thought it was cute.

"How did you do it?" I blurted. I had to know, before we went any further, what happened last night with FFG. "How'd you get away with not kissing her?"

McKale's eyebrows came together and he was quiet a moment. "I did not get away with anything, love. I don' wish to recall a single moment of it, but ye should know. I hope ye can forgive me."

"You kissed her?" He nodded once. His eyes were strained. "*Really* kiss her?" Another nod.

Jealousy reared, but I didn't feel angry at McKale. I knew he did what he had to do to get the FFG to believe him and go back to the portal. But the thought of his mouth on hers... I buried my face in his neck, trembling. "How is your mind so clear after that?"

"'Twas strange, it was," he whispered. "I thought only of you. I kept ye at the front of my mind, noticin' how fragile she felt compared to your strength. I imagined ye stealing the ball from the lads, and wrestlin' me in the waters. As her magic o'ercame me, the focus of my passion was no' her. It was hard, I'll no' lie. And I was no' completely meself when I stumbled to the Clour land."

Amazing. I lifted my head and looked at him. "Do you think the plan will work tomorrow?"

His face became grave. "It must. Let's no' think on it anymore this night." He kissed me with tenderness and I put aside my fears. We had this night, if nothing else.

Together we untied each knot at our sides, making a neat pile of cloth bindings on the floor beside his bed. By the time he pulled the last strip from our thighs my heart was pumping rapidly. We were both sitting up. I almost made a move to untie our ankles, but I waited, remembering how he'd taken the initiative with our wrists like it was his job. Sure enough, he bent at the waist, undoing our last two bindings with graceful, gentle fingers.

He dropped the scraps of cloth on the floor and came right at me, slowly, never hesitating.

"Kale," I breathed.

"Aye." He was laying me back and I was breathing too fast.

"If I would've known we were binding tonight I would have cleaned up for you." And shaved, and worn the pretty bra and panty set I'd picked out in hopes of a happy binding night. But McKale only laughed and pulled his shirt over his head, throwing it to the corner. I swallowed.

"Ye can be certain, Robyn, I'll not be complainin' about the state of ya."

And then he kissed me without an ounce of tentativeness, like a man claiming what was his. A barbaric analogy, maybe, but in my heightened state of nervous expectancy, it felt crazy good to be claimed. My hands were all over him. Well, not *all* over yet, but all over his bared skin. I loved the way his lean biceps and triceps bulged as he held himself over me.

"You are so hot," I whispered onto his lips.

He pulled back. "Are ye too hot?"

I laughed and reached for him. "It's just a figure of

speech. I meant that you're really… good looking. Come here."

He kissed me again, but this time his hand found the bottom of my t-shirt. His touch, unlike his kiss, *was* tentative. My insides fluttered as his hand inched upwards, caressing my stomach and waist. I was insanely nervous about what he would think.

"Yer so soft," he said. He kissed me again and moved his hand up a little more. "Is this all right with ye?"

"Yeah. It feels good when you touch me." It was strange to hear myself say that, but the grim reminder that we might only have this night kept me from holding back. We had no time to be shy. I wanted to show him how I felt.

When his thumb brushed the underside of my breast, it was on.

I wiggled and tugged my shirt over my head, tossing it aside and propping myself up on my elbows as if presenting him a gift. I watched as his expression changed from the amazement of a boy to the need of a man. A sound of triumph rose from my throat as he pressed me back with a deep kiss, and the exploration of one another began. We took our time learning each other's skin, the sensitive spots, savoring each pleasurable response that our touches elicited. We refused to be rushed, not caring if we didn't sleep at all that night.

And we didn't.

When the sun dawned on the wide Irish sky, a crackle of magic split the air and a horn sounded. We jumped from the bed, stumbling for our clothes and laughing. Yes, laughing. The blasting horn should have scared us, but we were giddy in our newfound selves—our *bound* selves—not yet willing to let go of that exquisite feeling. With a parting kiss I ran for the door, only to be gently tugged back. He took my chin so I couldn't look anywhere but in his eyes.

"I love ye, Robyn of the Leprechaun."

It was his first time saying it. Moisture sprung to my eyes.

"I love you, too, Kale of the Chaun."

He grinned and let me go.

I got as far away from his bungalow as fast as I could. The cool morning air felt as fresh and crisp as ever during the mad dash back to my room.

It was prospectively the most terrifying day of my life, and yet, I'd never been happier.

TWENTY

THE HORN TURNED OUT to be a false alarm. It was only the Fae gatekeeper giving a message that the Summer King would, indeed, be honored to attend the binding ceremony this afternoon with several of his court officials. At that news, the mood in the clan became festive once again. The ovens blasted heat, cooking piles of mouthwatering pastries and savory delicacies. Wild flowers were strung together and strewn along tables. Tall, hanging lanterns with candles dotted the perimeter of the clearing, transforming it into a beautiful reception area.

I was smoothing out a large, round sheet of cotton in the middle of the clearing with Leilah, Cassidy, and Rachelle when I heard McKale whisper my name from the wooded area. I sat up on my knees and peered toward the sound, spotting him in the trees. I looked around, but only my sister and two friends seemed to have noticed. The girls snickered as I stood up and jogged to him, unable to keep the smile from my face.

He grabbed my hand and led me into the confines of leafy shade before pulling my face to his for a kiss.

"I've missed ye, *Bláth mo chroí.*"

Flower of his heart. It had only been five hours since we were snuggled warm together, but I'd missed him, too.

I let him walk me backward until I was against a tree. I savored the feel of him, and the taste of licorice on his tongue. I wanted to stay there all day and forget about what awaited us.

We broke away with reluctance at the sound of Cassidy calling from the entrance of the woods.

"Dad's looking for McKale!" she whispered. "It's time to get wired up."

"Okay, thanks," I answered with a sinking nervousness.

"Happy birthday, Robyn." He bent to kiss me one last time, nipping my lower lip between his teeth before pulling away and leaving me there to melt back against the tree, weak-kneed. Cassidy came walking into the forest, raising her eyebrows at the sight of me.

"Something tells me our little McKale's not so shy anymore."

"Not so much," I said with a sigh. Cassidy laughed.

"Well, come on, if you can manage to walk." She held out her hand and I took it.

We passed Leilah and Rachelle who were busy spreading flower petals all around the circle of cloth where McKale and I would bind again. They waved as we went by.

Mom, Dad, and McKale stood at the "technology station." Dad pinned something on McKale's shirt as we approached. A wire connected on the inside, snaking around his torso to the back where a thin device was clipped inside his pants.

"This is a video recorder. It should be the right height. Just make sure you remain facing the Faerie. What are you going to do when she gets here?"

"I'm going to pull her aside, Mr. Mason, sir, and get her to divulge her plan once again."

"Perfect. Really play it up. Get her to show how she feels. Make sure she states every sordid detail. Don't feel bad going for the kill. Flirt with her. Whatever you have to do to make her look bad."

"Except kissing her, right?" Cass asked, making a face. "Gah, please don't kiss her."

"A *little* touching might make it believable," Mom said. I glared at her and she quickly backpedaled. "Of course, avoid it if you can, but like Leon said, do what you must. Robyn will understand."

McKale cleared his throat, opening his hands straight at his sides and then balling them into fists—open, closed, over and over. I took one of his hands, interlocking our fingers. We both held tight.

Dad had given everyone a brief test performance of the technology earlier in the day, video-taping people, and then showing snippets on the large screen. Very amusing for the clan, indeed.

"Let's all stay positive," Dad said, adjusting the wires at the back of McKale's pants so they wouldn't show.

"We are," I whispered.

McKale nodded at me. I knew his pulse was working overtime, just as hard as mine. The time was approaching.

The plan was for McKale to get footage with FFG as soon as possible after the Fae arrived. Then, once everyone settled, the fake binding would commence, followed by the "special entertainment." Cue video footage of FFG revealing her master plan to Leprechaun and Fae alike. And then it was up to the Summer King to decide what to do.

My stomach hurt. I had to let go of McKale's hand to bend over with my hands on my knees.

A hushed whisper began throughout the clearing, growing louder.

"Oh, great," I heard Dad mumble.

I stood and looked toward the woods where everyone else was staring. It took a second to make out the lost boys blending in with the trees until they all took a further step out and stopped. All except Rock, who continued toward us.

He seemed like a different person. His face was made of stone. Around his waist was a leather band with what appeared to be an iron dagger sheathed at his side. Upon inspection, all of the Clour at the tree line looked to be carrying different iron weapons, their faces equally severe.

"Ronan!" Cassidy called. Mom took her by the arm, stopping her from running to this.

"We don't have time for this today," Dad said to Rock as he neared us.

"I will not be in the way for long, sir." Rock stopped within arm's reach of Dad.

"Rock," McKale said in a warning tone. "Don't do anything foolish, mate."

"It's the least foolish thing I've ever planned, Kale." He looked back at Dad. "I will no' let yer daughter be taken into Faerie, sir. Nor my best mate. Me lads an' meself are prepared to fight. I will offer me own self as a substitute fer Cassidy if it comes to that."

Cass's hands flew to her chest. "Ronan, no! You can't!"

"I can." His eyes seared into hers. "And I will."

Mom and Dad stared, shocked.

"It will no' come to that," McKale tried to assure him.

"Indeed, I hope it does no'. But if it does, I will be there." He pointed to the woods where his clan stood at attention. "Waiting."

Dad said nothing, just sort of balked as Rock turned and headed back to the woods, seeming to disappear out of sight.

Cass tried to tug from Mom's grip, but she held tight. "I need to go to him!"

"There's no time," Mom said.

I turned Cassidy to me and hugged her. Mom let her go and I felt Cass's arms grip around me for dear life. She let out a sob.

"Nothing will happen to him. Or you. This is going to work. Everyone will be okay."

Please let us all be okay.

What if the Summer King didn't care what shenanigans his daughter was up to? The whole plan could backfire if he was offended that we tried to make a fool of the princess. So much could go wrong. I lay my head on her shoulder and rubbed her back, taking as much comfort from the embrace as I was giving.

Someone rubbed my shoulder, and then a finger was under my chin, lifting my face. Mom. She gripped both of our shoulders tenderly.

"Cassidy, please take Robyn to the room and help her get ready while we finish preparing out here."

Cass gave a final glance toward the forest before swallowing hard and nodding.

McKale reached out for me and I wrapped my arms around his neck, breathing in the scent of his skin and hair. I didn't want to let him go.

"I'll see ye soon," he whispered, holding me tighter.

"Yes. Good luck," I told him.

We pulled away and gave each other one last peck before I left for my room with Cassidy. I really wasn't feeling well, but I had to be strong.

Pulling the gorgeous dress over my head lightened my mood a fraction. The silk was so smooth. Mom joined us, and she and Cassidy fastened tiny clasps and buttons up my back, then stepped away and "Ooooed."

Leilah and Rachelle showed up with a basket of flowers and hairpins. Together the four of them brushed, tweaked and twirled. I was a little worried for a second. I didn't want to be transformed into a giant flower-head, but Cassidy wouldn't let me walk out of the room looking bad. When they finished and Cass handed me the mirror, I smiled. It was pretty. They'd twisted strands of hair from my temples and hooked them together in the back. Flowers lined the twists of hair, looking like a peasant's crown, and waves of brown tumbled around my forehead and neck.

"*Áillidh.*" Leilah surveyed me with her hands on her hips. "Beautiful. McKale will surely be thanking his lucky stars he gets to bind with ye twice!"

"I love it," I told them. "Thank you. And thank you for last night, Leilah."

She shrugged it off and waved a hand, smiling. "Not at all, love. It's me who should be thanking you fer bringin' a bit o' romance and hope back into the village."

Rachelle covered her mouth and giggled.

Cassidy crouched in front of me and pinched my cheekbones to get a natural blush going. "Now all you need's a little make-up and you'll be set," she said.

Before she could stand again I grabbed her wrist and looked in her eyes. "I was wrong about Rock," I whispered. "He does care." Her eyes watered and she nodded. The two of them were quite a pair. A mess, for sure, but his willingness to sacrifice himself went a long way toward scratching out those bygone mistakes in my eyes.

I reached for my make-up bag and got started, making quick work of it while Cassidy changed into a summer dress.

"It's time," Mom said when I finished. "Are you ready?"

"Yes." I stood up. "I'm ready."

"Yeah, let's get this bee-otch!" my sister exclaimed. Mom glared at her. "Sorry," Cass muttered.

I wished I could share Cassidy's confident zeal for what was to come.

Our timing was impeccable because at that moment a draft of powerful magic shook the room. I rubbed the bare skin of my arms. All eyes went round, and Rachelle covered her mouth with a tremor.

"The Summer King," Leilah whispered, a look of terror on her face.

Cassidy grabbed my hand and I grabbed Mom's with my other one. We couldn't avoid this forever. Time to go. We all nodded at one another, and then filed out into the warm, overcast afternoon.

As we entered the clearing a wave of heat like sunshine warmed my skin, though the sun hid behind clouds. The Leprechauns were all gathered, standing in silence and watching as a procession of Faeries glided up from the field. There were at least ten of them, forming a semicircle around a taller male who seemed to shine. The heat, I realized, was emanating off him. His hair was golden platinum, like his daughter's, but unlike the other men he did not wear it down. His was pulled back at the nape of his neck and tied with twine, which accentuated his metallic crown, interwoven with vines and leaves. He was draped in a silky robe the color of a blue summer sky.

I was glad I hadn't eaten anything that day because my body felt like a wreck on the inside. I fought to appear well and not ill.

We stopped at the edge of the clearing and watched as the Fae halted in front of Brogan, Dad, and McKale. I couldn't stop staring at the Summer King. He held the same mesmerizing quality as Khalistah, only stronger. This was a being who could manipulate nature with a wave of his fingers. His power hummed through the air. The King's freaky eyes did not stay one color. Even from a distance I could see how they changed like a kaleidoscope, blending from fresh green grass, to bluebird feathers, to lavender lily petals.

With great effort I moved my eyes away from him to scan the other Faerie faces. Six male, four female; however, no tiny, angelic face with platinum hair was present. I stared in the direction of the portal, but it was closed, invisible. Nobody else was coming out.

Heart. Pounding. Oh. Crap.

Where the frick was FFG?

McKale craned his neck until he found me. His confusion and worry morphed into admiration as his eyes swept up and down the gown, but when he met my eyes his trepidation returned. Khalistah had not come. Our entire plan was ruined.

Brogan bowed low with a swoop of his forearm across his waist. The other male Leprechauns also bowed, and the women curtsied. Cassidy, Mom, and I dipped curtsies to the guests as well, and then looked at one another, covert questions in our eyes. *What will we do if she doesn't show?*

"Shoe Master and King of the Summer, we are humbled and honored by yer presence here today for our meek celebration," Brogan said.

"Indeed, it has been too long since last I visited the cobbling folk." The Summer King's voice rang over us like a bursting rainbow. Songbirds from neighboring fields and woods fluttered skyward, drawn to the outskirts of our gathering, a cacophony of chirping. The King laughed gaily at the sight and sounds of them. The light rumble of his voice gave me a heady sensation, as if surrounding trees were photosynthesizing overtime, sending a rush of pure oxygen into the air.

Brogan cleared his throat, looking uneasy. "And will the lovely Shoe Mistress be joining us today, as well?"

"Ah." The Summer King linked his fingers together behind his back. "The previous day has brought change, as is necessary from time to time. The princess has requested a new venture and I have allowed it." At an outburst of whispers, the King continued. "But do not worry. A new Shoe Mistress will be presented and I trust you will find her agreeable."

Brogan looked shaken. "Of course, King of the Summer, but we've not offended the former Shoe Mistress in any way, have we?"

The Summer King laughed again, sending the birds around us into a frenzy of flight before they settled.

"Not in the least, master Brogan. You know the whims of youth. How easily they tire. Roles must change in Faerie, just as the seasons on earth."

Brogan nodded, his eyes heavy. "Indeed."

A Faerie woman approached and stood next to the King. Her hair was as long as Khalistah's, but wavy and dark like glittering spices. Mom stiffened next to me and it felt like she might squeeze the blood from my hand. The Fae woman peered around at us with eerie eyes like the yellow of dandelions.

"Which two are to bind?" she asked.

McKale and I looked at each other and stepped forward. I had to wrench my hand from Mom's grip. Without thinking twice McKale and I grabbed hands and stood before them. Mom and Dad moved up next to us. The sight of the King's eyes up close scared me so bad that my instinct to flee was in full effect. The King nodded his approval and the female grinned with pride.

"So this is the tiny, beautiful babe whom I saw in Faerie years ago…" Her head tilted as she examined me with interest. Then she noted our linked hands. "An extraordinary pair. I knew it would be so. How divine that she was brought to me that fateful day. And see how they have taken to one another? Adorable." Now she gazed at the Summer King as if seeking his praise.

"Yes, Martineth, dearest, you have an exceptional eye for detail."

I caught Mom sending a death glare toward the King's consort.

"Well, then." Brogan cleared his throat. "Without further ado, let the celebrations commence. We hope ye will enjoy yerselves and let me know if ye be needing anything at all."

Brogan clapped his hands twice and the musicians

skittered into place, lifting their instruments and beginning an upbeat tune, which seemed out of place, given the fact that everyone remained unmoving. Brogan let out an embarrassed laugh.

"Well, go on then!" he called to his people. "Don't be shy. Let's show our honored guests a nice time, then, 'eh?"

There were nods and forced smiles, and then people appeared to relax and fall into fake celebration mode. Platters of food and vats of beverages were presented. Dancing broke out beside the binding circle, though everyone was careful not to disturb it.

I locked eyes with McKale as a trickle of despair crept into me. Leave it to Khalistah to ruin our plan. She had us in her grip. Of course she wouldn't want to see us bind. But I had no doubt she'd be expecting McKale to waltz into her den and fulfill the agreement at the end of the day. I hated her self-assurance.

Brogan waved Cassidy forward so my whole family stood before the Fae. I swallowed hard and looked up at the King.

Cassidy sidled close and clung to my arm with a death grip caused by her own fear, and it kept me grounded to the spot.

Brogan introduced each member of my family, starting with Dad. We each bowed or curtsied, and the King seemed to nod with a flicker of his eyes. Martineth, the King's consort, watched Mom's stoic front with a victorious grin. Mom, however, would not look at the smirking Fae woman.

"This appears to be a very good match," the Summer King stated. "And what say you about this union, Brogan?"

"King of the Summer, truly, the coming binding of McKale and Robyn has brought our lot joy beyond measure.

We believe 'tis the start of a new era for the cobbling folk. We wish future generations of our clan to serve ye with as much delight as we have."

The King's mouth softened at the edges, and I sensed a genuine fondness there.

"I wish you many generations to come, Brogan of the Leprechaun."

Brogan bowed in response. When he straightened, he held an arm toward the festivities.

"Won't you join us?" Brogan asked.

"I believe I shall," the King responded. He held out his elbow and Lady Martineth slid her slender hand in the crook.

Four Chaun boys carried out a massive wooden chair and set it facing the party. Bright purple cushions were placed on it and fluffed. The Summer King took a seat and his entourage flanked him in a semi-circle with his consort at his right side. Their faces remained chiseled masks, but their eyes shone with amusement as they watched the Chaun men and women dance.

My family, McKale, and I stood a distance from the festivities in tense, silent thought.

Think, Robyn, think! How the heck could we get Khalistah to come out of the portal?

"She's not coming," Dad said in a low voice.

"What are we gonna do?" Cassidy whispered.

"I'll go into Faerie for the footage," McKale stated.

Wait… excuse me?

"No!" I gripped his forearm. "No way. She'll never let you back out of there."

He began to shake his head but Dad cut in, saying, "I'll go."

Uh, *no*. I shook my head. "That won't work, Dad. She won't answer to you. It has to be me. The sight of me will make her talk. She hates me."

"Exactly," Dad said. "Maybe she won't let *you* back out." We all thought about it, then Dad said with reluctance, "You and McKale will go together. That's your best shot. She knows her father will expect you both back for the binding."

We were all silent, staring around at one another as the change of plans set in. McKale and I were going into Faerie. Being that it was our only chance—our last hope—a strange sense of calm determination shrouded me.

"Let's get wires on Robyn, too," Dad said. "Just in case." His voice was strong, but I could see the panic behind his eyes as he jumped into action. He glanced over at the celebrations where the Fae and Leprechauns were busy, paying us no mind.

Mom stood still with a hand covering her mouth. She'd almost lost me to the Fae as a baby, and now my fate would once again be in their hands.

"Shitballs. You can't go in there," Cassidy whispered, thinly veiled panic in her voice.

Mom, Cass, and I faced one another in a triangle.

"We'll be fine," I whispered. "Everything will be okay." My words did not relax them. Dad came up behind me and started hooking wires under the seams of my dress.

"Don't piss her off," Cass warned me. "She'd probably prefer revenge and take her chances on punishment if she has any idea we're trying to pull one over on her."

"I know," I whispered. I wouldn't put anything past the FFG at this point.

"What will you say when you see her?" Mom asked.

"I don't know," I admitted.

I motioned for McKale to join us just as Dad placed the finishing touch around my neck.

"This necklace has a video camera in it," he said. It appeared to be an ornate, round Celtic knot.

"They had this in that small town?" I asked.

Dad chuckled. "No. I used my satellite phone and called in some expedited shipping."

Satellite phone? I shook my head. Apparently he had lots of secret tricks up his sleeves.

"How will we get into Faerie?" I asked the group. "It's not like the Summer King won't notice when the portal's opened."

"We get his permission," Dad said. "Come on. We can't stand here any longer. We're drawing attention. Just follow my lead."

McKale and I linked fingers and followed.

TWENTY-ONE

APPROACHING THE SUMMER KING with our request was terrifying, and I wasn't even the one expected to do the talking. If he refused to help, or if his anger was roused, it could be disastrous.

The King's eyes swirled with power as we drew near. Waves of heat branched out from him, and the once-deadened grass beneath his chair, trampled by years of dancing and foot-traffic, was now vibrant and green with life. He was a force of nature confined to a body.

Dad stopped several feet away with our group flanking him. He dipped his head in a gesture of respect and the Summer King raised his brows with interest. Brogan joined our group.

"King of Summer," Dad began. "Please forgive us for being so bold, but we were discussing how distraught we are that Princess Khalistah will not be joining us."

The King's head tilted to the side with further interest, and Dad continued.

"McKale, especially, was hoping to see her one last time."

One of the Fae females sniggered and shared an amused glance with the other Fae girl, and it burned my blood.

"Is that so?" The King turned his attention to McKale, whose stance shifted.

"Aye, King, sir." McKale cleared his throat. "I wanted to properly thank the Princess for her years of service to the clan as Shoe Mistress. And… she left behind a trinket I wished to return."

McKale pulled the shining chain with the golden talisman from his pocket and several of the Fae gasped. The Summer King's eyes flashed through several dark colors and the grass beneath our feet began to whither. As his mood settled, his eyes remained a vivid gold to match the trinket, and the grass sprang to full life again.

"I find it hard to believe the Princess would be so careless with her favorite charm," the King murmured.

I watched McKale swallow at the same time the nerves in my body frayed.

"Aye, King, sir. 'Twas quite the chaotic moment."

The Summer King surveyed McKale for a moment before saying, "The Princess is occupied at the Summer Gala. My people will return the trinket and carry forth your message to her."

The bronzed Fae male stepped forward to McKale and placed his hand out. McKale's fingers clamped around the chain and he looked from the male to the King. *No, no, no! This has to work!* I gave McKale a nervous glance, and I could see the gears turning in his mind just before he spoke.

"Er… Summer King… might Robyn and I enter Faerie and return the item ourselves?"

Every set of Fae eyes widened and snapped to him. A

stillness fell, as if the air molecules had stopped moving around us. The King's face was a mix of shock and humor.

"I understand humans are not meant to enter the sacred Faerie realm," McKale forged on. "And we would be ever so respectful, sir." He looked up at the sun. "We have several hours before the binding will take place. We would seek the Princess and return immediately. 'Tis very important to me."

The King gazed at McKale like he was dealing with a precious, albeit naïve, toddler whom he couldn't quite understand. When the King let out a chuckle, neighboring flowers brightened and butterflies burst forth from their cocoons. Dancing Leprechaun and their women paused in awe to watch the newborn flutters all around them.

"Lucky for you, McKale of the Leprechaun, I am feeling exceptionally giving this day. Consider this a binding gift. You may enter my realm so long as you return at once at the conclusion of speaking with my daughter. I will even have one of my guards guide you. One bit of warning, however…" His freaky shimmery eyes moved back and forth between McKale and I. "When humans enter, they seldom wish to leave. Are your minds strong enough to resist? It is quite a risk given your importance to this clan."

I held back a derisive sound. We were not in danger of the realm's lure, but I'd never have the nerve to say that to its proud ruler.

McKale let out a rush of breath and nodded his understanding. "Aye, King, sir. We can only imagine how difficult it will be to leave yer magnificent realm once we've set eyes on it. 'Tis why Robyn agreed to accompany me."

The King waved a hand at the male with a sheen of bronze hair and skin, who then stepped toward McKale and I.

"Take them. Do not linger."

My stomach dropped and Mom gave a tiny whimper. This was really happening.

"Follow me," the bronzed Fae said.

I know my family wanted to embrace me and say things, but caution prevented them. With a final squeeze of my hand from Cassidy, and shared glances of fear with my parents, we were off.

Stepping into the slice of sky to enter Faerie was like deliberately walking into my own worst nightmare. It was the hardest thing I'd ever done. McKale went first behind our guide, keeping his fingers linked with mine. The force between realms felt as if we were pushing against a strong wind, though there was no movement of air.

When we were finally through I found myself breathing hard with a pounding heart. It was dark, but I could make out the portal guard in his glinting armored uniform, who'd stepped aside to let the three of us in.

"Summer King's orders," our guide said to the guard. "They're to see the Princess." The two Fae shared disbelieved shakes of their heads.

I felt McKale's grip tighten around my hand and it gave me strength. I took a deep breath and let it out slowly. We were in, and so far I didn't feel any different.

"Let us be on our way," said our guide. Now that we weren't in the King's presence, the Fae male allowed annoyance to creep into his voice about the task of babysitting humans.

We followed him down the darkened corridor which was squishy underfoot and smelled of wet earth. When we came to the opening, our surroundings brightened and our feet halted. I'd assumed we were below ground, but I could see now that we weren't. We were in a labyrinth of sorts—a series of intricate tunnels. The walls were formed by twining growths of plant-life, greens and browns, like aboveground roots that had looped and braided. And through spaces between the twists of vines I caught glimpses of a clear, pink sky.

McKale pulled my hand to keep up with the bronze guide. The Fae wasn't waiting for us, and if we got lost in here we'd never find our way out. McKale's other hand reached around his back as we walked and slipped to his waistband, pressing the button to activate his video equipment. I followed his lead, reaching up to rub the spot on my necklace that would turn it on. Now we just had to hope and pray that nothing in the strange land of Faerie would keep the electronics from recording. Dad assured us that his watches and other electronics had not stopped working or been broken when he'd entered in the past to deliver reports.

We wove our way through tunnel after tunnel, some tight and confining, and some wide open. Voices and magical music filtered down halls as we passed, and my steps grew lighter at the joyous sounds. Pleasant, foreign scents swirled past, as fragrant as spun sugar and budding blossoms. It hit me with a jolt that Faerie was messing with my mood in a good way, which was frightening in its own right. The air held the magical feel of a theme park, encompassed by promises of fun and adventure. It prodded me to let go and enjoy. After weeks of heavy, burdensome worries, the lightness was welcome.

Without my permission, a smile stretched out on my face as our tunnel widened and we came upon an opening filled with laughing voices and music more wondrous than any I'd ever heard. It sounded like songbirds and chimes and instruments that rang out in a way that caressed the wind. The sky burst with luminescent color above us—pastels shifting like clouds.

Our guide stopped to speak with a guard at the tunnel's exit. I sidled closer to McKale, wishing we could dance. I wanted to spin and leap. McKale let go of my hand to shake out his limbs. He rubbed his ears before glancing at me.

"Robyn?" he whispered. "Is it affecting ya? Get a hold of yerself, love."

What was he talking about? I was fine. I gazed at his multifaceted hair, autumn colors enhanced by the Faerie sky. How could I not appreciate the beauty of it all? No harm could come from enjoying the sensory of this enchanting land. Standing there in my gown, I was more feminine and alive than ever. I knew if my feet began to dance, each movement would be filled with unfamiliar grace. I wanted the bronzed Fae to hurry his chat with the other guard so we could see the Gala up close.

After our guide had finished debriefing the tunnel guard about our situation, the guard took an interest in me. His gaze held me in place, intense. Silky black hair spilled around his amour, and I couldn't look away from his silvery eyes.

He held out a perfectly masculine hand to me, palm up. "This is a pretty one. So much taller than our Fair females. I think I might enjoy curves such as these. Greatly…"

Without thinking I reached out to take his hand, not wanting to seem rude. The last thing I heard was McKale hissing my name in warning.

Touching the Fae's hand was like submersing my palm in hot peppermint water—it gave me warm tingles that shot from my hand up my arm and cartwheeled to the core of me. My entire body tightened and pulsed with a sensual charge. I was filled with need and want and—

My hand was torn from his and I was shocked by the volume of my own gasp for air. I closed my eyes against the image of the grinning Fae guard, far too gorgeous to deny if he reached for me again.

I fought to catch my breath and shake away the unhealthy desire. Was that what McKale felt each time he and Khalistah touched? It's a wonder he hadn't run off to Faerie long before I arrived. That was... wow. I shivered in horror at my own weakness.

"With all due respect," I heard McKale say. "The Summer King expects us back soon, so we cannot dally."

The guard's only response was a low chortle.

McKale grasped my hand in his when our guide began to move around the outskirts of the Gala.

"I'm sorry," I whispered, shaken.

He squeezed my hand.

Though the moment of lust had passed, I couldn't seem to rid myself of the light happiness coursing under my skin.

The Gala arched in a wide circle, surrounded by tunnels of flowering vines, which all led to this spot. Breathtaking Faeries twirled in every direction to the delightful music. Each female was petite and graceful, but I appreciated their beauty so much I couldn't bring myself to be jealous. I was only glad to be near them. Every curious glance in our direction brought a surge of appreciation.

I wanted to stop and watch, but McKale's incessant pulling kept my feet moving. His grip became so hard that I almost cried out. He never stopped walking, but I followed his stare toward a group of Fae sitting in a lush garden. Fae of both genders were lounging on plush cushions with young men and women, humans, surrounding them: lying at their feet while staring up with adoring eyes, dancing for their masters, feeding the Fae with their fingers.

While all of the Faeries seemed to take a mild interest in McKale and I passing through, the humans never once looked our direction. Their eyes were only for the Fae. The dancing girl, no older than Cassidy, turned our way, but her gaze passed right through us, her expression full of physical bliss, but empty of life.

A revolting tremor shook my whole body and McKale glanced back at me, worried.

Oh, my gosh, was my first coherent thought. *That could be McKale or Cass. Or me if I don't get myself under control!*

"I'm okay," I whispered to McKale, though I wasn't sure. I struggled to push through the fog in my mind.

McKale gave me a tight nod and turned forward again, pulling us faster to catch up. He kept rubbing his ears with his free hand, I realized he was attempting to muss the affects of the music. I dropped my eyes and refused to look at the Gala revelers. I hummed *Twinkle, Twinkle, Little Star* to clear my head of the magical sounds. I'd thought I was too strong and level-headed to be led astray by the land of Faerie. I'd been wrong, and that terrified me. I wanted to call off the whole thing and turn back before I lost my wits again. My breathing quickened.

You can do this, Robyn, I told myself.

I'd been allowing McKale to lead me with my eyes closed, but I opened them when I felt his body go rigid and his step faltered. He righted himself and kept going, tugging me along, but when I dared a peek out at the Faerie I understood. There, in the middle of the revelry, was a hill lined with strange trees. Their trunks were bent in different directions, branches with willowy green leaves swooping the ground as if caught in dancer poses. Through the trunks and branches on the hill was Khalistah, dancing alongside other Fae who held the same regal airs. I felt no appreciation of her beauty like I had the others. All I felt when I saw her was a renewed urgency to ruin her efforts.

The bronze male led us around a mound of earthen steps to the upper courtyard lined with the dancing trees. I dropped McKale's hand, not wanting to spark the FFG's fuse any worse than necessary. The entire group of about a dozen Fae stopped as we entered. They stared, unabashed. One, in particular, wore a look of pure shock and malice.

I'd never seen the FFG divulge as much emotion as she did in the brief moment after she noticed us. Her icy eyes flashed from light blue to bright white and my stomach dropped with fear. In an instant her features were soft and languid again. She joined the others as they gathered nearer.

"Has the Summer King sent a couple of Gala gifts?" asked a Fae girl with hair as black and wavy as ink in water. The way it flowed around her reminded me of a mermaid.

"I daresay not, Melindalah," Khalistah answered. "This is McKale of the Leprechaun and his… *betrothed.*" Her eyes raked me from bottom to top. At the sight of my binding gown, she covered her lips with two fingertips and a giggle slipped out. "How quaint."

My face heated and I dropped my eyes to disguise my anger.

Another girl who looked to be Melindalah's mermaid-esque twin stood on the FFG's other side. "Is this the one who fancies you to pieces, Princess?"

"The very same, Mirandalah." Khalistah eyed McKale with a sort of lazy ownership before snapping out of it and linking her fingers in front of herself. "I cannot imagine what brings you into our realm, McKale of the Leprechaun, but I must warn you to be on your best behavior while here. Humans have a tendency to lose memories when they speak unpleasantries among our kind."

Her warning was clear. We were not to humiliate her in front of her peers, or else.

"Aye, Princess. That I understand. I've only come to thank ye for yer time as the clan's Shoe Mistress. Ye'll be missed, ye will."

"Especially by *you*," cut in one of the mermaid girls.

McKale cleared his throat. "Aye. And... I've come to return something ye left behind when last ye visited."

He withdrew the golden chain and talisman from his pocket and everyone looked at the Princess, aghast that she'd be so careless. She stared at it, very still, but did not reach for it. In her stance it was clear that she knew, for sure, we were up to something now. For the Leprechauns, a returned gift was like a broken promise. A break-up.

With an uncharacteristic stiff movement she stuck out her hand and took the chain. There was a stillness to her body that made the others stare, wondering what was really going on here.

"You left your heartsong trinket with a human?" one of the girls asked, aghast.

"Do not be ridiculous, Melindalah!" The FFG laughed. "I was called back into our realm and…" Her throat seemed to close up and she gave a dainty cough. "A simple misunderstanding, is all."

She couldn't tell a lie! It was one of the many facts we'd learned about Fae from Dad over the years.

"Well, do be careful with it from now on," the other girl teased. "You may want to take the Prince up on his offer to bind for a time someday."

The girls glanced toward the bronze Fae male and smiled. Our guide was a Prince? He cast a warm glance at the Princess, whose eyes stared out at the distance. For that brief second I experienced a pang of pity for her. She'd given McKale a token that was apparently supposed to be given to someone she wanted to bind with, for a time. Fae didn't do anything "forever" except keep living. Temporary bindings were as close as they came to love and commitment. But I didn't feel sorry for her for long.

Khalistah's eyes suddenly widened. "Where is my Paulie?" Her head swiveled to scan the sky.

"Pardon?" McKale asked.

"Her Pixie," one of the M-girls clarified.

McKale and I shot a glance at each other.

"He's, erm, still in Chaun land, Princess," McKale answered. "I'm certain he'll return soon."

In a dangerous whisper she asked, "What have you done to him?"

Her friends took a step away and looked at us like we were in big trouble.

"He's not been harmed, I promise ye. He was causing no end of ruckus last night and the boys... detained him."

Her hand flew to her chest. "Not with iron?"

McKale dropped his gaze and shoved his hands in his pockets. In a swift move the Princess glided forward and slapped him across the cheek with a startling *whack*. He let out a muffled sound and stared at her, stunned. My hands balled into fists at my sides and I rocked forward before reminding myself not to move. She would use any excuse right now to finish us. She stood close to McKale with her chin lifted to his face. His eyes met hers.

"Let it be known, McKale of the Leprechaun: I do not take kindly to others touching something that belongs to me. You will take me to Paulie. *At once.*"

This was about way more than her stupid pixie. We'd flustered her. But it was good that she wanted to return to Chaun land. Now we just needed to somehow get her to reveal her plan again.

"Will you be joining us on the return journey, Princess?" asked the bronzed Prince.

"I will." She smoothed down the front of her dress and stood tall.

The Fae Prince held out a bent elbow to her but she ignored him, gliding past and leaving her court without a backward glance. The Prince glared after her, ego bruised, and then pointed to the steps.

"Go," he commanded us.

We followed the FFG with the Prince close behind.

I kept my eyes down and was careful not to touch

anything as we skirted the Gala festivities and made our way back to the initial tunnel. I made the mistake of looking up at the guard as we were passing through and he raised a perfectly sculpted eyebrow at me, silver eyes caressing my curves. My heart fluttered and I rushed to stay close to McKale. The Fae Prince was on my heels.

For a tiny being, the FFG moved fast. Even in her graceful gliding, the set of her shoulders gave the image of a female on a mission. As she moved along, buds from the tunnel's branches and vines turned to her and opened, then closed again and returned to their positions when she'd passed.

"Princess Khalistah?" McKale called out.

She didn't answer. My heart couldn't race any faster as I realized McKale was going in for the kill right now.

"Princess, might I speak with ye a moment?"

Without turning her head she said, "I cannot imagine what thing of importance you think is worthy of my hearing."

The Prince gave a snort behind me and muttered, "Your father gives the Leprechauns too much grace, Princess. He coddles them into believing they are equals."

McKale picked up his pace to walk at Khalistah's side, and I hung back. The Prince let out a huff of air like he couldn't believe McKale's tenacity.

"I wish to speak with ye about the terms ye set forth when last we met," McKale whispered.

A loud group of Fae turned down our path and Khalistah shrieked, "Move!" Her eyes flashed with a swirl of icy white and the Fae scattered out of her way. They bowed as she passed.

"I have not the slightest clue of what you are speaking,"

the FFG said to McKale once we'd left that tunnel and entered a smaller one.

The narrow path was confining, and I wanted McKale to stop pestering the FFG for information. I knew he felt pressure to get her confession soon, but I wished he would wait until we were on Chaun land again. We weren't safe here.

"What is that human blathering on about?" the Prince grumbled. Then he raised his voice and called out to McKale, "Leave the Princess alone."

The FFG answered without stopping or glancing back. "He has been like this since childhood. I am accustomed to his need for attention. Do not worry yourself, *kind Prince*."

The way she said "kind Prince" sounded as if she were just as annoyed with the Fae as she was with McKale. But McKale was undeterred. I chewed my bottom lip and practically jogged to keep up.

"I thought since a few days had passed… perhaps ye'd had time to think on it and change yer mind?" When she didn't respond he said, "Do ye still require me to come to ye after the binding—"

She halted in her tracks and the walls seemed to contract inward on us. The FFG pivoted to face McKale, eyes flashing white once again.

"You will come to me of your own free will." Her voice was level.

"What is the meaning of this?" the Prince asked.

Without looking away from McKale, the Princess held up her pointer finger at the Fae male and said, "Silence."

His perfect brow creased with confusion as he watched her address McKale with maddening calmness. She moved close, her chin jutting up to point those scary eyes at his face.

Each word she spoke was laced with a venomous punch of enunciation. McKale looked ready, hopeful.

"Nothing changed, McKale of the Leprechaun, until you dared to enter my realm with *her*. You are the one who has broken our agreement. Now I am forced to break mine. I *will* have you. And your precious betrothed *will* be punished. My Fair Folk will have her sister as a Gala gift this very night!"

Air caught in my lungs and I sucked in a choking breath. McKale, however, wore an expression of relief. The FFG had revealed herself, just as we'd wanted. But what if the video equipment didn't work? Or what if it did and the King didn't care? I would lose both of them. I reached out to steady myself against the wall, but the thick vine under my hand was wet and it squirmed at my touch. I yanked my hand away.

The Prince sputtered behind me and came forward. "Explain yourself, Princess."

She turned her frosty eyes to him and smiled. "How would you like a human girl all to yourself?"

"I..." He considered this. "Humans are a lot of work, and then they die. I have never seen the value in keeping pets. My only interest has been you; however, now I am not so certain. It seems you have been keeping unsavory secrets." He eyed McKale with disdain.

"I have wanted to do this for a long time," she whispered.

The Prince cocked his pretty, bronzed head to the side. "Do what?"

"Alter your memory."

His face paled at the sly grin on the FFG's face, and he took a step back.

"You cannot do such a thing without the King's

permission. He would never allow it."

"He will never know."

She stepped toward him and he stepped back. McKale and I moved to stand together. I was sickened by the entire spectacle taking place. I grabbed McKale's hand.

The Prince put up his hands and shook his head, a frightful expression contorting his immaculate face.

"*Ar oscailt intinn,*" Khalistah whispered to the Prince. *Open your mind.*

He dropped his hands and relaxed, captured by her eyes. She whispered everything that he would forget, and what he would remember in its place. His feelings for her had changed and would now only be those of friendly admiration. We'd never stopped in this tunnel to carry on a conversation. Once on Chaun land he would take a fancy to Cassidy Mason and request that he be allowed to have her.

I let go of McKale's hand and wrapped my arms around myself, chilled to my heart.

When the FFG said the closing words she spun and continued down the hall as if we'd never stopped. I was trembling uncontrollably. I glanced back at the Prince who was blinking, his face scrunched with mild confusion. The four of us followed down the twists and turns of living tunnel-work until we reached our portal with the brutish guard standing vigilant. He bowed low for Khalistah.

"A pleasure to see you, Princess."

"Open the portal," she commanded.

He obeyed.

TWENTY-TWO

WE PUSHED THROUGH THE thickened atmosphere between realms into the warmth of Chaun land. The light blue sky and sunshine seemed pale in comparison to Faerie's atmosphere. The green plants appeared duller and the scents too faint. I experienced a fleeting moment of longing for the beauty we'd left behind. Next to me, McKale shook out his arms and cracked his neck. Khalistah moved through the tall grass toward the clearing and the Prince gave McKale and I small shoves from behind.

A heightened sense of anticipation rose up from the crowd as we approached. The musicians didn't dare to stop playing, even as the dancers stilled, all heads pointed in our direction. Brogan and my parents stood beside the Fae King and his people. Cassidy jumped up from a nearby table and bypassed Khalistah to run toward me. I gave my head a frantic shake, but she didn't notice. She flung her arms around me just as I heard the Fae Prince whisper behind us, "Glory be. Is this Cassidy Mason?"

Surprised, Cass pulled away from me and looked at him. I tried to catch her eye. I wanted her to run like hell, but she was riveted by this bronzed article of perfection who knew her name, giving her a stare worthy of a Princess.

I tilted my head away from him and hissed at her between my teeth, "Get out of here!"

She spared a short, confused glance at me before taking a step back. Her movement was stopped when she met the Prince's golden eyes again. There was no passion in his glazed expression, only a robotic sort of fascination. He held out a beckoning hand to Cass.

I grasped her elbow.

"Pardon us a moment, er, Prince," I said.

"*Prince?*" Cassidy murmured as I pulled her a few feet away.

"He's been brainwashed by the FFG to take you back to Faerie!" I whispered.

I'd never been more relieved than I was in that moment when Cass's curiosity turned to mortal fear. Her tanned face paled and her forehead gleaned with sweat as she stared at me in disbelief. I'd been hoping she would run somewhere and hide, but instead she spun away from us in her summer dress and sprinted to my parents.

I cleared my throat and whispered to the Prince, "She's really high-maintenance for a human." I left him standing there, dazed.

Khalistah and McKale were just making their way to the King's presence where the Princess curtsied low and McKale gave a respectful bow of his head. I lifted the hem of my gown and rushed forward to be at McKale's side.

Mom and Dad formed steely towers around a cowering Cass who'd linked her arm inside Dad's. The three of them watched me for some sign that everything had gone as planned. I gave a small nod, and my parents' faces smoothed as they shed their tension.

I was not relieved in the slightest. I clutched the chain around my neck and closed my eyes.

Please work.

"Father, King." Khalistah's musical voice rang out.

"I see you decided to join us after all," he said. His fingers were linked in front of himself, at ease.

The FFG held her head high. "I have not come to join the festivities, Father. The Leprechaun are holding my pixie captive. I have come to retrieve Paulie from his iron prison."

Nobody in the entire clearing breathed as we waited for the King's response. He stared at her for a long while before tipping his head toward Brogan with a frown.

The leader of the Chaun bowed low, his beard sweeping the ground. "My apologies, King of the Summer. We intended to release him to ye this day. I assure ye no iron is touching the creature. His cage is lined with a pelt. 'Twas the oddest thing, it was. Last evenin' the pixie attacked our dear Robyn and we had to put a stop to it. We meant no harm to the Princess's pet."

In a slow movement the King nodded his head then chuckled. Khalistah's eyes grew wide. Near the forest and all around the field, brown and gray bunnies came out of hiding and hopped around like a fairy tale.

"Ah, dearest daughter. That pixie of yours has ever been a pesky thing. I cannot condone the torture of a Fae creature; however, you must keep a better watch over your pet."

Her tiny lips pursed. Brogan cleared his throat and waved a hand at Keefe.

"Release the pixie," Brogan told him then addressed the King. "He has not been harmed or tortured, King of the

Summer. I swear it."

"Fine, fine." The King waved off Brogan's assurances as if bored. "I have wished to cage the scoundrel myself more than a few times."

He chuckled again, and all the Fae except Khalistah joined his merriment. Colorful songbirds swooped through the sky overhead.

Seconds later Pauli flew in a slow, depressing buzz, landing on the FFG's shoulder and nuzzling her neck. He lifted his face long enough to send me a vicious show of teeth.

"There, there," she said to it with no warmth in her voice.

With the pixie returned and the King seeming unfazed, Brogan motioned for his people to continue their dancing and get back to celebrating.

Khalistah stared at me so long it was beyond creepy. I could all but hear the crank in her mind deciding what to do next. Her attention finally turned to the Prince, who was pondering Cassidy from afar as if bewildered by his interest in such an ordinary creature. She clung to Dad's arm, practically hiding behind him. I wanted to scream at her to run as fast and far as she could.

"See something you like, Prince?" Khalistah asked him.

His eyes slid from the Princess, back to Cassidy. The FFG's lips turned up in a vile expression of happiness.

"I believe I do," he answered. "The sister…"

The King and other Fae noted the Prince's interest and I swallowed hard. McKale cleared his throat next to me as the Prince began to make his way slowly to Cassidy. She moved further behind Dad and his jaw set in a frown at the bronzed

Fae. Khalistah gave a wickedly happy laugh.

Just as the Prince neared, causing Dad to walk backward, an angry voice hollered from a distance like a war cry. All heads turned toward the trees where the Clour showed themselves, looking fierce. Rock was sprinting toward us, iron dagger in hand, yelling, "Ye can't have her!"

McKale and I met each other's eyes with mutual shocked expressions.

Before Rock could make it the last ten feet to us his feet were suddenly halted and his upper body jolted forward. I watched in horror as grass shot up from the ground, long and wide, winding around his legs and up his torso. He struggled in anguish against it.

"No!" Cass yelled.

Dad held her back. Grass twined, squeezing his arms to his side, and then wound around his face to cover his mouth. His head thrashed, curls everywhere.

"Drop the weapon." The cool voice came from the Summer King, causing an uproar of delighted bird chatter that contrasted the dismay of everyone in the field.

Rock's eyes blazed at the Prince and he fought for short breaths through his nose. He had enough good sense to drop the dagger at his side. The other Clourichaun retreated a step back toward the tree line, as if frightened that their approach might make things worse for Rock. Their poor faces were filled with fear.

"The Clourichaun?" Summer King murmured. "How many of their kind remain?"

McKale cleared his throat and said, "Twelve, sir."

"Only twelve..." He seemed to ponder this with something regret for what could have been, but it only lasted a moment before being replaced by disdain. "A pity."

Martineth piped up next to him. "They deserve every moment of punishment they have received. Worthless pups. This one should die for coming near us with a weapon."

The King lifted a hand toward Rock and the blade of grass peeled back from his mouth. "What is the meaning of this outburst, Clour boy?"

Rock attempted to suck air into his lungs, panting. "I meant no disrespect to ye, King o' the Summer. But I cannot sit back an' watch Cassidy Mason taken from her family."

The King looked genuinely baffled. Khalistah glided to her father's side with a sweet smile. "Do not listen to this fool, father. Unlike this Clourichaun, the Prince has been your good and loyal servant. If he seeks a simple gift I am certain you would agree that he has earned it."

The King's attention went to the Prince as it all came together. "Is it a human you fancy? I find that rather surprising, given your efforts the past few centuries for my daughter's affections."

Several of the Fae sniggered.

"I…" The Prince was still puzzled. His head swiveled toward Cassidy. "Such an urge is quite strange and unfamiliar to me, but I believe I would like to have this human."

"Ne'er!" shouted Rock. "Take me instead! I will go!"

"Oh, my God." Cassidy covered her mouth.

The Prince's face contorted. "I do not want *you*!"

"Ye can't take her! Ye—" The blade of grass slapped back over Rock's mouth before he could finish and the King sighed at the trivial issue.

The FFG clapped her hands, elated. "What fun!"

"She is of magical blood," the Summer King pointed

out. "We do not have a wealth of magical humans to spare."

"Oh, go on, Father. Do let the Prince have her!"

Martineth ran a slender finger up the King's neck. "He has been such a good boy. And never asked for a thing."

No! No, no, no, this could not be happening.

Rock thrashed against his bindings. I stepped closer to McKale until our arms were up against each other. I thought I might pass out from anxiety.

Brogan shifted uncomfortably and looked at the sky, which had darkened a bit as the sun dipped behind the trees.

"Er, Father," McKale noticed it too. "Should we perhaps begin the pre-binding entertainment for our esteemed guests?"

"Fabulous idea, son!" He looked at the Summer King. "Aye, King o' the Summer, we have prepared a video for ye to view using a sort of 'human magic.' Completely harmless, of course."

"Entertainment!" said the King. "How lovely. It will give me time to think."

Khalistah did not look pleased, but she didn't complain. She shot me a glare that told me it wasn't over, though.

Brogan beamed. "'Twill only take a few minutes to prepare. Excuse us, please." He motioned to his people. "Music!"

Brogan backed away from the group as a new round of music rose up. Cassidy never let go of Dad's arm, and Mom took her other hand, sending a hostile glance at the Prince. He was too busy staring at Cass to notice. My parents came up behind McKale and me. Mom's hands were cold and shaking when she removed my necklace. Dad unhooked McKale's wires and pulled them from the backside of his shirt. The Fae, clueless about the nature of our doings, continued their conversations and watching the festivities. Rock remained in his confined place nearby while the other Clour kept to the trees, their demeanors void of any playfulness.

McKale and I turned our heads toward the technology table, watching Dad connect wires with Mom and Cass at his side. A maelstrom of emotion swirled inside me. I reached for McKale's hand and we both held tight.

This was it.

Blue light suddenly flickered to life on the giant screen. Leprechauns gasped and clapped at the sight. Fae conversation halted as they turned toward the screen. The music stopped and the clearing was momentarily silent. My stomach tightened into a ball, pinging around inside me like an arcade game.

Please let this work!

"What a grand contraption," the King murmured. "Quite peculiar."

Brogan addressed the King. "We've recently found ourselves in a fearful bind. Please accept my apologies ahead of time for any offense occurred from this show, King of Summer. That is not our intention. Ye have ever been gracious to our kind, and I can only hope ye'll understand when ye see it fer yerself."

Once again, the King looked utterly confused. Brogan turned abruptly and strode away.

I held on to McKale's hand for dear life. His eyes found mine and we shared a mingling of hope and love that clashed with fear and worry.

A loud, muffled sound burst from the speakers and

everyone in the clearing jumped then laughed at themselves. Dad adjusted the volume as darkened images appeared on the screen—the back of the bronzed Prince as we followed him down the dim tunnel.

Yes!

I let go of McKale's hand to hug his arm. His video and audio worked! He grinned at the screen. All around us Fae and Leprechaun speculated over what they were seeing.

"…appears to be the Prince," a Fae girl said.

"Why, it's Faerie!" another exclaimed. "However is this possible?"

"What is this?" asked the FFG, her voice thick with suspicion.

The King raised a hand to shush his entourage, his rapt attention on the screen.

Dad gave me a discreet thumbs-up and I beamed at him. But it wasn't over yet. Not by far. We'd made our way over a giant hurdle, but more were in our path. Our fate rested on the King and his daughter's reactions to the video.

The Leprechaun were silent as images of human pets filled the screen. The Fae were fascinated; all except the FFG, who wore a mask of dread as realization began to dawn. If we'd somehow captured all of this, then that meant we'd captured the events to come as well. Her head swiveled to McKale and me, eyes flashing an arctic white. The patch of grass beneath her feet shriveled in a miniature version of the effect her Father had. I clutched McKale's arm harder.

When it got to the part where we followed Khalistah away from her court, she cried out.

"Make them stop this nonsense at once, Father! This is unseemly. They wish to make a fool of me!"

He gave her a withered expression as if she were a child interrupting his nightly program.

"They have managed to capture things exactly how they are, dearest Princess. Do you find the truth so unseemly?"

"I question their intentions, Father. Make it stop!" she demanded. She moved to stand in front of him with her hands on her hips.

The King sat up straighter and the sun was covered over by a momentary storm cloud. "I will not. Stand down and mind yourself."

The Princess appeared taken aback, as if not used to being scolded. But the King's word was final and she shot me one last hate-filled glance.

"It is not utterly—" Khalistah mumbled, but her words, her attempted lies, died on her lips. "They have somehow—"

Her father ignored her.

It didn't take long until we came to the part of the video where Khalistah lost her temper, revealing her ultimate plan and then altering the Prince's memory. She lifted her head and squared her petite shoulders, even as those around her sucked in breaths of admonishment and a few Fae laughed at her desire to have McKale. But their reactions did not matter. It was the King I watched. His face had gone hard and his back was rigid. By the end of the video the entire field of grass crackled dry beneath us. The tall grasses of the field tipped back, lying dead as if blown by a lethal wind.

Dad turned off the video and every eye settled on the Summer King.

"Father," the FFG began. "It is not…" Again her tongue seemed to swell at the attempted lie and she brought a creamy hand to her throat.

The King stood with grace and his light blue robes swirled around him as if tiny tornadoes flanked his body.

He looked directly at McKale and I. "Have you somehow altered reality and replicated Faerie and its occupants?"

"Nay, King o' the Summer." McKale stepped forward. "The human device records things exactly as they happen. What ye saw was real and true. I swear it."

His head slowly swiveled to his daughter in disbelief. She shrank back.

"There is more, Father. This—" she waved her hand at the screen, "—*contraption*, does not reveal all. What I did was necessary. I can explain."

"You are born of me, Princess Khalistah, however you are as bound to my laws as all others."

"But of course, King Father."

"You would interfere with my plans to continue my race of cobblers?"

"I had a plan which would ensure—"

"Silence!" The ground and trees shuddered at the King's booming voice.

The FFG pressed her lips together.

"You would use forbidden magic against a brother Fae?"

We all looked at the Prince for the first time and found his disdainful stare pointed at the Princess.

"I admit it was wrong," Khalistah said to her father. "I was overcome by a rare fit of temper when I discovered the two humans were attempting to trick me and harm my reputation. We had an agreement."

"An agreement that you would take a *human* consort?" her father bellowed.

A Fae girl made a gagging sound and the FFG's cheekbones filled with a rosy blush.

"He has ever wanted to please me," Khalistah explained. "He would be my pet, just as other Fae have."

"That is not how it appears. This is a disgraceful moment, daughter of mine."

She stepped toward him, pleading with her eyes and words. "Please, Father. Erase the memories of these witnesses so they will not know my shame. I had a weakness for the boy. Even *you* cannot help but feel affection toward the wee folk!"

The Prince let a sound of disgust escape and the Fae took steps back. Their faces were filled with fear at the prospect of having their memories taken, and aversion to the idea of affection toward humans.

"I am displeased, Daughter. You have left me no choice but to do that which I abhor."

Khalistah shook her head and held out her palms. "Not me, King Father!"

"*You, especially.*" His voice sent a heated gust through the clearing and we all covered our eyes against it.

Martineth looked rattled for the first time all night. "My love. Do as you must to them. But not I."

Just as she reached out for him, the King lifted his arms, encompassing each of the Fae before him. They all stiffened as if locked in place. The Summer King's eyes flipped through colors, and sparks of static light flashed from his outstretched fingertips like a summer storm. Warm winds whipped around us. McKale and I stepped away, terrified. The Fae beseeched their King with their eyes, but their mouths could not move.

The King roared, "*Ar oscailt intinn!*" and sudden silence fell.

The wind settled and we watched as the Summer King wove his magic over the Fae, carefully saying the exact words to erase the video from their minds. He then paid special attention to Khalistah.

"You will forget you ever longed for the Leprechaun son of Brogan. Instead, you will now find yourself feeling affections for the Prince."

I wanted to fall to the ground and weep.

The King's attention shifted toward Rock. He turned his hands and the grasses unwound, retreated back into the earth. He beckoned Rock, who came forward with stiff movements.

I saw Cassidy try to rush to him, but Mom and Dad both grabbed her.

"Do you fancy yourself in love with the young Mason girl?"

Rock turned his head to her, and watching her face with a pained, heartbroken expression, he nodded.

The Summer King clenched his jaw. We were all so still. The relief I felt moments before had slipped away as tension filled my body again.

"I cannot have your kind interfering with those who would actually work. You will forget you ever loved her. You will forget any time you had with her. Your kind are not welcome at this ceremony."

Rock's eyes went blank and his body slackened. Mom pulled Cassidy's face to her chest and she let out a horrible, muffled screech. I felt like I might be sick.

The Summer King ignored all this, done with the drama. He flicked his wrists and the spell ended with a *zap*. The Fae rocked back on their heels, stunned. Rock turned and ambled back toward the trees, glancing back once to stare at the scene with puzzled wonder. And then he was gone, along with the other Clour. Cass buried her face into the crook of Mom's neck. It took all of my will-power not to run to her and embrace her.

The King painted a smile across his face for his people. "Ah, well, it seems as though the so-called human magic has failed. Our only entertainment shall be this merry dancing and the binding itself."

The Fae shared disappointed nods, all seeming as if they'd missed something but were too afraid to ask. Khalistah gazed around at the decorations with bemused interest. For one fearsome moment her eyes landed on McKale and I, but slid past without remark. I exhaled and felt McKale relax next to me.

Brogan bustled forward.

"Would our honored guests care to dance, then?" he asked.

"Go on," the King said, waving a finger at his people. "Enjoy the hospitality."

The Prince stepped forward and extended a hand to Khalistah. She curtsied and took his hand. Martineth still stood there, seeming stunned and distrustful, until the King reached for her hand and kissed it, causing her to relax.

"Will you not dance, my love?" he asked. "You know how much I enjoy watching."

She gave him a seductive smile, and without a word turned to the dance circle.

As the Fae filtered out to dance among the Leprechaun, the King gave his attention to McKale and me. His frown and shifting eyes caused my heart to falter in its rhythm. I felt the warmth of my family as they joined behind us. I reached back and found Cassidy's hand, pulling her close behind me. I felt her face lean against the back of my shoulder. There was nothing I could do to help or comfort her. Rock's memories of her love might be gone, but the fact that her memories of him would remain was heartbreaking.

The King eyed our group and I focused on him now. Would he punish us?

His voice was pinched and frightening. "You have brought shame to my daughter and forced my hand."

"King of Summer," McKale began. His head was bowed. "We ne'er wished to bring shame to the Princess or yer people. We were powerless against her demands and didn't know what else to do."

The King pondered this. "Khalistah is quite keen on getting what she wants. How unfortunate that her desires led her astray. I would not have believed it if I had not seen it with my own eyes. But know this…" His eyes flipped through a rainbow of colors. "I allow you to keep memory of this day only because you were wronged. Let us hope you will never find yourselves in a position where you feel you must fool our kind again."

McKale dipped his head. "Thank you, King. I am so very sorry fer all that's happened. Truly."

"Humans are often careless of their affections," the King responded. "Such is the nature of beings whose lifespan are so short… and speaking of that, I have another matter with which to discuss." We stood still and quiet, waiting for him to continue. "While you were in Faerie my consort and I discussed a proper gift for your binding, considering how fond you seem to be of one another. I understand that you will live considerably longer than your binding partner—am I correct?"

"Er... yes, King, sir." McKale scratched his cheek.

McKale would live approximately seven hundred years longer than me.

"Instead of a gift, I have an offer." The Summer King surveyed Brogan, McKale, and all of us Masons. "If you and your people can assure me that you will keep this indiscretion between us from now until forever, I will increase the magical ability of the Masons, thereby allowing them to live as long as the Leprechauns. I do not make this offer lightly. If I find you have spread word of Princess Khalistah's shame outside of these clan lines the price you pay will be more than lost memories. Do you understand?"

We all nodded. Incurring his wrath was not something we wanted. I was certain the only reason we still had our memory was because his daughter had offended him more than we had.

"And does this offer appeal to you?" he asked.

I looked at my family. Dad and Mom shared grateful glances. Cassidy, still sad, gave me a single nod. I looked at McKale, whose eyes shone with hope.

"Definitely," I said.

"We would be honored to serve you all of our years," Dad told the Summer King. "Thank you for showing mercy. Today's events will never leave our lips. You have our word."

McKale and Brogan stepped away. The King lifted his arms as he'd done to his Fae minutes before. A moment of fear shot through me as I wondered if this was a trick—if he'd decided to erase our memories after all. But the words never came to open our minds. Instead he sang a stream of magical words that enveloped us. I felt power constricting every cell of my body, blooming from my core outward, strengthening every fiber of my existence. Next to me Cassidy made a sound of surprised bliss.

As the spell ended with another *zap*, I inhaled, revived.

"There," the King of Summer said. "Let us be finished with unpleasantries this day. I came to see a binding. Shall we have one?"

McKale came forward and took both my hands in his.

"Aye," he said. "We shall."

TWENTY-THREE

UNFORTUNATELY, THE TALES ABOUT Fae dancing all night were truth. They didn't leave until dawn, which meant I couldn't run off to console Cassidy when she left the party. As McKale and I finally headed to his, I mean *our* room, I peeked in at Cass but she was already asleep.

I'd awoken the next morning with a start in McKale's arms, sunlight seeping through the drapes of cloth. Trying not to wake him, I slipped my dress back on and quietly left the room. But when I got to my old hut Cassidy wasn't there. I ran around the nearly empty village. It had to be close to noon, but most of the Leprechauns were still sleeping after being danced to exhaustion the night before.

Panic began to rise as I burst back into my new room and found McKale sitting on the edge of the bed rubbing his eyes. He looked up at me blearily.

"I can't find Cass."

Without a word he dressed and we both ran. No need to discuss where. We headed to Clour land.

We were both breathing hard as we splashed through the shallow part of the stream, my dress getting soaked at the bottom despite my efforts to hold it up. Finally, at the edge of

Clour land we found her. She must have heard our loud approach, but she didn't turn to look at us. She leaned against a tree, one arm around it, watching as Rock, Blackie, and the blond twins gathered sticks and twigs at the other edge of the forest.

"I've been debating whether or not to say goodbye," Cassidy said to the air.

I came up to her side and put a hand on her shoulder. For once, she wasn't even crying. I wrapped my arms around her waist from behind and rested my chin on her shoulder. She rested her hands on mine and turned her face enough for us to press our cheeks together. I had to shut my eyes against a wave of emotion.

I had no words—no method of taking this pain from her.

A shout from the Clour boys made us look again. Blackie and the twins were playing around, but Rock wasn't joining. He tossed his sticks onto the pile and sat on a log, staring out at the trees.

The poor guy looked... depressed.

McKale stepped up next to us, his eyebrows drawn together as he watched his friend from afar.

"He's not forgotten ye, Cass. Perhaps he does no' have the exact memories, but look at 'im. His soul remembers. He knows he's lost somethin'."

Cassidy sniffled, and her tears came now. McKale drew back as if he'd said something wrong, and I rubbed his arm to tell him he did okay. Then I held Cass tighter.

"Sweetie," I said. I needed to be real with her. "We can introduce you to him again. You can have your goodbye, but it's not going to be easy when you remember and he doesn't.

It might make it hurt even worse."

"I know." She wiped her eyes and sucked in a breath. "I spent all night thinking about it. I don't think I can handle him not remembering. I know I have to go back home and finish school. I know I have to go to college or start working with Mom and Dad next year. I keep telling myself Ronan is just another ex-boyfriend who I'll eventually stop thinking about."

But he was so much more than that.

I heard her swallow. "It'll be okay, right, Sissy?"

"Yeah, chickadee. It'll be all right in time." Inside I was cringing. I knew Cass, and I knew she would be hurting for a long time. She had many bygone boyfriends, but she hadn't loved any of them. Only Rock. Only the boy who wouldn't remember.

"Come on," I whispered. I moved to her side and took her hand. She let me lead her away.

"I'll be 'round in a bit," McKale said. I gave him a grateful nod as he turned to seek out his Clour friend.

"Wait!" Cassidy said. Her eyes were wide. "I have to try. I have to see. Just this once."

Her eyes pleaded with me, and I nodded. I would not stop her. "Just... be careful what you say. He might be feeling confused and I don't want you to accidentally make things worse for him."

She agreed, and the three of us walked through the trees.

Blackie noticed us first. "Oy! Lads, we have guests!" He ran a hand through his hair and grinned at us as the rest of the Clour rushed out of the rundown cottage.

Cass's hand was cutting off the circulation to my fingers. Rock was slowly standing. Looking between the three of us.

We greeted the Clour boys, who weren't nearly as boisterous as usual. Like McKale and I, they kept glancing furtively between Cassidy and Rock.

Rock stepped up, pale.

"Feeling ill, mate?" McKale asked him with concern.

"Aye. 'Tis a strange feeling about. Bad magic or somethin'. Can ye feel it?"

"Aye," McKale whispered. "I can."

Rock shook his head, then looked straight up at Cassidy. All movement stopped as they locked eyes. And then Rock turned to McKale and said, "Have ye been hiding the lasses from us? Afraid the ole Clour charm will steal 'em away?" This was asked half-heartedly, and even the chuckles from the other Clour were weak.

Cassidy slumped and my heart sank.

"'Tis been a busy summer," McKale told him. "This is Cassidy Mason. Cass... this is Rock."

"Hi," she said softly.

The look on Rock's face as he watched her was pitiful, like his mind was frantically trying to grasp at something right out of reach. His entire summer had been spent with Cass— that was a lot of memory to take. As grateful as I was to the Summer King, I was also angry that he addled the mind of a young man in such a dangerous way.

Rock pressed two fingers to his temple and closed his eyes. "Me head..."

"You should have a lie down, mate," McKale said, reaching out to steady him. Rock nodded and hung his head, heading indoors.

"It makes it worse for him to see me," Cass said with sad realization.

"Should we try to remind 'im?" Blackie asked. "A bit at a time—"

"No." Cass's voice was strong. "I'm afraid it'll strain his mind. I need to just… stay away."

We looked around at each other, at a loss, awkwardness and discomfort spreading. Cass turned from us and rushed away, tearing into the trees. I would have chased her, but I was sure she needed some time to herself. I pinched the bridge of my nose.

"We still have three more weeks before my family goes home," I said. "This is going to be hard."

They all nodded. It was strange and wrong to see the Clour forlorn.

"Take care of him, 'kay?" I said to the guys.

Again they nodded, and McKale escorted me away, back to Leprechaun land.

Three weeks passed in a dizzying mix of joyful love with McKale, and sorrowful silence with Cassidy. She had changed—matured overnight. Not once did she try to see Rock after that day on Clour land. She woke early every morning to help with chores, spent afternoons devouring classics from her AP summer reading list, and went to bed early each night. I actually missed the carefree, spontaneous, giggling girl who'd come to Ireland with me.

On another note of drastic change, Mom and Dad had spent the last three weeks on Clour land helping the boys till the land for a late summer garden, fixing up the cottage, and teaching them to do basic things to better care for themselves and their home. Dad had even talked Brogan into allowing the Clour to begin helping with Shoe House responsibilities again once they were gone. He said the boys needed more responsibilities to feel like men. They were young when the Fae had cursed their clan. The older generations of Clour who'd caused all the problems were now gone. Dad wanted these boys to have a second chance to be better than their ancestors.

On my family's last morning I sat behind Cassidy french-braiding her wet hair while she finished reading *Pride and Prejudice*. My stomach had been hurting for days at the thought of them leaving. I loved McKale and would follow him anywhere, but I was going to miss my family like crazy. Especially my sister—my best friend.

Cass closed the book with a sigh just as I snapped the rubber band into place.

Someone knocked quietly on the door before pushing it open. Mom and Dad stood there, dressed for the day. Cassidy and I stood.

"Listen," Dad said. "We need to go into town to return the tech stuff and van and get our rental car back. We'd also like to get some things for Robyn—necessities to hold her over here for a while."

I nodded at that. There were several things I wanted to stock up on.

"And, um…" Dad swallowed and Mom slid his arm through his, encouragingly. "We were thinking of inviting McKale and Ronan to come along. But only if that's okay with you." They looked at Cass.

Her face stayed neutral, but I saw her chest rise and fall faster. "Okay."

An hour later Cassidy and I were holding hands and turning the corner around the back of the village. Our hands were sweating, but we didn't let go. The front of the white van came into view and then we stopped in our tracks. McKale and Rock stood there, waiting for us, looking so cute with anticipation. They both looked clean, with haircuts and shaven faces.

McKale's face lit up when he saw me, filling me with familiar, welcome tingles and forcing a smile to my lips.

Next to him Rock gave a rueful grin to Cassidy. "There ye are again. I was beginnin' to think ye were only a figment of me imagination and dreams, I was."

Cass gave a nervous laugh and blushed. "No, I'm real."

Rock grinned at McKale, then at my sister and I. "So, we're goin' on an adventure today, aye? One last day to try and win the heart o' me best mate's sister. I'd best take advantage."

Though his words were playful, there was something almost cautious about his demeanor, as if he still felt strange in her presence although he was clearly drawn to her.

Cass crossed her arms and pursed her lips to hold back a smile. "I should warn you that I'm kind of hard to win over."

I covered my mouth to hide a snort and McKale came to my side, nudging me with his shoulder and giving a chuckle.

"Is that right?" Rock asked, sidling closer to her. "Well, I'll take that as a challenge, Cassie-lassie. We'll see if yer no' in love with me by the end of this outing." He winked and pulled away, causing Cass to blanch and flush. I bit my lip.

Dad ambled up carrying a speaker and the guys rushed to help him.

I watched Cass stare at Rock and thought to myself that she was way ahead of him. I think Rock's heart was way ahead of his mind, as well. For once I didn't want to tell my sister to be careful. I wanted her to enjoy this day and this boy.

One at a time, Dad, McKale, and Rock carried equipment to put in the van, and each of them gave us a wink in passing. Cassidy and I broke into laughter and it was so good to hear her humor that my eyes watered.

"Come on," I said, pulling her arm. "Let's grab some stuff."

Our steps were lighter than they'd been in over a month as we jogged to the equipment pile and took armfuls of "human magic."

I looked at the technology that'd saved us, and my sister walking in front of me, and the guys joking with Dad at the van. I marveled at how things worked themselves out.

Mom had walked up to see us off, kissing us goodbye. She would stay behind to pack. All around us Leprechaun people were filing out and holding hands, watching us in gratitude. My heart overflowed.

Cassidy stood next to the van with Mom, smiling. So pretty. McKale passed me, going back for the last bit of gear. I jumped and squealed as he pinched my butt and laughed under his breath. Some of the Leprechauns giggled at this show and I shook my head, blushing.

Yes, the Fae were stronger. They could force us to work for them. Force us to bind with strangers. They could alter our minds and take our memories. But they couldn't take away our will to live or our choice to love. We would endure, and then we would die, but our hearts would be full along the way. I pitied the Fae with all their power and beauty and their lack of love.

I wouldn't trade places with FFG for anything—nay, not even for all the pots of gold in the world.

ACKNOWLEDGEMENTS

THANK YOU, THANK YOU, thank you. Yes, YOU.

No matter what you thought of this little book, I thank you for giving it a chance.

Thank you to all of the readers who cheered me on, and whose support spurred me out of a major funk. Small kindnesses have big effects.

Thank you Nathan for laughing at me and saying there was no way a leprechaun could be sexy. I love a good challenge. And I love you. *winks*

Huge gratitude to my early readers and late proofreaders: Morgan Shamy, Evie Burdette, Kelley Vitollo, Jolene Perry, Nicola Dorrington, Brooke Leicht, Carol Marcum, Carrie McRae, Gwen Cole, Sharon Johnston, Courtney Fetchko, Carolee Noury, Hilary Mahalchick, Jill Wilson, Valerie Rinta, Meredith Crowley, and everyone on Inkpop who read it and gave feedback in the early days. You all have my heart.

A special thanks goes to Evie J., not only for reading the manuscript twice and providing priceless feedback, but also because she did a rockstar job on my website. I'm so lucky to have you, girl!

Thank you to my beta readers for their time and

thoughtful critiques: Jenny Zemanek, Samantha Wilson, Kayleigh Gore, Maya H., Jamie T., Brooke D., Luce, Tiffany B., and Julie B.

Thank you Angela McLaurin for your gorgeous formatting skills!

Carrie McRae, I'm in love with the covers you made. I can't thank you enough for all the time and talent you put into this project!

Thank you Mom (Nancy Parry) for your unrelenting devotion to this story, and for reading it to Grandma in her final days.

Many thanks to my agent, Jill Corcoran, for your help, praise, concern, and faith in me.

Big hugs and smooches to the best friends a girl could have—cheers to my Dugout Girls and FoFs.

Lastly, all my love goes out to my family, near and far, especially my babies (Autumn and Cayden) who put up with my absent-mindedness on a daily basis when I'm lost in story land.

ABOUT THE AUTHOR

WENDY HIGGINS RECEIVED HER degree in Creative Writing from George Mason University, and a Masters in Curriculum and Instruction from Radford University. She taught high school English until becoming a mom and full-time writer. Wendy is the author of the *Sweet Evil* trilogy from HarperTeen. *See Me* is her first independent YA publication. Wendy lives in Virginia with her veterinarian husband, daughter, son, and their doggie Rue.

Website: http://www.wendyhigginswrites.com
You can contact Wendy at wendyhigginswrites@gmail.com

Made in the USA
San Bernardino, CA
21 April 2014